Also by Sherrilyn Kenyon:

League Series

Born of Night
Born of Fire

Dark-Hunter World
(in reading order)

Fantasy Lover
Night Pleasures
Night Embrace
Dance with the Devil
Kiss of the Night
Night Play
Seize the Night
Sins of the Night
Unleash the Night
Dark Side of the Moon
The Dream-Hunter
Devil May Cry
Upon the Midnight Clear
Dream Chaser
Acheron
One Silent Night
Dream Warrior
Bad Moon Rising

The Dark-Hunter Companion

By Sherrilyn Kenyon writing as Kinley MacGregor:

Lords of Avalon Series

Sword of Darkness
Knight of Darkness

New York Times bestselling author **Sherrilyn Kenyon** lives a life of extraordinary danger…as does any woman with three sons, a husband, a menagerie of pets and a collection of swords that all of the above have a major fixation with.

Writing as Sherrilyn Kenyon and Kinley MacGregor, she is an international phenomenon with more than twelve million copies of her books in print, in twenty-eight countries. She's the author of several series including: The Dark-Hunters, The League, and Lords of Avalon. Her books always appear at the top of the *New York Times*, *Publisher's Weekly* and *USA Today* lists.

Visit Sherrilyn Kenyon's award-winning website
www.darkhunter.com

Praise for Sherrilyn Kenyon:

'A publishing phenomenon…[Sherrilyn Kenyon] is the reigning queen of the wildly successful paranormal scene'
Publishers Weekly

'Kenyon's writing is brisk, ironic and relentlessly imaginative. These are not your mother's vampire novels'
Boston Globe

'Whether writing as Sherrilyn Kenyon or Kinley MacGregor, this author delivers great romantic fantasy!'
New York Times bestselling author Elizabeth Lowell

BORN
OF ICE

SHERRILYN
KENYON

piatkus

PIATKUS

First published in the US in 2009 by St. Martin's Press, New York
First published in Great Britain as a paperback original in 2009 by Piatkus
Reprinted 2009

A CIP catalogue record for this book
is available from the British Library.

ISBN 978-0-7499-0899-7

Printed in the UK by CPI Mackays, Chatham ME5 8TD

Papers used by Piatkus are natural, renewable and
recyclable products sourced from well-managed forests and certified
in accordance with the rules of the Forest Stewardship Council.

Mixed Sources
Product group from well-managed
forests and other controlled sources
www.fsc.org Cert no. SGS-COC-004081
© 1996 Forest Stewardship Council

Piatkus
An imprint of
Little, Brown Book Group
100 Victoria Embankment
London EC4Y 0DY

An Hachette UK Company
www.hachette.co.uk

www.piatkus.co.uk

To the readers, past and present. Thank you for the support. As always, to my friends, family, and staff, a special thanks for all you do.

Much love,
Sherrilyn

AUTHOR'S NOTE

To everyone who's read the previous version of this book, the book you hold in your hands has been completely rewritten. It is my original vision for the worlds I had all of those years ago. If you've read the first one, you'll be surprised at all the changes, the new characters you'll meet, and the turns of events that take place. I hope you enjoy *Born of Ice*.

For *Born of Ice* bonus material, please visit

http://livetheleague.com

BORN
OF ICE

PROLOGUE

"That right there is the meanest son of a bitch ever born."

Devyn Kell jerked his head up from his paperwork as he heard that deep, familiar voice coming from across the room.

No. It couldn't be . . .

He barely bit back his smile as he saw the newcomer instantly through the group of milling soldiers who separated them in the mess hall.

Adron Quiakides. Braggart. Womanizer. Lunatic . . .

And his best friend since birth.

Only a handful of years older than him, Adron had snow-white hair that fell in a braid down his back. A League assassin, Adron wore the uniform well. So black it absorbed light, it was a stark contrast to his hair and molded itself to every muscle the assassin possessed.

His eyes were covered by a pair of opaque shades, but even so, Devyn knew their color better than his own. As a kid, he'd saved the right one from blindness after they'd had a race through a briar patch that had all but ripped it out.

Devyn had won the race. But Adron claimed it was only because he'd almost lost his eye.

As if that could ever slow one of them down . . .

He hadn't seen Adron in almost six months, a record for their tight friendship. He was definitely glad to see him now.

"You mean Kell?" Devyn's commanding officer choked as Adron draped his arm over Quills's shoulders. "Are you high, Commander? He's a friggin' doctor. The only part of me he scares is my tonsils."

Adron *tsk*ed at Devyn's CO, who'd done nothing but rag on him for the last two months since Devyn had been reassigned to this unit. The man really was lucky Devyn had learned to control his temper.

Most days, anyway.

Adron cuffed the CO on the back so hard, Quills actually staggered from the blow. "Yeah, that's what he wants you to think. But trust me. I know his skills firsthand. His father was the notorious filch and assassin, C.I. Syn. His mother the legendary Seax, Shahara Dagan."

Devyn clamped his jaw tight to keep from drawing his blaster and shooting his best friend for letting out a secret he'd done his damnedest to keep.

You asshole.

Quills gaped at them both. "He . . . *Kell* is *their* son?"

"Oh, yeah. And I'll do you one better. He was

trained from birth to fight by the best assassin The League ever created."

Quills scoffed. "You mean there's someone out there better than your father?"

Adron shook his head as he shoved Quills away from him. "No, idiot. My father trained him." He flashed an evil grin at Quills. "Just FYI, my father is also his *god*father. So you want to be real nice to Dev. All of us take it personally when people aren't."

Devyn rose to his feet as Adron closed the distance between them. He held his hand out and let his friend pull him into a tight man-hug. "It's good to see you again, *aridos*. But really . . . some discretion would have been nice. Out of character for your rotten ass, but nice."

Adron laughed good-naturedly as he released him. "C'mon, Dev. You need to let these assholes know what you can do. Who you really are. They think you weak, they'll step all over you."

A true assassin's philosophy, but it wasn't in Devyn's nature to push people around. He was too easygoing for that.

Well . . . again, most days.

Devyn glanced around the room, noting they were the recipients of way too much attention.

Yet true to Adron's words, the soldiers in the room now held a respect for Devyn in their gazes that they'd never had before. "Being an arrogant braggart just doesn't work for me."

Adron took his insult in stride. "You should try it. It really does grow on you, trust me."

Devyn laughed at his friend, who was much more like an older brother to him. "So what brings you here?"

"People needed killing." Adron's tone was completely stoic about his brutal trade. "I was actually on my way back to The League and heard your unit had been dropped here. I just wanted to say hi before I left."

"Who was your target?"

Adron leaned in to whisper so that no one else would know who he'd killed. "Emperor Abenbi."

Devyn was surprised by the name. "The Probekein leader?" Abenbi had once ordered the rape and death of Adron's mother. It was a story they all knew well, and it was how Adron's parents, as well as his own, had met. "Was it personal?"

"It was an assignment . . ." A tic worked in Adron's jaw. "And it was personal for what he put my mother through. Too long in coming, in my opinion, but it was legal, so my father should be proud."

"He's always proud of you, Adron."

Adron didn't comment. "How long are you here for?"

"We're evacing troops out of a hot zone and have some supplies for the civs. A few days and we're clear."

"Good. I don't want to be taking your body home to your mother."

"Yeah, she'd probably hurt you if you did."

"Probably so." Adron grinned roguishly. "In all the universe, your mother is the only thing that truly scares me, especially where you're concerned. I don't ever want to be on her dark side."

"Ha ha. And need I remind you my mother wasn't the one screaming at the pool when you got shoved in."

"Yeah, all right, so we both have screwed-up, irrational mothers. Anyway, I've got to get out of here. I took a little longer on assignment than I should have and if I don't make check-in . . . I don't want to be hunted and have to take out another assassin dumb enough to come after me." He gave Devyn another quick hug. "Take care, little brother."

"You, too, A. I'll see you around."

Adron inclined his head to him before he made his way back toward the doors.

As soon as Adron was gone, Quills stepped forward. "Was he full of total shit about your parents?"

Devyn had to force himself not to roll his eyes. If the man only knew the truth. Lethal venom ran through his blood from both sides of his family. He'd been bred for survival and had cut his teeth on skills this man couldn't even imagine. "No, sir."

"Then if your parents are Syn and Dagan, why is your name Kell?"

Because he was the grandson of one of the most ruthless criminals ever born and his parents had done everything they could to shield him from people who would judge and discriminate against him based on his ancestry alone. That paternal connection to a madman had ruined his father's life twice before Devyn's birth, and it had been hammered into him that he must always keep it a secret.

And it was none of Commander Quills's business.

"Have to ask my father, sir. I didn't pick my name. He and my mother did." Gods, how he hated being obsequious to these pricks. Why had he joined the military again?

To help people . . .

Yeah, but it was getting harder and harder to take their crap and thank them for ramming it down his throat.

His CO narrowed his gaze at him. "Are you being smart with me, Captain?"

Devyn arched a sardonic brow. How stupid was Quills that he couldn't tell that was a major affirmative?

Before he could answer, Quills's comlink went off. "Commander? There's an attack on the road twelve miles down. We have orders to move out. Now."

Quills took off and left Devyn alone with the lieutenant who'd been sitting close to him. The young man's face was pale and drawn.

Devyn frowned. "You all right?"

"I've never been in a battle before."

Poor kid, but he'd learn. "Don't worry, Lieutenant. Your training will kick in and you'll be fine."

"And if not, I'll have you there to patch me back up. Right, Doc?"

"Absolutely."

Inclining his head, the kid took off.

Devyn grabbed his pack and weapon. He didn't like the thought of battle anymore than the rookie, but this was what he'd signed up for . . .

This was so not what he'd signed up for.

Devyn was furious as he knelt on the ground where a boy lay in a bloody mess. No older than ten, his body had been shredded by a mine as the kid and his town had been caught in the crossfire of League troops trying to flush out a group of rebels. One arm was missing and his left leg would never be the same again . . .

Provided he didn't lose that, too.

"I don't want to die," the boy cried. "I want my mommy."

Unfortunately, Devyn was pretty sure she lay among the bodies that littered the road and village.

His hands shook as he tried to slow the boy's bleeding. "What's your name, kid?"

"Omari."

"How old are you?"

"Nine." Omari sobbed, trying to rub the blood out of his brown eyes. His dark brown skin had been savaged by his multitude of injuries. "My birthday's next month. I'm not going to die before my birthday, am I? My mom said I could finally have a puppy if I was good, and I've been real good so that I could have one. I don't want to die without my puppy."

Devyn's throat tightened at the boy's panic and fear. He had to get him calmed down. "You go to school, Omari?"

He shook his head. "The League blew it up. I was home sick that day. All my friends were killed." He broke off into fierce sobs again as he continued to call for his mother at the top of his lungs. Baleful shrieks that were drowned out by the sounds of lasers, blasters and bombs exploding around them.

Devyn had to bite back a curse. He'd joined The League to protect people. To keep predators from doing what their own soldiers had done to these people.

Anger burned through him so raw and fetid that he could taste it.

"Kell? What the hell do you think you're doing?"

He looked up at his CO as he reached for another bandage. "Trying to save a life." He had to force himself to finish the sentence. "Sir." But there was no way to keep the venom and disgust he felt out of his tone.

Quills kicked dirt at them. "He's nothing to us. We have soldiers bleeding. Get your ass moving and tend to them."

Devyn glanced at the men who were hurt, but nowhere near as badly as the kid in front of him. If he didn't stop the bleeding, the kid didn't stand a chance. "I'll be there in a minute."

"You will do as you are told, soldier. Now move!"

Devyn refused to budge. "In a minute."

Then Quills made the worst mistake of his life.

He pointed his blaster at him. "Move or die."

Devyn scoffed bitterly as he heard his mother's favorite phrase run through his head. He narrowed his gaze at his CO. "Never give someone a choice that doesn't leave them with any way out except to hurt you."

"What?"

"You want me to move?" Devyn shot to his feet and had the blaster out of Quills's hands faster than he could blink. "How's this?"

"Arrest him!"

League soldiers came at him from all directions. But Devyn didn't care. The only thing that mattered to him was the kid at his feet.

Omari.

He hadn't donned this uniform to slaughter civilians. To cut off town supplies and punish miners who were protesting The League's cruelty to them. This was wrong, and he refused to be a part of a system this corrupt.

He slammed the butt of the blaster into the first man to reach him. Another shot at him. He dodged the blast that cut down two other men before he took down the man aiming for his head. He pulled out his knives and went for the next one who tried to kill him.

Turning around, he caught another attacker in the chest, and the next in his arm and throat.

One by one, using the skills his parents and uncles had taught him, he brought down every soldier dumb enough to attack him until he stood alone.

His conviction solid steel, he moved back to his commander, who lay sniveling on the ground. "You should have listened to Adron. I *am* the meanest son of a bitch ever born. And you . . ." He blasted his commander into unconsciousness. "Are a worthless piece of shit."

And Quills was lucky Devyn had enough of his Aunt Tessa in him to have mercy right now when he really wanted to kill the SOB. Either one of his parents would have cut his throat where he lay. But he wouldn't be so cold . . .

Tonight.

Devyn paused as he looked over the men he'd wounded. Those who weren't dead, anyway. They lay holding their wounds, but made no more moves to attack him.

He'd made his point. Just because he was a doctor didn't mean he was a wimp.

They'd learned a valuable lesson tonight about attacking people they didn't consider a threat.

But as he stood there, reality hit him. By what he'd done, he'd declared war on The League. There would be no going back. They would hunt him like an animal and come for him, night and day.

So be it.

After all, he was a Wade through and through. And if Wades were anything, they were staunch survivors.

May the gods have mercy on anyone dumb enough to come at him, because he wouldn't.

Turning around, he picked Omari up from the ground. "Don't worry, kid. I'll protect you. No one's ever going to hurt you again."

Because he would kill anyone who ever threatened this kid.

CHAPTER 1

Nine years later

Devyn Kell is the devil himself. He will not take mercy on you, and he will kill you if he finds out who you are and why you're there. Trust me. I've buried every agent we've sent in after him—male, female and everything in between. Since he can spot an operative three seconds after he meets one, maybe a civ can bust his ass wide open.

Do not *fail.*

Alix Gerran held those words close to her heart as she entered the hangar bay where Kell's ship was docked.

I don't want to do this . . .

But she had no choice. It was either find the evidence to bring Kell to justice or watch her mother and sister die. She had three weeks before the Rita-darion Chief Minister of Justice executed them. And every day that passed, her family sat in a prison cell, rotting.

She was their only hope.

You can do this.

She still didn't understand why Merjack didn't just kill the man if he hated him so much. But the CMOD had been adamant that Kell have a public trial and execution. For whatever psycho reason, an assassination contract wasn't good enough for Kell.

Maybe Kell had run over Merjack's dog . . .

We've already taken care of his engineer, so he has an opening on his crew tailor-made by us for you. You are to bring him to justice, alive for trial, or so help me, I'll rape your family myself and then throw you to the class-three felons and watch them take turns with you.

Whatever Kell had done to the CMOD had to have been fierce. There was no other reason for a hatred so strong.

"How did I get in the middle of this?"

But then, she already knew. Her father had been a freighter until six months ago, when his first mate had absconded with all of their savings. With no reserve, her family been forced into smuggling.

Unfortunately, her father had seriously stunk at that career, and had been apprehended two weeks ago and executed within twenty-four hours of his conviction. Because she, her mother and her sister were slaves, they'd been bound for the auction block to pay for his trial and execution.

Until Merjack had seen Alix.

Apparently, she bore a striking resemblance to

someone in Kell's past he'd cared about, and that alone had kept her from being sold to a brothel.

So here she was . . .

I'm so going to die.

Stop it, Alix. You can do this.

She was getting tired of that worn-out litany. The least the voice in her head could do was not sound so despondent when it said it.

You can do it!

Yeah, now she sounded like she was on drugs.

Swallowing her fear, she headed for bay Delta Alpha 17-4, where Kell's ship, the *Talia*, was docked.

Just don't let him kill me three seconds after meeting me. It would seriously screw up her already messed-up day.

She passed numerous freighters and fighters, the majority of which were outdated and barely legal for flight. Typical, really. Most of the people who visited the Solaras station were outlaws, grifters, prostitutes, fringe dwellers or pilots who needed the extra hazard pay that was offered to anyone dumb enough to fly through the Solaras system. Money for them was every bit as tight as it was for her.

But as she rounded a corner, she froze at the sight of what had to be the prettiest ship she'd ever seen. Her jaw dropped.

What I wouldn't give for something like that . . .

It was absolutely stunning, with gentle lines and no sharp angles anywhere on her. Painted a dark vermillion with gold highlights, she dominated the hangar. That ship was definitely a lady who shamed every single spacecraft that was docked here. For that matter, she shamed *every* ship Alix had ever seen outside of ads and online catalogues.

Letting out a slow, appreciative breath, she forced herself to not even dream about that one and started looking for the *Talia*.

It's probably a rusted-out tanker or freighter no better maintained than your father's ship was. You're definitely going to have your hands full keeping her in space.

Just let Kell not be as disgusting as my father's crew.

That was the worst part about runners and smugglers. They were a low-hygiene bunch. It was like a badge of honor for them to out-stink each other.

Look on the bright side—at least this way you don't have to sleep with his smelly hide.

True. With this mission, she only had to find or fabricate evidence to convict Kell before he killed her.

Go, me!

Pushing that frightening thought away, she counted off the bays as she passed them. "One . . . two . . . three . . ." She stopped as she came even with the ship that had caught her eye.

No. It couldn't be.

She double-checked the numbers and sure enough, it was.

The *Talia*.

Whoa . . . A rush of excitement went through her until she remembered that she wasn't really here to work. She was here to either frame or apprehend a vicious felon.

A killer.

"Dammit, Vik. How can you not know what's wrong with this thing? Can't you commune with it or something?"

She hesitated at that deep, rumbling voice that sounded like thunder. Lightly accented, it sent a shiver down her spine. Her heart pounding, she peeked around to the back and froze dead in her tracks.

If she'd thought the ship was something, it was nothing compared to the group of men who appeared to be its crew . . .

Oh. My. God.

The one who'd spoken had to be a good six foot four in height. Built in perfect proportions, he was lean and ripped. Broad shoulders tapered down to narrow hips and what had to be the finest butt she'd ever seen in her life—she could bounce a credit off that.

Or break a tooth biting it . . .

His black hair was cut short, but the front of it fell down into a pair of eyes so dark they blended perfectly into his pupils. Dark brows slashed parallel to sharp cheekbones, and his jaw had a becoming tic in it.

Oooh, that was totally lickable, too.

Power and strength bled from every pore of his

body. An image that was perpetuated by the black Armstich suit hugging every dip and curve of his muscles and the holstered blasters that were strapped to his hips.

Yeah, this guy meant business and was ready for trouble.

And the men with him were no different. There was one, a Hyshian by the looks of him, to his right. A few inches shorter, the Hyshian was no less ripped. His black hair fell in long braids to the middle of his back. He seemed to be around the same age as the first man she'd noticed.

Instead of black, he wore dark brown with even more weapons strapped to his body. His long coat was sleeveless, showing his bulging arms. Thick gold bracelets encircled both of his wrists and one thin band wrapped around his left bicep—a mark of marriage in his world.

Yeah, he was every bit as deadly.

The third she suspected was a mecha. A good two inches taller than the one who'd spoken, he had dark blue hair and lighter blue skin. With his skin tone, he looked like a Rugarion, but their lips and eyes were black instead of the darker blue his were. As with the others, he was absolutely gorgeous. Well-muscled and perfectly sculpted.

He also seemed remarkably peeved—something impressive, since it was hard to get emotional programming perfected in an AI.

The mecha glared at the one who'd spoken. "My name is not 'Dammit, Vik' and I find it ironic that you think I can commune with all metal beings when you can barely communicate your point of view to your own parents. And they birthed you. I did not give birth to this ship. Last time I checked, I was male and that would be impossible on a multitude of levels."

The other man laughed. "What do you think, Dev? Can we make a mod on Vik so that he *could* give birth?"

The mecha scowled at him. "Careful, Sway, I could easily lock you in your room again . . . accidentally, of course."

The Hyshian pulled out a blaster and angled it at his head. "I knew it, you metal bastard."

The man he'd called Dev let out an irritated breath before he disarmed the Hyshian. "Are we just going to stand here taking pot shots at each other? Or can we focus our collective ADD on getting us off this shit hole?"

Sway glowered at him. "Look, no one wants off this hole worse than I do. I'm open for suggestions, Captain I-Can-Do-it-Myself. Do you have any idea what's sending off a warning?"

Dev gave him a droll stare that sent a chill down her spine. "Yeah, the malfunction system that won't let us launch."

Vik snorted. "I suggested we hire a new engineer, but someone ignored me." He slid his gaze to Dev.

Dev grimaced. "And what was I supposed to do? Shit one out? In case you haven't noticed, there's not a plethora of engineers here."

"Plethora?" Sway mocked. "What kind of girl word is that?"

Dev went for his throat, only to have Vik come between them.

Vik shoved the Hyshian back. "Sway, do not bruise the sacred entity. I don't want to get dismantled because you desecrated the magic seed. Now both of you behave like you're actually grown men."

Alix scowled. It *was* like watching a group of kids on a playground.

Deadly, scary kids, but . . .

You have to get in there and get on his ship.

I don't want to go.

Just do it.

Taking a deep breath, she forced herself to walk forward. *Please don't let them shoot me.*

"Excuse me, scary people. Your rear stabilizer's down."

Three pairs of eyes turned to her with an intensity that was absolutely terrifying. She had to fight the urge to run.

Instead, she held her ground as she faced them.

Devyn froze at the sound of the husky female voice that reminded him of a soft, cool caress sliding down his naked spine. Without conscious effort, his mind flashed on an image of what the woman who possessed such a voice must look like. His body roared to life at the prospect of spending some time with her.

Suddenly, the idea of staying on this stifling station for a little longer seemed appealing. A sly smile curved his lips as he turned toward the woman of his dreams.

His smile faded as an electrical shock jolted him and he saw the face of a woman he hadn't seen in years . . .

The last face he'd *ever* expected to see again.

It's not her.

She's dead.

You killed her . . .

No, this wasn't Clotilde. While they shared very similar features and coloring, Clotilde had been tiny and short. The woman in front of him was almost as tall as Sway and built for battle. Her body was well-honed and strong. Not to mention she looked like a lost puppy—something Clotilde had never been. Even first thing in the morning, she'd always been dressed to perfection. Always in complete and utter control of every situation.

Except for the night you killed her . . .

He shoved that thought away before it ignited his temper.

A faded red cap covered the woman's head, shielding her eyes from him. Her pale blonde hair fell over one shoulder in a thick braid hanging to her waist. She wore a baggy brown battlesuit that had seen far better days. Even her boots were scuffed and worn out.

"What did you say?" he asked her.

An intriguing blush spread across her cheeks

while she kept her head down as if looking at his feet. She pointed to the rear of his ship. "Your back stabilizer is down. I think that might be what you're looking for."

Devyn was grateful someone knew what was wrong with the damned thing. He moved to check on it.

"Are you Captain Kell?" She followed a step behind him while the rest of his crew exchanged wide-eyed stares.

Worthless bastards . . .

Devyn slammed the stabilizer plate back into its original position and locked it down. Suspicious, he turned to face her. He'd learned a long time ago to be extremely cautious of people who came looking for him, no matter how harmless they might first appear.

Especially someone who looked like Clotilde.

"And you are?"

She extended a small hand out to him, her features stern and determined. "Alix Gerran. I heard you were looking for a new engineer, and I'd like to apply for the job."

He took her hand and noted the calluses there as he shook it. She might not appear much older than an adolescent, but her hands told him she was used to hard work.

Normally, he wouldn't consider someone so young for a member of his crew, but right now he'd take on the devil himself so long as he could operate the flight checks and get the *Talia* back into space. "You got any experience?"

"Well, I was born on a freighter and worked on one since I was old enough to hold a wrench." She shifted the backpack on her shoulder and lifted her head with an arrogance he found admirable for her age. "I know how to run preliminary flight checks, keep logs, and I can fix any engine malfunction with a piece of string and a drop of sealant."

Devyn arched a brow. For some reason, he didn't doubt that last boast in the least.

He leaned against his ship with one hand and narrowed his eyes on her. "My last engineer was killed in battle. I don't run from fights with anyone. Ever. You sign on with me, you have to share that one basic conviction. You got a problem with that?"

She met his gaze unflinchingly, and he noticed the strange dark blue shade of her eyes—very different from the hazel green pair that haunted his nightmares. The fire inside that intrepid gaze said she was a scrapper, too, and wouldn't be scared to face whatever hell was thrown at them.

That was something he could respect.

"I don't have a problem with it."

Devyn pushed himself away from his ship, pulled a cloth out of his back pocket, and wiped the grease from his hands. "How old are you, anyway?" He didn't want to assist a young runaway.

"Twenty-seven," she answered without hesitation. He raked her slim frame with a scowl. He wouldn't have placed her at any more than sixteen. "You got any ID?"

She reached into her back pocket, pulled out a small wallet, and handed it to him.

Devyn studied the picture and the birth date. He had a good eye for forgeries, and this ID was either the best he'd ever seen or authentic. Deciding on the latter, he handed it back to her. "You're a long way from Praenomia."

She shrugged her thin shoulders. "My birth was registered there, but I've never spent more than a few days on a planet in my life."

"Then you're used to recycled water and air."

"And bad food, boredom, and stuffy noses," she added with a wistful sigh.

"Then why do you want to sign back on to a ship?"

She put her hands in her pockets and looked up at him with probing eyes that struck a long-forgotten chord inside him, a chord he'd hoped was forever severed.

She's not Clotilde . . .

Still, that part of him that hated the bitch wanted to lash out at the woman in front of him. Luckily for her, he had enough control to stop it.

"It's home to me, and I have to make a living. I don't know how to do anything else."

That was one reason Devyn understood. Something about the dark tranquility of space seemed to comfort even the most troubled of souls.

Even his own.

He scanned her competent stance. She seemed honest and capable enough. At worst, she had to be better at maintenance than his current crew of incompetents.

Speaking of, he looked at them to see what they thought of her.

Vik gave him an agitated stare. "I would voice an opinion, but since you never care what I think, I won't waste the energy."

He looked at Sway, who shrugged. "Nera's only four days away. We can give her a try, and if she's not as good as she claims, dump her ass off there. If she annoys us before we get there, we can always toss her out an airlock."

Devyn looked back at her to see her horrified gape. "The job's yours if you want it."

But at this point, he wouldn't be surprised if she told him where to stuff it.

A puzzled look crossed her face. "Don't you want some credentials or references?"

He shrugged. "Most people don't have any for this kind of work. You spotted the stabilizer with hardly any effort. Hell, I've wasted almost half an hour looking for it." He looked back at his crew. "And don't get me started on how long Team Worthless over there spent with it. You obviously know something about ships."

Sway made an obscene gesture at him.

Alix smiled, and he became entranced with a dimple in her left cheek.

Devyn braced himself as his own hormones

fired. What was wrong with him that she could affect him so easily? Especially given how much she favored a woman who made his blood run cold and his fury run high.

Maybe Sway was right and he needed to get laid. "We're getting ready to launch, so if you have any gear or good-byes jus—"

"Just this gear." She shrugged her backpack off her shoulder. "And no good-byes."

Devyn frowned at the catch in her voice. "None?"

She clenched her teeth, and he had the strange sensation she fought against tears, but her eyes betrayed nothing except the fiercest of spirits. "My father died very recently. I . . . I don't have anyone else."

He nodded in sympathy. He'd never lost anyone close to him, but he could imagine how hard it would be to lose one of his parents. "I'm sorry."

She looked around the bay as if his words embarrassed her. "Don't worry. It won't interfere with my work."

"Well, then, uh . . ." Devyn paused in an effort to remember her name.

"Alix," she supplied with an odd half-smile. "My dad wanted a son." She looked down at her body and pulled at the loose material over her breasts. "I guess he didn't miss by much."

Devyn noted the bitterness in her voice, and a strange surge of protectiveness ran through him.

"You don't look like a boy to me." Her smile returned and sent a wave of heat straight to his cock.

Yeah, he definitely needed to get laid.

Before he could comment, his link buzzed.

Sway snorted in utter disdain. "Let me guess. Mom?" His tone rang of ridicule.

"Shut up, Sway." Devyn checked the ID and flipped off his friend. Yeah, it was his mother . . . probably because his heart rate was elevated.

Sighing in frustration, he put the silver link on his ear, but didn't answer it. "Alix, meet our first mate, Sway Trinaloew."

Sway shook her hand. "Nice meeting you, Alix."

"Vik is our—"

"Man-bitch," Sway inserted with an evil grin.

Vik gave him a lethal, cold glare.

Devyn ignored his interruption. "Security and techspert."

Instead of shaking her hand, Vik kissed it. "I'm enchanted by your beauty, my lady. Welcome aboard. You make a most welcome addition to our acerbic company . . . a lovely-smelling one, too."

"Thank you, Vik." Stepping back, she took her cap from her head. She brushed her hand through her damp bangs and tucked the cap into her back pocket. "Don't let me stop your normal routine. Consider me a ghost."

Devyn inclined his head as his link buzzed again.

Sway laughed.

"I better take this." He gave a menacing glower

to his first mate. "Sway, show Alix where to bunk. And you"—he indicated Vik—"get the ship ready to launch." He tapped his ear to open the channel. "Hi, Mom . . . No, you're not bothering me at all. It's always good to hear from you."

Alix scowled as he walked into the ship while politely talking to his mother, of all people. How strange. It seemed so incongruous that a man so feral would be that respectful of his mother.

Sway grinned at her. "You'll get used to it. Dev's his mother's only child and she's extremely protective where he's concerned. For that matter, his dad's even worse. He lost his oldest son and panics every three seconds Dev's out of his sight."

"Don't they know what he does for a living?"

"Yes, which is why they call all the time to check on him. Hell, I'm surprised he's not backjacked." Backjacked was a slang term used for the chip inserted into pets, League soldiers and slaves so that their owners could locate them.

A chip she had embedded in her own arm, which was one of the reasons she had to do what Merjack said. There was no running from a back chip. So long as Merjack knew her frequency, he could find her.

If only she knew some way to dig it out, but they'd made a mistake when they put hers in, and it was now embedded in her bone.

Sway glanced askance at her as he led the way into the ship. "You completely horrified by us?"

"Not . . . completely." But she was scared of this gruff crew. While there was a playfulness to their caustic barbs, there was also an aura of "I'll kick your ass back to the Steel Age if you so much as breathe my air the wrong way."

So she wanted to be careful until she either knew them better or had them in custody.

"Follow me."

Alix walked down the narrow corridor of the ship, her heart hammering against her ribs. She hated being on a new ship, surrounded by strangers. For the first time in her life, she didn't know every crevice of machinery, every chink in the cold, titanium walls.

She wanted to go home. But the only home she'd ever known now belonged to whoever had bought it at auction. Her throat tightened. She clenched her teeth, refusing to cry any more tears over her lost ship. She'd done what she had to, and there was no going back.

Now she had her remaining family to worry over, which meant she'd have to find evidence of Devyn's illegal activities quick so that she could free them. Every minute they were in prison was her fault.

"You can bunk in here." Sway pushed the controls to open a door.

Alix's eyes widened at the large sleeping compartment. The bed in the room occupied as much space as her entire private chambers had on her father's freighter. Rich, blue carpet lined the floor.

She'd thought only aristocrats had ships with carpet in them.

Without a word, she stepped inside and ogled the rest of the furnishings.

"I'm sure Devyn will want to run over the ship with you, but he'll probably wait until after we launch."

She found it strange that he referred to Kell by his first name. Normally the crew was more formal than that. "So how many other people make up the crew?"

Sway leaned his back against the open doorframe and folded his arms over his chest. He eyed her suspiciously. "Just what you met. You got a problem with that?"

Alix pursed her lips as she scanned Sway's body. He reminded her a lot of Captain Kell—both of them had attitude problems and a lethal undercurrent that said they could take down even a League assassin without breaking a sweat.

They also had the same tough, muscular build, but Sway wasn't quite as handsome to her. Of course, she'd never been partial to Hyshians, and Sway's yellowish eyes unnerved her.

"I've never had much of a problem with sober men chasing me around decks, if that's what you mean. As long as none of you gets desperate or drunk, I think I can manage."

Sway laughed. "I think you'll fit in pretty well with us." He tucked one of his multitude of black braids behind his left ear. "This isn't sexist or any-thing, but can you cook?"

Alix wondered at the strange question. "Noth-ing fancy, but I do all right with the basics."

"Oh, thank God. I'm sick of eating synthetic food."

"And I'm sick of listening to you bitch about it, you old woman."

Alix's heart sped up at the sound of Devyn's deep voice. She told herself not to feel this way. Her heart and body had done this to her before and she'd been crushed.

To this day, she could see Edwin's mocking sneer. *"Trust me, baby. There ain't enough woman in that boy's body of yours to ever entice a real man."*

Yeah, that had taught her to never again let a man know she was interested in him. And Edwin hadn't been anywhere near as handsome as Devyn.

Besides, she was here to ruin the captain. Some-thing that would get her killed if she wasn't careful.

Devyn knocked Sway lightly on the arm. "If you two don't mind, I think it's time we get out of here."

Sway inclined his head and left.

Alone with the captain, awkwardness consumed her. Alix studied her feet, wishing she could think of something to say. But as usual, when she was around a hot man, her brain couldn't focus on any-thing except the way his shirt clung to his muscles.

Gah, she could lick that man all night long, and she wasn't the type of woman to have those thoughts. Too many years of being the sole "entertainment" on her father's ship had left her disgusted with men in general and with sex in particular.

But then, none of her father's crew had *ever* looked like this. And that made her wonder if Devyn would actually be good in bed . . .

Stop it. He's your captain and *the man you have to frame.*

He cleared his throat. "Your cooling unit isn't stocked, but we'll take care of that at our next stop. There's plenty of water and other liquids in the galley if you start dehydrating . . . Take your time unpacking and whenever you're ready, the bridge is at the bow of the ship."

Alix nodded, still not willing to even glance at him.

She heard the door slide shut. Swallowing the lump in her throat, she finally looked at the door and sighed. She'd seen the disbelief in Devyn's eyes when she'd told him her age. His reaction was normal, but for some reason, it bothered her more that he'd done it.

"What's wrong with you?" She dumped her backpack on her bunk so that she could put her things away. "You ought to be happy you're with men who know how to actually use a shower."

Her father's mocking voice echoed in her mind. *No man wants a woman like you. Hell, you're more man than most of us with a penis. And look at yourself . . . all grimy and greasy. What man wants that? You're lucky the crew gets desperate enough to use you, though to be honest, I'd rather mastur-bate.*

She flinched and toughened her resolve. What did she care, anyway? She had no interest whatsoever in men. Love was give and take—the more you gave, the more people took. Just look at her parents. Her father could have freed her mother at any time, but no . . . he'd kept them all as slaves so that they had no choice except to put up with him. Now that he was dead, they were subject to the whims of their next owner.

Bastard.

She didn't have any use for men or love—both were selfish to the end. Or even people, for that matter. Life was hard enough without their drama.

Putting her thoughts on her task at hand, she ignored everything else.

It didn't take long to unpack her two pairs of pants, three shirts, shorts, two tanks tops, and two pantsuits from her backpack and place them in her closet. She folded her backpack up, stored it in the closet next to her clothes, then decided to join the men for the launch.

Slowly, she made her way down the corridor, dragging her finger along the sleek, cool titanium wall. Everything was so clean and new. This was such an impressive ship . . .

A soft tilt told her they were leaving the station, but the smoothness of the ride astounded her. On her old freighter, no one could stand, let alone walk, during a launch.

As she neared the bridge, she heard . . .

Was that . . .

Music?

It thrummed into the corridor at a pitch she knew must be deafening from the interior. The beat was heavy and the lyrics in-your-face. Not the kind of music she listened to, but it seemed to fit with what the captain was doing.

Frowning, she pushed the control to open the door and was almost thrown back by the force of the beat. Devyn glanced at her over his shoulder. "Hope you don't mind my taste in music. I like a little backbeat when I launch."

Sway scoffed at her. "Just wait until you're in battle with him. That shit'll make your ears bleed."

Devyn rolled his eyes. "I swear you're a woman."

"I would respond to that, but I don't want to distract you while you're attempting to drive and I'm dependent on you for my life."

"Yeah, right."

Alix hesitated. "Do you guys want me to go back to my room?"

Devyn shook his head. "You might as well get used to us. Better to find out on a short trip if we're going to get on each other's nerves. I hate taking long trips with people who annoy me." He passed a pointed stare to Sway.

Sway made an obscene gesture at him.

Devyn ignored it.

What a strange crew. Her father would have had Sway beaten for that. But it was obvious Sway was more friend than employee. Or maybe "friendly enemy" might be a better term for their relationship.

She leaned back in the cushy, plush engineer's chair that molded to her body. Oh, yeah, she could get used to this.

But she did notice someone was missing. "Where's Vik?"

Sway answered. "He's top deck. He likes to watch the colors as we shoot down the launch tube."

Okay . . .

Alix ran over the ship's settings, amazed at the updated equipment. The *Talia* had the latest of everything. She'd never even dreamed of being in something this nice. "You've got a great ship, Captain. I know you're proud of her."

Sway grinned. "If you're going to fly, only fly the best."

The ship leveled out as they entered the shipping route through the system.

Devyn flipped on his autopilot and stood. "C'mon, Alix. I'll show you around the ship."

"Ooooh," Sway breathed. "Mark the date, Vik. Dev's trusting me to fly."

Devyn made a rude sound. "No offense, but I want to live. Vik, take the helm."

Vik's insidious laugh came through an intercom over their heads. "See, Sway, that's what you get for flunking your pilot's test six times . . . which I'm pretty sure is a record of some sort. If not for the actual flunking, definitely for the persistence in pursuing that which you obviously have no talent for. Personally, I wouldn't let you fly a remote-control kid's plane."

Sway curled his lip. "Shut up before I find a can opener."

Stifling a laugh at his sullen threat, Alix left her chair to follow after Devyn. He led her around the ship, explaining various engine specifics and the location of gauges she'd be responsible for checking and maintaining.

As he ran over the logs, she frowned at their final destination for this trip. "We're flying into Paradise City?" A tremor of nervousness ran through her.

"Yeah, we'll stop on Nera VII in four days, then head out to PC. Something wrong with that?"

Well, yes. She, too, wanted to live. "I've heard it's a rough place since the rebellion broke out. Not even runners or assassins are safe there. The rebels have been rounding them up and executing anyone they deem a threat."

Devyn shrugged. "No worries. They don't scare me."

Alix cocked a brow at him, doubting his mental abilities. He'd seemed sane enough at first, but now she had to wonder. "All right, but if my brain matter ends up smeared against a wall, I'll never forgive you."

Devyn leaned across the panel in front of her, his head less than three inches from her own, and pressed a couple of switches. The fresh, manly scent of his skin and hair filled her senses. She stared at the planes of his face, wondering how it would feel to touch the sun-darkened skin with her fingertips and feel that jaw flex . . .

How his lips would taste . . .

He glanced up at her and she looked away, embarrassed by her thoughts.

"I don't let my people get hurt," he said with a tough sincerity.

"What about your last engineer?"

Laughing, he dropped his gaze back to the panel. "I lied about that. He ended up in a fight and was arrested by the yokels. I tried to get him out, but they refused bail. Poor bastard. There was nothing I could do for him."

She raised her brows, shocked by his confession. "Why'd you lie about it?"

He continued to program coordinates into the computer log. "I thought you were a kid trying to leave the station because you were mad at your parents. I figured my words would make you think twice about signing on to a ship, especially with a crew of men you don't know."

Alix smiled at his kindness, but before she could say anything, a whistle rent the air.

"Devyn!" Sway's anxious voice broke in. "I've got League ships asking for the captain. Get your ass up here. Now!"

Devyn pushed himself away from the panel. "Better get strapped in. Looks like we're going to have a bit of trouble."

Alix went rigid, knowing all too well the type

of trouble he meant. "You want me to take the guns?"

He shook his head. "No. We're runners, not smugglers."

"Is there a difference?"

He gave her a strange look that she couldn't define. "Runners are motivated by a lot more than money." He dashed down the corridor.

She followed after him.

As they took the bridge, the hailing channel buzzed in her ears. The captain of the lead ship demanded their call letters and manifests. Devyn disregarded the strident tone and strapped himself in while Vik started playing another heavy song.

Alix looked at Sway. "How much questionable cargo are we carrying?"

"Enough to put all of us in jail until we're bent double with old age." Sway turned around in his chair and tossed her a bag. "Keep that handy."

"Why?"

Before he could answer, Devyn took the controls, and the ship lurched to the right at an angle she hadn't thought possible for a craft of this size. Grateful she hadn't eaten a large lunch, she gripped the arms of her seat.

Laser canons exploded as League ships opened fire on them. For close to ten minutes, the ship bucked and dipped like some crazed beast trying to sling off a rider. Sweat covered her face as she struggled not to undignify herself with her heaving stomach.

All of a sudden, Devyn fired the retrorockets and the ship jerked to a crawl. Alix looked up with a frown, only to wish she hadn't.

Before them, three battleships waited with a tractor net spread out in two directions. The other tracers were closing in behind them.

A trickle of sweat ran down her cheek. She swallowed the lump in her throat and tightened her grip on the armrests.

They were about to be caught and jailed.

CHAPTER 2

"Surrender your ship, crew, and cargo," a gruff voice demanded over the hailing channel.

Devyn's response was curt and to the point. "Bite my ass."

The ship fired a warning blast across the bow. "This is your last chance. The next one will be through your bridge."

Devyn didn't even flinch as he laughed at their threat. "Come get some."

"Shall I concentrate extra power to the shields?" Vik asked.

"Yes!" Alix and Sway shouted in unison.

Devyn shook his head like they were pansics.

Sway pulled his legs up to his chest, laid his head on his knees, and covered it with his arms. "Dev, I really hate it when you do this."

Alix swallowed in fear. By now she'd learned enough about the captain to realize he wasn't going to surrender. In fact, he stared at the surrounding ships with a look on his face that told her how much he was enjoying the threat. Though to be honest, she had no idea how they were going to get out of this. The League ships had their hyperdrive blocked, so they had no hope of outrunning them.

They couldn't escape.

And they were seriously outgunned.

But none of that seemed to stop Devyn from trying.

"Alix," Devyn said. "Put your head down and take a deep breath."

He didn't look at her, but from the tone of his voice she could just imagine the gleam in his eyes. Quickly, she duplicated Sway's position.

Devyn's hands flew over the control panel, making adjustments to the ship's settings. "Vik? You ready?"

A dry, arrogant tone came through the ship's intercom. "Your stupidity is what I live for, Captain. Shall I make calculations on the usual?"

"If you want to live, yes."

"Done. Releasing safeties in three . . . two . . . one."

Devyn took control from the computer as all electronic controls and safeguards were dropped and the ship switched to complete manual control.

Ah, God, we're going to die . . .

Nothing would keep them from slamming into something or banking too hard or . . .

Don't think about it.

Through a miracle of his piloting abilities, the ship dropped straight down at the same instant The League opened fire on them. Alix's stomach lurched straight up. The ship's gravity field switched off automatically, and the unexpected weightlessness hit her like an asteroid.

She gripped her legs, her body rigid in expectation.

Fighters moved in to shoot and cut them off. Devyn banked as two shots impacted against their side. A battle cruiser launched its tractor net. Devyn hit the retrockets, allowing it to shoot past their prow, narrowly missing them.

Two more ships moved in.

Devyn plunged them straight down, spinning the ship to avoid the blasts aimed at them.

Then, just as she thought she'd definitely be sick, they stopped descending. They drifted for half a heartbeat before Devyn fired the rear engines. The sudden force lurched her back against the seat with an impact she was certain would leave a long bruise down her spine.

Shots fired all around them, some hitting the ship dead-on. Luckily, the shields held and all it did was cause them to rock and spin.

Within a minute, they hit a natural hyperspace opening and were slung out of the sector.

Alix held her breath until she was sure their pursuers hadn't followed them in. She checked the gauges, which confirmed her relief. It appeared they were safe.

"Everyone all right?" Devyn asked as he flipped the gravity back on.

Sway growled irritably as he unwrapped himself. "I think I just gave birth. Damn. And I'm the one who flunked the pilot's test?"

Vik let out his own noise of agitation. "If you really want to get him into trouble, capture one of his stunts and email it to his mother. She'd have his ass in traction over it."

Devyn shook his head. "Any more bitching from the geriatric crew? What a bunch of old women. Should I hire another crewmate to change your bed diapers while I'm at it? Next time I'll let The League have you." He clicked the sublight panel on. "Vik, I'm relinquishing control back to you."

"It's what I live for. By the way, ye organic life forms aren't the only ones who've soiled themselves. Can I have a minute to attend my needs, Captain Asshole?"

Devyn let out a sound of supreme disgust. "You would think one of you could say, 'Great flying, Captain. Thanks for saving our worthless asses.' "

His words amused her, but she couldn't quite bring a smile to her shaking lips. He was right, though. That was some of the best flying she'd ever seen.

Sway wiped an arm across his sweat-covered brow. "One day, someone's going to make the markings on this ship, and then we're going to be absolutely screwed."

Devyn shrugged off the warning. "They might, but there's never been a League prober born who could outmaneuver a Dagan and you know it."

Alix looked up at the mention of the Dagan surname. Everyone in the shipping or running business knew of the infamous family of smugglers. Their exploits were legendary, especially Caillen Dagan. That man had been a god among smugglers and had vanished mysteriously in the prime of his career.

And Devyn's relation to them was something extremely important Merjack had failed to tell her during his briefing. Anyone related to that family was indeed someone to be reckoned with.

Sway scoffed. "Your aunt and uncle would be proud of you, no doubt. But your mother would have your head if she ever saw you do what you do."

Devyn swung his chair around to face Alix. "Any complaints you want to add to his?"

Startled by his sudden attention to her, she focused her gaze on his dangerous brown eyes. She wasn't used to men who joked about life and death, and the things in between.

Her father and his crew had possessed no sense of humor whatsoever.

A strange surge of emotion filled her, but she couldn't quite name the sensation. She shook her head. "No complaints, Captain, but as soon as my legs can walk again, I think I need to lie down."

Sway shook his head. "See, Dev, you've already crippled our new engineer. Good job, dumbass."

Ignoring him, Devyn unstrapped himself from his seat. "C'mon, I'll help you to your room."

Alix started to protest, but the words stumbled on her tongue as she looked up at him standing over her. Maybe it was the lighting, or her shaky nerves, or maybe her leftover fear. She wasn't sure what caused her sudden muteness, but as she watched him, she could barely breathe.

Gracious, he was sexy and disturbing.

He unstrapped her and helped her up from her chair. A half smile played across his lips with a devastating effect on her. No longer sure if her shaky legs were a result of the flight or the man, she slumped against his long, lean body.

Devyn draped her right arm over his shoulders and held her wrist with his right hand. He wrapped his other arm around her waist. She swallowed at the intimate contact.

"I think I can manage to make my way on my own."

His gaze burned into hers, and for a moment she feared he might be able to see past her defenses and detect the way he unnerved her.

Or worse, see her deceit.

"C'mon. It's not often I get to play a gallant hero to a damsel I distressed. Don't interfere with my good deed for the decade. I assure you, they're few and far between."

Well, since he put it that way . . .

The heat of his body warmed hers as he led her from the bridge and down the corridor. Goodness, but he smelled delectable. It was such a sharp, spicy scent . . .

All man and all good.

She swallowed as she tried to think of something

that could distract her from her thoughts. "That was some really good flying, Captain. How'd you know a hyperspace opening was there?"

That devilish grin returned. "I inherited my uncle's star charts that detail every opening in the trigalaxies. Most of them are unknown by anyone except my family. I've found them immensely helpful whenever The League thinks they've got my hyperdrive locked down." His eyes twinkled in the dim light. "They can block our ship, but they can't block the entire galaxy."

Alix frowned. "Your uncle?"

"Caillen Dagan."

Her stomach hit the floor. Caillen Dagan was the baddest of the bad. Even though he'd vanished when she'd been in diapers, smugglers and League officials still wet themselves whenever his name was mentioned. His reputation was the stuff of legends. "I heard he was dead."

He didn't respond to either confirm or deny it.

She narrowed her gaze on him. "Are you really a Dagan?"

Devyn nodded, his features serious. "Son of a Dagan Seax and the equally notorious C.I. Syn. Only fitting I ended up on the questionable side of the law."

Alix came to a complete stop. C.I. Syn was the most infamous filch and assassin who ever lived. Again, his name alone sent terror through the hearts of anyone who heard it.

And here she was, standing next to his son.

How much of his father's brutality had Devyn inherited?

He gave her a gimlet stare. "You got a problem with my history?"

Nice attitude. Obviously he was defensive about his parents. Not that she blamed him. She'd be a little waxed, too, if she had a genetic link to people like that.

She shook her head in honesty. "No, but I'm curious about how your parents met."

The question seemed to amuse him. "My mom was hired to track my dad down and arrest him."

"I take it she let him go."

"No. She shot and stabbed him the first time they met and did, in fact, hand him over to the authorities . . . twice."

She was completely stunned by what he described. "And he let her live?"

He shrugged. "My dad's a forgiving man where my mom's concerned."

Obviously. Still, how could anyone be *that* tolerant? She couldn't imagine ever forgiving someone for shooting her.

"And I thought my parents had a screwed-up relationship."

Devyn cocked an eyebrow. "I know your father ran a freighter. What about your mom?"

She squelched her sudden burst of panic before she gave herself away. He must never know about her mother or her sister. She couldn't even think about that right now without her head becoming light and her sight dimming in mortal terror.

She had no doubt that this fierce man would absolutely *kill* her if he ever learned she was here to betray him and his crew.

"She . . ." Alix paused while trying to think up a believable lie. She shifted her gaze to the floor, hoping he couldn't detect her deceit. "She disappeared when I was just a kid. I don't really remember her."

Skittish about the turn in their conversation, she let go of him and sprinted the rest of the way to her room.

Devyn scowled at her hasty departure. "Alix?"

She didn't even pause.

How weird was that? But there had been no mistaking the frightened look he'd seen on her face when he asked about her mother. Tempted to go after her, he decided it would be best to give her time to get used to all of them slowly.

Trusting strangers wasn't easy for most people. In all honesty, he envied her that suspicious nature. Blind trust had gotten him screwed more times than he could count.

All right, Alix. Keep your secrets. So long as they don't threaten the crew, I'll let you live.

Alix sat on her bed, dreading what she was going to have to do—scan the ship's logs looking for proof of Devyn's criminal activities, then transmit them to

Merjack. But honestly, she was scared of being caught. What would they do to her?

Kill you.

Most likely. *It'll probably be brutal, too. They might even feed you to the dog.*

He doesn't have a dog.

Yeah, well, he might get one just to feed you to it.

She'd never been the kind of person to let something as ridiculous as rational logic interfere with her fear. And while she sat in indecision, her parched throat begged for something to drink.

Well, she didn't have much choice. She had to go find something to drink before the dehydration made her sick.

She got up and decided to try the bridge first. If her luck held, Sway or Vik would be there, and Devyn would have gone on to do something else.

Reaching the door, she pushed the touch-activated lock. The portal opened and she sighed in disgust. Since when had luck ever been on her side? Devyn stood to her right, leaning over a panel where he worked. He glanced up at her. "I'm glad you're here. I thought I was going to have to wake you."

Alix frowned at his tone, which landed somewhere between frustration and relief. "What's wrong?"

"I've got a fluctuation in the radiation shielding and I think gamma rays are leaking in. Vik can't pinpoint it."

Alix's eyes widened. She didn't like the sound of

that at all. Stepping up to the panel, she ran over the gauges. They had pulled out of hyperspace and were traveling at fifty-percent light speed. She glanced over the diagnostic test Devyn was running and saw the leak.

"Out of curiosity, where did Vik go? I haven't seen him since we launched."

"He's plugged into the ship." Devyn looked up. "Vik, say hi to the lady."

"Must I when I'm trying to find a leak? Contrary to your beliefs, just because I'm a mecha, I'm not immune to it. It could melt my wiring as easily as it can mutate you."

Devyn rolled his eyes. "He's a surly bastard. You'll get used to him."

She wasn't too sure about that, and if he was part of the ship, that made her job a lot harder. Vik would know the instant she started pulling up data on Devyn. "So where's the shield's power source?"

"I'll show you." Devyn led her back to the corridor.

Halfway down the hall, he stopped and pushed the controls for a lift to the lower deck. "The air gets a bit thin. If you start getting sick, let me know."

"Believe me, if I start getting sick, you'll be the first to know since I'm sure it'll be all over you."

Without responding to her sarcasm, he stepped into the lift. Alix followed, but quickly wished she hadn't. The small compartment forced them together in an intimate proximity she found horribly unsettling. She bit her lip and tried not to brush up against his hard, muscular body. All too well, she remembered how it felt to be in his arms.

"When did you notice the leak?" she asked, trying to distract herself from those thoughts about him.

"A few minutes ago. I was about to buzz your room for you to come investigate this." He looked down at her and smiled. "So what brought you out?"

She licked her dry lips. "Dehydration."

A deep frown creased his brow. "Why didn't you say something before I brought you down here?"

The anger in his voice startled her. "Why are you growling at me?"

"I don't know. I'm frustrated, and you should have told me you were thirsty. That's not something to play around with out here." For such a reasonable response, the tone of his voice wavered on violence.

"Well, I'd rather die of thirst than radiation poisoning. I daresay it's less painful."

Devyn relaxed a little. "I guess you're right."

Alix stared up at him. Never in her life had she been so attracted to a man. Maybe the knowledge that she couldn't have him caused the strong attraction. Or was it his feral reputation that enticed her so? She knew he was capable of killing anyone who got in his way . . .

Especially her.

Whatever the source of her attraction, all she

wanted was to taste his lips and feel his arms around her once again.

With a soft whir, the door opened. Relieved, Alix walked out first. Stepping past her, Devyn led her to the engineering room and punched in a sequence of keys to open the door. "The code to enter the room is ClAria 1-8-4-9-3. Capital on the C and the middle A."

A wave of disappointment ran through her at the mention of a woman's name and the note of obvious affection in his voice when he spoke of her. Was that the woman Merjack had said she favored? "Claria?"

"Sway's wife."

She'd known from the gold band on his arm that Sway was married, but it still caught her off guard. "Is she not part of the crew?" Since runners could spend months at a time on a mission, it wasn't unusual for a married man to have his wife on board.

"No. Claria's a junior senator for the Hyshian government. Since she travels so much, and they don't have any children for him to watch, Sway stays with me."

Alix frowned at him. "That sounds odd."

He shrugged. "Only by most humans' standards. The Hyshians are obscenely matriarchal. The males can't do anything without female consent. The men even take their wife's name."

She found his good humor infectious as he looked at her with those dark eyes. Still, the thought of owning someone, even in marriage, was revolting to her. Having been a slave her entire life, she couldn't imagine voluntarily subjugating herself to someone else. "How does he stand it?"

"He loves her more than his life. But it can be hard for him to submit. Hyshian males are as aggressive as any other. I've been told that some wives drug their spouses to keep them in line. Some even surgically alter them."

"And their culture allows this?"

He held his hands up in surrender. "I hear you. Believe me, I'm grateful to the gods that I'm not one of them. But in defense of their culture, Sway's mother was never like that. Probably because her father was human. Jayne has always been respectful of her husband and sons, and Claria's the same way . . . most of the time. It's why she allows Sway to travel with me even though she takes a lot of shit from her family and others for not riding herd on him. She's a good woman, so I stay out of it."

He entered the room and started checking over the system's gauges. "That being said, because of their laws, I'm Sway's legal chaperone—which is why he gives me such grief about my mom's calls. He considers it justice over the way I taunt him."

Alix wondered at his words. "So how did you end up as his chaperone?"

"Our parents are close friends and we grew up like brothers. When he married, Claria wanted to keep him happy, so she asked me to take custody of him. It felt kind of weird to have custody of someone older than me, especially at first, but I didn't want him forced to live with Claria's mother, who would have driven him mental with her bullshit rules for his behavior." He glanced up from the panel. "What about you? You have any siblings?"

A cold, twisting lump coiled in her stomach, and she feared for a moment she might be sick.

Don't think about it. Because when she did, she wanted to cry. Her sister was only fifteen, and she'd do anything to keep Tempest safe.

Not to mention her mother.

But she couldn't tell Devyn about them. If she did, he'd want to know where they were and why she'd left them.

Alix dropped her gaze and looked over the control panel for the shield's leak. "I told you I don't have any family ties."

"Sorry, I forgot."

She hadn't meant for her reply to be so curt. She tried to ignore her guilt—and his presence—as she concentrated on her task, but it wasn't easy.

It didn't take long to isolate the leak and correct it. "There." She stepped back to show him. "It's all fixed."

Devyn checked the gauges.

She studied his frown of consternation and smiled. "How is it a pilot of your abilities doesn't know anything about ship maintenance?"

He shrugged. "My dad tried his best to teach me engineering all through my childhood, but I'm missing that gene—too much like my mom. For some reason, I can't wrap my mind around mechanics. All I know is how to check things, fly them and shoot them when they really piss me off. What about you? Can you pilot?"

"I can do a launch sequence, but that's about all. I couldn't get near the directional controls unless my father passed out."

She bit her lip in shock at the slip she'd made, but she couldn't seem to help herself. There was something about Devyn that stripped away all the careful barriers she'd built for herself. In spite of the fact that he was lethal, he was way too easy to talk to.

A flicker of anger touched Devyn's eyes but quickly vanished, and it made her wonder why.

"Is that why you became an engineer?"

She brushed her hand across her cheek, skimming the tiny scar just below her right eye from when her father had slung her against a control panel a few years ago after she'd made a simple mistake. "No. My father didn't like paying the extra money to hire an engineer, so one day he handed me a wrench and a manual and told me to fix the side stabilizer or get off the ship."

Devyn stared at her in disbelief. The blasé tone of her voice told him more about her than the words themselves. Her father had been a real bastard. Even so, she hadn't let him hold her back. A surge of admiration ran through him. "I bet you fixed it like new."

She gave an undignified snort. "No. It went out

before we could even complete the launch. Ended up busting one of the cargo bays and losing half our shipment. Not one of my finer moments or memories, to be sure."

Devyn studied her halfhearted smile. "I'll keep that in mind if one of ours ever goes out."

She gave him a guarded look that made him regret his words. He'd meant them as humor, but obviously she didn't appreciate it. So he filed that away as a topic to never mention again, even in jest.

As she stayed beside him, he stared at her eyes. They were such an unusual shade, probing, intelligent, and pain-filled. For some reason, he wanted to soothe away the agony that blazed in defiance of him and the whole universe.

In spite of her rough, prickly defenses, she was an attractive woman with a quiet assuredness he found refreshing.

The women he'd known had all played major head games, but she didn't seem to. She was very straightforward and professional. He liked that.

Unlike Clotilde . . .

It was all he could do not to wince. Even dead, she wasn't quite dead enough. Her viciousness lived on in his memory and made him want to dig her up just so he could kill her again.

And right now, he knew he should walk away from Alix. She was a member of his crew, and business and pleasure shouldn't mix. But he couldn't seem to stop himself from touching her soft cheek, or brushing her lips with his thumb.

This is sexual harassment. You're going to get sued.

Yet right now . . .

He really didn't care.

Alix opened her mouth to speak, but no sound came out. Her cheek burned under the weight of his fingers. She wanted his kiss, and a small voice inside told her it was more than mere want. She needed it.

Her experience with men had been severely tainted by her "duties" with her father's crew. None of them had ever kissed her worth a damn. But she suspected Devyn Kell wouldn't be clumsy with his attempt. Nor would he try to give her a tonsillectomy.

She would lay money that his kiss would be the stuff of legends . . .

His hand paused on her cheek. He closed his eyes and dipped his head toward hers.

"Dev? Where are you?"

Silently, Alix cursed Sway's Hyshian hide for the interruption. Just a few more seconds and he could've called without her wanting to strangle him.

Was one decent kiss in her life too much to ask?

Devyn blinked in confusion, as if he were waking from a dream, then dropped his hand from her face and took a step back.

Her skin still tingling, Alix wanted desperately to return to the mood, but it was too late.

Sway had destroyed it.

She sighed in disgust. Luck would never be her friend.

Devyn moved to the wall intercom. "What do you need?"

"I need you to get your ass up here and assure Claria that Alix is human and that you're not going to leave me alone with her. She's stroking over stupid jealousy. I swear I should have lied to her."

Devyn rolled his eyes in obvious frustration.

Alix laughed.

"I'm on my way."

She stepped away from him. "Ever wish subspace transmissions were impossible?"

"Only every time my mom or Claria calls."

Her smile widened.

They remained silent the whole way back to the main deck. Devyn stepped out of the lift first. "The galley is all the way down the corridor on the left. Search through the cooling unit until you find something you like."

Alix stared after him as he walked toward the bridge, amazed he'd remembered her thirst.

Her throat tightened as longing raced through her.

You're not here to hook up with him.

No, she was here for something sinister, and the guilt of it was unbearable.

Maybe you could trust him . . .

Yeah, right. People were crap and they betrayed. She knew that better than anyone. If she told him what was going on, he'd kill her and let her mother and sister burn.

She'd lived her entire life under dire, soul-wrenching threats, and that had been from the man who fathered her. The man who was supposed to love her.

Just imagine what a stranger would do to her.

With a determined stride, she crossed her arms over her chest and headed to the galley.

What she wouldn't give for the type of friendship Devyn and Sway shared. Someone she could talk things over with, release the darkest secret of her soul.

Don't. As long as you keep your mouth shut, no one will ever know what you are. You'll be free.

Free. It was the one thing she'd always wanted. And if it was the last thing she did, she would be emancipated.

Even if it meant Devyn's life.

"What are you doing?"

Alix jumped at her desk as Vik's booming voice startled her. It came through the speaker in the ceiling above her head. "Nothing." Gah, she hoped he didn't hear the panic and fear she felt in her voice.

"You're not authorized to view the captain's logs or any of the files you're trying to access. They are strictly locked."

She'd been afraid of him saying that, but at least he wasn't trying to arrest her or notify Devyn. "I was just curious about the types of missions we carry out."

There, she almost sounded normal.

"Then you can ask about what you want to know."

But that wouldn't get her the proof she needed to hand over to Merjack. Damn Vik for being so alert.

"So what kind of missions do we carry out?"

"Not me, bonebag. You'll have to ask Devyn."

Yes, but he might get suspicious and then where would she be? Launched into space, most likely. "Wouldn't it be easier for you to tell me?"

"Not for me it wouldn't, and I'm not here to make *your* life easier."

Which made her wonder what he *was* here for. "So what is your programming?"

"To protect Devyn at all costs and against all enemies."

That was a scary prospect. "Even at your own risk?"

"I'm here to die for him if need be. Not because it's my programming, but because I love him. His survival is far more important to me than my own."

That didn't make any sense. He was an AI and should have no real feelings. Only simulated ones. Yet there was no mistaking the loyalty she'd heard in his voice.

But that was neither here nor there.

She had to find evidence to use against Captain Kell. "Is there anything you *can* show me?"

He popped up a live feed of her sitting at her desk in her quarters.

"You're not exactly helpful, Vik."

"Not true. I'm extremely helpful. Just not to

people I don't know. Which, in case my subtlety is lost, would be you. No one accesses our records until they pass my security clearance and Devyn authorizes it."

"And how does one do that?"

"Take a shot for Devyn and we'll talk."

In other words, the metallic bastard wasn't about to trust her at all.

What am I going to do?

"You don't like me very much, do you?" she asked him.

"I don't know you. Therefore like and dislike are inapplicable terms. However, I love Devyn and Sway. So I think you will forgive me for being protective of my charges. They are all that matters to me."

She smiled sadly. How she wished she had such loyalty in her life from a friend, even an artificial one. "I forgive you, Vik, and I respect you for it. You're a good man."

"Mecha, you mean."

She looked up at the intercom he was speaking out of. "No, you're more man than most of the ones I've known. Good night, Vik."

He hesitated before he spoke. "Good night, Alix. Shall I adjust your environment before you retire?"

His offer touched her. No one had ever cared before if she was comfortable or not when she slept. "No, thank you. I'm good."

Still, he dimmed the lights for her. "Don't worry. I won't be peeping into your room while you sleep or move about. I'm a paladin, not a perv. I only have the monitors on now because you were acting suspiciously."

She let out a nervous laugh. "Thanks. I appreciate that."

Pushing her chair back, she stood and then froze in place as the reality of her current surroundings hit her. She was on board a ship that was top-notch with a crew of men who treated her like a human being. Men who seemed to be looking after her.

Not in her wildest dreams had she ever thought to have even a single day of this.

And I have to betray them all.

It was so unfair. But then, that was life. Injustice had been rammed down her throat since the moment she'd learned to swallow.

Somehow she would have to learn to bypass Vik's security system and get proof of Kell's illegal activities.

Maybe when they landed on Nera, she'd be able to stay on board while he followed them to their meeting. Then she could scan the files without Vik being any the wiser.

She hoped.

The next day flew by as she acquainted herself with the ship and its subtle nuances and quirks.

Machinery was like people, each a unique entity that had to be learned. But that being said, Vik had to be the most irritating thing ever created. No matter how she tried to find evidence on Kell, whether it was scanning their cargo or trying to get a shipping manifest, he was there to question her over it.

Like a spider.

And because he was a mecha, he didn't sleep or go to the bathroom. He didn't shower.

Nothing.

Ugh!

They're going to die and it's going to be all my fault. She couldn't stand the constant pressure that hung around her shoulders, threatening to pull her into insanity.

What am I going to do?

She had to find or plant something incriminating, but every time she went near a computer to run their inventory, Vik stuck his nose in it.

Unable to cope, she went to the rec room, hoping to find some workout routine that could help take the edge off her panic. But as she stepped into the darkened room, she froze.

Devyn was there.

Wearing a tight black VR suit that was trimmed in green and silver, he appeared to be running through a training exercise. Mesmerized, she watched as he fought against enemies only he could see.

Wow . . . his entire body was a symphony of sinew and grace. And he moved like lightning.

Fierce. Strong. Fluid. Honestly, she'd never known that a man could move like that. She doubted if even an assassin could match his skill.

I don't ever want to be on the receiving end of that . . .

The lights in the room flashed before Devyn came to a stop. His breathing labored, he pulled his helmet off.

Damn . . .

Sweat made his tawny skin glisten, and his black hair was plastered against those perfect features. The sight of him like that made her instantly wet as he licked his lips and brushed his hand through the damp strands to push his hair out of his eyes.

And when he saw her, the smile that spread across his face did the strangest things to her will.

"I didn't hear you come in. Sorry." He unzipped the VR suit and peeled it off until he wore nothing but a sleeveless gray T-shirt and a pair of tight black shorts.

She wanted to respond, but her tongue was too thick to cooperate. All she could focus on was how incredible that ripped body was.

I so want a piece of that . . .

Alix, get a grip.

Yeah, but the problem was, she only wanted a grip on him. Oh, dear lord, he was fine.

He's a killer. A felon.

He's the hottest thing on two legs.

There was definitely no denying it.

He picked up a towel to dry his hair. "You coming to work out?"

"Yes." True, her voice was breathless, but at least this time she managed to speak a whole cognitive syllable.

"You want me to reset the machine?"

No. I want to ride you until you're begging me for mercy. Clearing her throat, she tried to shove that image out of her mind. "That would be great. Thanks."

And strip off the rest of your clothes while you're doing that.

She clenched her teeth in frustration at herself for those thoughts she couldn't seem to stop. Why was her body doing this to her? She never reacted to a man like this.

You're a frigid bitch. I swear you have ice in your veins.

She cringed at the memory of Irn's voice in her head. He'd been a nasty bastard. Taking all of her father's money had been the least of his crimes. Truth was, she'd been relieved when he left. Her biggest fear had been of him raping her sister while they slept. She was still amazed they'd managed to survive without that happening.

Probably only because her mother slept in the room with them and everyone knew Alix slept fully armed. She would never willingly be a victim to anyone. Her father might have made her the crew whore, but she refused to be raped.

Devyn frowned at Alix's continued silence. He

glanced at her, only to have her look quickly away. A slow smile broke over his face as he realized she'd been eying his ass. While she was distracted, he traced her curves with his gaze. Though she wasn't the kind of skinny women strove for, she was none-theless stunning. It was obvious she worked out and had the kind of body a man would love to have wrapped around his for days on end.

And her hair . . .

He'd always been a sucker for long hair. Yet for some reason, all the women he'd dated had always cropped theirs short. Alix's looked so soft that his palm itched to feel it.

More than that, he wanted to bury his face in it and inhale until he was drunk on her scent.

You have been way too long without a woman.

That was certainly true. After the last few women he'd hooked up with, he'd decided he was tired of the drama that came in most shapely pack-ages. He liked his life uncomplicated and his rela-tionships honest.

And short.

Yet for some reason, he kept finding women who wanted to stir up shit and lie to him about the most basic of things. After he'd finally man-aged to get the last cloying beast off his back, he'd decided he'd rather handle himself than deal with their issues.

And still, Alix appealed to him on a level he'd forgotten existed.

Shaking his head to clear it of the image of her

going down on him, he finished resetting the program.

"I had a fight sequence going. You want something more mundane?"

She pulled her hair back from her face and
secured it with a band. "Yeah. Running."

"Desert, urban, beach, country . . ."

"Countryside."

He frowned. She didn't strike him as a rural
kind of woman. "Really?"

She nodded. "I like the greenery and foliage.
When I was little, I used to try and grow plants on
my dad's ship."

That had to be tough. Most living things didn't
like the recycled air and lack of natural daylight.
"Didn't work?"

She shook her head. "I never could get the hy-
droponics or lights right."

"Sorry." He stepped away from the machine and
picked up his suit. "If it makes you feel better, I
once tried to grow a monkey."

"A monkey?"

He laughed at the memory. "You know the
candy, Monkey Seeds?" They were nothing but
chocolate-covered raisins—a nasty candy, really,
but it was one his dad loved and it was something
Devyn's mother always kept in large supplies for
him.

"Yeah."

"I thought if I planted them, they'd grow monkeys."

Alix laughed at the image of the fierce captain trying his hand at farming. And for something so ridiculous . . . He must have been adorable. "How old were you?"

"Five or six. I would run out every morning to see if my monkeys had sprouted. My mom didn't have the heart to tell me I was wasting my time. So my dad created a monkey body for Vik and buried him in the garden. He crawled out one afternoon while I was watering the seeds."

"No, he didn't."

"Yeah, he did. Since my dad had also altered his voice track, it took me a full hour before I realized my monkey was Vik."

"Were you angry?"

"Nah. But Vik, being Vik, finally explained to me why he was the only monkey I'd ever have."

"And I've been your monkey ever since."

A charming grin broke across Devyn's face as he looked up at the speaker. "Nah. You're not my monkey, Vik. You're my bitch."

"Of course I am. And I'll remember that the next time your shower door is stuck and you want me to open it . . . Wait. That does make me your bitch, doesn't it? Damn, I'm whipped."

Alix's humor died as Devyn drew near and she saw the awful jagged scar on his left arm that twisted from just above his elbow all the way down to his wrist. "That looks like it hurt."

He glanced down and shrugged. "It did."

"What did you do to get it?"

"Knife fight with a Partini."

She was impressed. The Partanai were renowned for their fighting skills. "And you lived?"

"Obviously so."

"What about your opponent?"

"He wasn't so lucky. I don't like to be attacked, especially when it's unprovoked. That never goes well for the aggressor."

"You actually killed him?" It was virtually unheard of for a human to kill a Partini.

He gave her a bland stare. "I was a League soldier, Alix. I've killed a lot of people in my career."

That was another thing Merjack had failed to mention. "How long did you serve?"

Devyn fell silent as he remembered his stint. He still couldn't believe he'd been so stupid as to sign up. Gah, what an idiot he'd been. "Almost four years." The most miserable years of his life.

He hoped.

"No wonder you can fight so well."

He snorted at that. "Trust me, that wasn't from The League. I knew how to fight long before I joined."

"Your father?"

"Among others. I was raised by The Sentella."

Alix took an involuntary step back. The Sentella was the only group that had ever successfully stood against The League. Started long before she'd been born, and run by outlaws and criminals, it was legendary. "You're not joking."

"Why would I?"

Yeah, why would he? It wasn't like he was trying to pick her up or impress her. "I don't know. A lot of people do that sort of thing."

"Not me. I hate lies."

And he will never forgive you for the lies you're speaking.

What does that matter? Her sister and mother were the only people she loved and she would do anything to keep them safe.

Devyn paused next to her. Given his sweaty condition, she expected him to stink. But he didn't. His body held a warm, delicious scent.

Mmm, she could breathe that in all night long.

She looked up and caught the hungry light in his eyes. It was mesmerizing and made her even hotter.

Wetter.

All she wanted was one single taste of those gorgeous lips . . .

Devyn told himself to walk on, yet he couldn't. When he looked at her, he remembered those early days of being with Clotilde. That sense of wonder and discovery.

The sex that had set him on fire.

She's not Clotilde.

No, she was Alix. Competent and sweet. There had never been anything sweet or even kind in Clotilde's makeup. She'd been vicious and lethal. At times he couldn't remember why he'd even wanted to marry her except for the fact that she was incredible in bed. That woman had had a way with her mouth that was unrivaled and she had blistered his sheets.

But as he looked into Alix's dark blue eyes, he felt like he was drowning. And all he wanted to do was taste her lips. To feel her hands on his skin.

I'm losing my mind.

"Devyn . . . Omari's calling."

Vik's voice snapped him right out of it and grounded him back to the real world where captains didn't make time with their engineers. "Tell him I'll be right there."

Alix scowled as Devyn literally ran from the room as if he'd been shot out of a proton cannon. Wondering about his actions, she looked up at the intercom. "Vik? Who's Omari?"

"Devyn's son."

The words hit her like a sledgehammer. Devyn had a son? "His son lives with his mother?"

"I'm not at liberty to comment on Master Omari or his whereabouts. You'll have to ask Devyn about him."

"Okay, but can I at least ask if the captain is married?"

"No."

That wasn't exactly helpful, and she had a feeling Vik liked being difficult. "No he's not married, or no I can't ask about it?"

He laughed before he answered. "He's not married."

"Thanks, Vik." Alix went over to the player to

turn it on while her thoughts stayed on the fact that Devyn was a father. Every time she turned around he was another surprise.

Just who was this man she was going to have to send to jail? How old was his son? She didn't want to leave someone without their father. While hers had sucked, at least he'd been there, and to hurt a kid . . .

Stop it. It doesn't matter.

Think of Tempest. She was barely more than a child herself, and the last thing Alix wanted was to see her sister raped by a madman.

You will hand him in and never think about it again.

CHAPTER 3

Alix grunted as she tried to get enough torque to loosen the screw on the panel she was attempting to open. Why couldn't she get this stupid thing to budge?

Out of nowhere, Devyn appeared.

"Need a hand?"

She started to turn him down, but he took the wrench from her hand and popped the panel open with a frustrating ease that disgusted her. Oh, to have one minute of that strength . . .

"Thanks, Captain."

"You know you can call me Devyn. We're not exactly formal around here."

She didn't comment as she stuck her head into the opening to look at the pipe she'd been eyeing on their schematics. Since she was trying to frame the man, she really didn't want to get that familiar with him.

Devyn sighed at her cold aloofness. He really didn't understand her. Sometimes she looked at him as if she were imagining him naked and other times, she was absolutely frigid. It was like she was trying to keep some kind of wall between them. And for some reason that bothered him.

His gaze dropped down and went straight to her shapely ass as she strained to reach something inside. Heat surged straight to his cock, which hardened instantly at the prospect of what he wanted to do to her.

Damn, I need to get laid.

Because right now all he could think of was stripping her clothes off and tasting every inch of her lithe body. What would she taste like?

Was she a screamer or more calm?

She pulled back to look at him.

He brought his gaze up to her face and had to stifle a smile as she blushed.

"We have a problem. There's a defect in two gaskets that are causing the radiation leak. We need to replace them."

Great. He looked up at the camera where Vik kept watch on the ship. "Vik?"

"Yes, my lord and tormentor?"

"Do we have any spare gaskets for the reflectors?"

"No."

"Any particular reason why not?"

"Sway's an idiot who didn't order them when we used up the last batch."

"Isn't that your job?"

"No. I'm the sub-idiot. Sway's head idiot because the company refuses to deal with mechas. Since I'm not organic, they think I can't pay."

"Thanks, Vik."

"Ever my pleasure to irritate you, sir."

Devyn looked at Alix. "And the sarcasm just keeps on coming without end. Makes me proud. Really." He sobered. "Is it something that can wait?"

"Depends on how much radiation you mind being exposed to. The levels are class two."

He arched a brow as the doctor in him kicked in. "We don't want to have any three-headed children."

"I'd like to do without it and keep my hair, too."

A smile toyed at the edges of his lips. "Vik? Where's the closest stop?"

Vik let out a dramatic sigh. "Not like you couldn't run a search for yourself, is it?"

"Just run the damn search."

"There's one on Miremba II. A couple of hours from here."

He growled at the aggravation. Miremba IV was owned by the Gourish, but II . . . "That's Rit territory, isn't it?"

"Last I looked."

Devyn cursed.

Alix was confused by his anger. "What's wrong with the Rits?" Other than the fact that Merjack, the Ritadarion Chief Minister of Justice, wanted to torture and kill him.

"Bad family history with the Rits. I try to stay out of their territory if I can . . . Vik? Is there anyplace else?"

"Don't you think by now that I've learned how to read a map? If there had been another place to go, I would have suggested it. Yes, there are other places, several days from here. But that wasn't what you asked me."

Devyn let out another feral growl. "Set the course and stay alert."

"Yes, Captain Courageous."

Alix pulled the panel closed. Devyn held it in place as she tightened the screws. "May I pry as to what happened with the Rits?"

Devyn started to tell her to mind her own business, but what difference did it make? If she did even a modest search on his parents, she'd find it all out, anyway. "My parents brought down their ruling house a few years before I was born. As a result, the Rits are holding a grudge against any Dagan or Syn they can find. Being their only child, I'm a special nubby treat for the Rits."

"But your last name's Kell."

His grin was even more charming. "And now you know why. My parents were paranoid that one of the Rits would take revenge on me for what they did, so I've never had their names. Hell, their real names aren't even listed on my birth certificate."

She gaped at that. In this day and age when IDs ruled everything, how had he gone to school or even owned anything? "Then how—"

"They had fake IDs they used whenever I had to register for something as a kid. Keeping me safe and alive has always been their primary objective."

She couldn't fathom that kind of love. Her father

would have gladly thrown her to the worst predators to keep himself safe.

And it went a long way in explaining why Merjack was so gung-ho to get him. He was in a grudge match with the ones who'd taken down his family. "Have you ever done anything to the Rits?"

"No. As I said, we stay out of their territory. While I'm pissed off over what they did to my dad when he was a kid, the ones who tortured him are long dead by his hands. I'm not one to take my anger out on the innocent."

He was a better man than Merjack, and it sent a wave of guilt through her. But she refused to listen to her conscience. That same conscience would be screaming even louder if something happened to her family because she failed them.

Which reminded her . . .

"You have a son?"

A proud smile curled his lips. "I do. He's a great kid, in spite of having been around me."

"But he doesn't travel with you?"

"Normally he does—he's actually my co-pilot. He's been off with some friends for a couple of weeks and he's the most important thing we'll be picking up on Nera when we get there."

She loved the way his face lit up while he talked about seeing his son. It warmed her in a way she would never have thought possible. "Ah, gotcha."

"You'll like Omari. He's a lot like me, only much better-looking."

That she couldn't imagine. "I'm sure I'll adore him."

Devyn didn't know why those words seared him, but they did. More than that, they caused an image of her holding a baby to flash through his mind. That would probably scare most men, but having partially raised Omari, he wanted more children. He'd thoroughly enjoyed watching Omari grow up and learn things while becoming one hell of a man. If he could ever find the right woman, he'd love to have a house full of kids.

And that thought turned his mind to what it took to create a baby . . .

Which brought him back to an image of Alix naked.

I have so got to get laid . . .

This was getting ridiculous. "I'm heading back to my office. Let me know if you need anything."

"Thanks."

Alix watched as Devyn walked away from her. Damn, he had the best backside she'd ever seen. She could stare at that man all day long.

It was getting harder and harder to reconcile his ruthless reputation with a man who loved his son so much. One who was so easy to talk to and who looked after her.

Sighing, she headed back to her room to get ready to de-ship and buy the part they needed.

As soon as they docked on Miremba, Alix met Sway and Devyn at the ramp. Sway was dressed in dark gray while Devyn, freshly showered, was delectable in black. The mere scent of him was enough to make her hot.

Sway smirked at Devyn, who refused to even look at her. "Happy hunting, buddy. May the gods be with you."

"Fuck you, Sway," he snarled. He shot down the ramp as soon as it finished extending.

Alix passed a puzzled frown to Sway. "What was that about?"

Sway laughed evilly. "Devyn's got a bad case of blue balls, which, while common for me, is an extremely rare condition for him. He's hoping to find some relief from them while you and Vik get the part and repair the ship. I'm staying behind to make sure no one here screws with the *Talia*."

"Ooookay," she said, emphasizing the word. "More than I needed to know about the captain."

"Not really. You're the one who gave them to him." Sway laughed again as he walked off.

Alix could only gape as Vik joined her. Her face exploded with heat.

"You should be flattered."

She arched a brow at Vik. "How so?"

"One, that Devyn wants you that badly and two, that he thinks enough of you not to come on to you—another thing that is rare for him. Usually when he wants a woman he's lusting after, he gets her pretty easily."

She gave the mecha a droll stare. "You know that could just mean he's not attracted to me but that I'm the only female on board, thus reminding him of sex."

"You keep on believing that, cupcake. I'm the one who monitors his biometrics and I've noticed that every time he gets near you, his heart rate and breathing elevate and his blood all rushes to a certain part of his anatomy. Trust me, I know the signs of sexual arousal when I see them. And it only happens when he's near *you*. Which is really good because I definitely don't want him coming on to me. Definitely not in my programming or job description."

Now she was so embarrassed, she wanted to crawl under something. "You don't monitor my bios, do you?"

"Not at all. No offense, don't care if you live or die. You're not my responsibility."

"Way to prop up my self-esteem there, Vik. Appreciate it."

He led her from the ship. "Well, if the truth offends . . ."

Rolling her eyes, she followed him through the hangar and toward the parts sector that had been set up for the convenience of the crews who traveled through here.

It didn't take them long to find the part and purchase it, but as they headed back, she couldn't keep her thoughts from drifting to Devyn and what he was looking for.

You don't care who he sleeps with. He's nothing to you.

It was true, and she knew more about men and their baser urges than she wanted to. That had been the part of her duties on her father's freighter that she despised the most.

I need their attention focused on their jobs. Go handle them, Alix. Make yourself useful for something.

Not to mention if she kept them happy and drained, they didn't turn their attention to Tempest. Something that had become harder and harder over the last year. In truth, she was almost happy her father was dead. Her biggest fear was that he'd do to her sister what he'd done to her.

Turn her into the crew's whore.

"Are you all right?"

She looked up at Vik. "Yeah, why?"

"You're suddenly very sad. Did I hurt you with my comments? It wasn't my intention."

"You didn't do anything, Vik. I was just thinking of something else."

"Then I'm sorry for whatever thought gave you so much pain. You seem like a very nice woman and while I know I'm a bit thoughtless at times with my comments, I would never want to cause you so much sorrow."

His sincerity touched her. "Thank you, Vik."

He opened the door to the ship for her. "My pleasure."

Devyn paused as he scanned the women around him in the bar. Half of them were prostitutes and the other half were like him—here to find someone to ease the ache in their loins.

One seriously built redhead in a skimpy leather halter top and slacks walked up to him as he ordered a drink. She scanned his body hungrily and smiled. "You interested in female company?"

Yeah . . . but while he could easily take a bite of that apple, he knew he'd be hungry again as soon as he finished.

Because he wasn't craving apples.

He wanted something spicier.

I am so messed up. How could he crave a woman who looked just like the bitch who'd almost killed him?

The redhead rubbed her breasts against his arm. "What do you say?"

He looked down at the deep cleft between her breasts and imagined what it would be like to bury his face there. His mouth watered. "I say you are one of the finest pieces of ass I've ever seen and I would love nothing more than to screw you until you beg me for mercy."

She pouted seductively. "Why do I sense a 'but' in there?"

Devyn sighed. "Because it wouldn't be you I'd be seeing while I did it."

She ran her hand down his chest to his hip, then lower until she cupped his swollen cock in her hand. "I don't mind, baby. You can even call me her name if you want to."

He ground his teeth as her hand teased him. *Oh, yeah . . .* That's what he'd been craving.

"There's a room in back if you want privacy."

The problem was he was so horny, he could screw her right here in front of everyone.

But with that thought came an image of Alix. More than that was the memory of Alix's scent. And while the woman in front of him was truly beautiful—far more so than Alix—she didn't have those guarded dark blue eyes or long blonde hair.

Determined to forget about that, he pulled the woman against him and kissed her. Her tongue swept against his.

She nipped his lips as she pulled back. "Come on, baby. Let me eat you up."

He took one step with her, then cursed. *I don't want to be with her.*

Are you out of your fucking mind? Look at her body.

It's. All. Yours.

And still he didn't move. He knew from experience that eating something because it was convenient didn't make it satisfying. This wouldn't quell anything. As soon as he got back around Alix, he'd be horny again.

He pulled the redhead into his arms and gave her a gentle kiss. "You are a stunning, beautiful woman and I am an idiot for doing this. But as much as I'd love to be inside you right now, I can't."

She gave a wistful sigh. "Your girlfriend must be something else."

"Yeah . . . she is."

She reached up and toyed with his earlobe. "I hope she knows how lucky she is." She leaned forward to blow and whisper in his ear. "For the record . . . you're passing on one of the best fucks of your life."

He almost whimpered as she walked away and headed for another guy. *Sway's right, I am a woman. Even worse, I'm whipped by someone I haven't even kissed.*

Disgusted, he turned around and knocked his drink back with one gulp, then motioned for the bartender to return. "Keep them coming until I'm unconscious."

Alix lowered herself from the engine well and descended the ladder. That repair had been a pain in the butt. But at least it was done. Wiping the grease from her hands, she used her elbow to push the button to close the hatch.

She was so intent on making sure it sealed, she was oblivious to everything around her.

At least until someone grabbed her from behind.

Assuming it was Devyn, Vik or Sway messing with her, she didn't react until rough hands squeezed her breasts.

"What are you doing here all alone? Stealing parts from someone's ship for your father?"

Alix's blood went cold at the sound of a voice

that sickened her. Irn Soilent. The man who'd ruined her father and had cost them everything.

He tightened his grip on her, his hand sliding inside her shirt. "Now where's that whore sister of yours? I still want a piece of her before someone else beats me to it."

Shrieking in outrage, she attacked him.

Irn cursed as she busted his lip with her fist. "You worthless slut!" He returned her blow with one that caught her along the jaw. Her head snapped back so hard, it dazed her for a moment.

Until he went to hit her again.

She punched him in the stomach, wishing she had a weapon to carve his fetid heart out of his chest.

"Get her!" he snarled at the men who were standing nearby.

Alix panicked as she realized there were ten of them altogether. And while she was good in a fight, she couldn't win against that number.

She ducked the first one to reach her and ran for the ship's ramp. Another man cut her off.

Kneeing him in the groin, she shoved him away. But before she could step past him, a huge burly bear of a man grabbed her from behind and lifted her off her feet. He slung her around to face Irn, who glared his hatred at her.

Irn spat blood on the ground. "You're going to pay for that, bitch."

Alix tried to kick and twist out of their hold, but couldn't do anything more than hurt herself. Even so, she didn't let up as they laughed at her.

"Since when did you get discriminating?" Irn passed an evil smirk at the others. "I know she don't look like much, but trust me, there's enough of her to satisfy us all, and it's free for our taking." He moved to kiss her. Shrieking in anger, she tried to turn her face away.

He grabbed her chin to hold her still while the man behind tightened his grip on her arms, keeping her locked between them.

Just as Irn's lips would have touched hers, his head was jerked back and he was spun about to confront the devil himself.

Alix froze as she stared into the face of Devyn's fury. *This* was the man Merjack had described. Cold. Lethal. Terrifying.

There was no mercy in his dark gaze. Nothing in his expression except the promise of death to those who'd pissed him off.

One man went for him. Devyn raised his arm, blocking the punch before he slugged the man so hard, he fell to the floor whimpering. The next one to attack was flipped over Devyn's back. Devyn slammed him on the ground and twisted his arm, breaking it. The man screamed out in pain.

Devyn turned and caught the next burly attacker by the throat. He shoved him into two more before he whirled on Irn again and backhanded him.

The man holding her shoved her to the ground before he bellowed and rushed for Devyn.

Devyn ducked his blow, then head-butted him.

There were no emotions on Devyn's face as he pummeled the man.

She pushed herself up, but before she could rejoin the fight, Sway and Vik were there. Irn's "friends" ran off, leaving the burly man who'd held her and the man Devyn was trying to kill—Irn.

Sway pulled him off Irn. "Let it go, Dev. You've almost killed him."

Devyn stomped Irn one more time before he snatched him up from the ground. He dragged Irn to stand in front of her and held him there so that she could see the rivulets of blood that ran from his brow, temple and nose. "You apologize to her right now, you animal."

"I ain't apologizing to no whore."

Rage descended over Devyn's face to such a degree that she was sure he'd murder Irn where he stood. "You don't *ever* treat a woman like that. You apologize to her or so help me I'll gouge out your eyes and shove them down your throat."

Irn whimpered before he glared at her with a promise in his eyes that one day he'd make her pay for this. "I'm sorry."

Devyn slung him away. "Get out of here. If I ever see any of you again, you won't live long enough to regret it." He didn't move until they were gone.

Then he whirled on Vik and Sway with a fury that made Alix take a step back. "Where the hell were you two?"

Sway's eyes darkened as he tensed and stood his

ground. "Don't come at me with that, boy. You know better."

But Devyn didn't back off or back down. "Know better, my ass. She almost got raped while you two were jacking off. Why weren't you out here watching her?"

Before they could speak, Alix intervened. "I told them I was all right on my own."

Devyn scowled at her then. "You what?"

She held her throbbing arm to her side. It was sore from the way the burly man had grabbed and held her. All she wanted to do was go hide from his anger, but she couldn't let Vik and Sway get into trouble over something as worthless as her. Determined to defend them, she steeled her spine. "Please don't blame them. It was all my fault. I told them not to worry about me. There wasn't anybody here at the time, and had there not been so many who attacked me, I could have handled it on my own. I'm really sorry I caused this to happen. I'll be more careful in the future."

Devyn's heart lurched at her apology after the way she'd been so forcefully attacked. Her cheek was swollen with a bruise already forming under her left eye. And still her eyes blazed with restrained fury and pain.

He saw the shame in Vik's and Sway's gazes that she was protecting them. "You didn't do anything to apologize for."

"I should have been armed or called for help. It

just happened so fast . . . I was caught off guard. I promise it won't happen again, Captain." She held her chin high, but even so he saw the tears in her eyes as she made her way back to the ship.

Sway shook his head. "I'm really sorry about this, Dev. I was talking to Claire. Had I known . . . You were right. I should have been watching her."

Devyn clapped him on the back as his anger dwindled into some tender emotion he couldn't even name. "Don't worry about it. I'm mad at myself for not being here and taking it out on you two. I should have never left."

Vik cleared his throat. "Speaking of . . . we better get out of here before one of the ass-kickees goes to the authorities and reports the assault. I don't think any of us want to be arrested in Rit territory."

Yeah, no kidding. That wouldn't go well for any of them. "Good point. Let's tel-ass while we all still have one."

Alix leaned back against her closed door, shaking. That had been close on so many levels. What if Irn had told Devyn she was a slave? Had he not been so rattled by the ferocity of Devyn's attack, he probably would have.

And Devyn . . .

Now she knew the full extent of his abilities, and they were truly frightening. He'd torn through those men single-handedly.

Oh, my God . . .

What would he do to her if he ever learned her secret? An image of him stomping Irn went through her mind so clearly that it made her chest tight.

"I can't believe you didn't even get laid after all that. Damn, Dev, you're an idiot."

She froze as she heard Sway and Devyn walking past her room.

"Don't go there, Sway. I'm pissed enough."

"You don't smell pissed, you smell drunk. Are you?"

"Wouldn't be if I'd gotten laid, but I needed something to take the edge off—not that it helped even a little. I swear to the gods I'm about to burst my seams."

Sway laughed. "No wonder you tore them up the way you did."

"They're lucky I didn't rip their arms off for touching her."

Sway tsked. "You know there are ways of relieving that pain on your own."

"It's not the same, and you of all people know that. Gah, I don't know how you stand it. I have a whole new respect for you . . . Actually, that's not true. I still think you're an idiot, but I'm too drunk to care right now."

They continued talking, but she could no longer discern their words.

She stood in her room, floored by that revelation. So Devyn hadn't slept with anyone while he'd been gone . . . For some reason, that thrilled her.

Don't go there.

But she couldn't help it. No man had ever defended her before. No man had ever cared who hurt her or slept with her.

Not even her own father.

Devyn had protected her from Irn and his fetid friends. That knowledge shattered something deep inside her. She tried to tell herself that he'd have done the same for any member of his crew. That it meant nothing to him, and yet . . .

"They're lucky I didn't rip their arms off for touching her."

It was the kindest thing anyone had ever said about her. Holding those words close, she pushed herself away from the door and went to put ice on her swollen cheek. She'd barely reached her new cooling unit when she heard a light knock on her door.

She went to open it and found Devyn standing in the hallway, looking contrite.

Why? What did he have to apologize for?

"You need something, Captain?"

Devyn savored the deep contralto of her voice that made him even harder and more desperate for her. *Damn, I am drunk.* He held up his med kit. "I wanted to take a look at your cheek. Make sure they didn't crack the bone."

"It'll be okay."

"I'm a doctor, Alix. I want to see it and there's no arguing with me."

Alix blinked in confusion at his words, not sure she'd heard him correctly. "What?"

He gave an arrogant nod. "Certified and schooled in human, Andarion, Hyshian and Trisani medicine and surgery. I can go get the degree if you really want to see it. Now let me in."

She stepped back, awed by yet another discovery where he was concerned. "Why would a doctor be a runner?"

He didn't answer as he moved her to sit down on the chair beside her bed. Pulling a scanner from his bag, he ran it over the throbbing side of her face. She could smell the alcohol on his breath, but unlike with her father, she couldn't tell he was drunk. He seemed completely sober.

Devyn tried not to think about how soft her skin was under his fingers as he gently tested the swelling on her cheek. It wasn't broken, but they'd given her one hell of a bruise. He ground his teeth against the burst of anger that wanted him to tear them apart over it. "I should have killed those bastards."

"I don't think they'll forget their encounter with you anytime soon."

He didn't respond as he ran his hand over her split lip. "Did they knock any teeth loose?"

"I don't think so. I don't have that much blood in my mouth."

His rage darkened. The fact that she knew what to look for and that she wasn't sobbing over what had been done to her made him wonder how many times she'd been hurt like this in her past. Obviously it was nothing new.

"If you want, I will go back and kill them."

One brow shot up. "I don't . . ." Alix caught herself before she finished that sentence. She'd started to say that she didn't want him to go to jail because of her and yet, that was what she was about to do to him.

The hypocrisy stung her.

"You don't need that trouble," she finished weakly.

"All right. But if you change your mind, let me know and we'll get 'em."

"Just how drunk are you?"

He flashed a devilish grin at her. "Enough that Vik wouldn't let me launch the ship."

She was completely amazed by that. "You really can't tell you've had any drinks at all."

"Yeah, I know. I get that from my dad. At least that's what my mom tells me. I've actually never seen my father take a drink. But my entire family swears he was raging alcoholic for many, many years."

Like her father . . . only his father had been kind to his child. "What made him stop drinking?"

Devyn returned the scanner to his bag. "He loved my mother more than the bottle and he told me once that he never wanted to take the chance on doing something stupid while drunk that might cause him to lose her."

"Really?"

"Yeah. My parents have the kind of marriage that everyone dreams about. Even after all these years, they're still like two teenagers stealing kisses and holding hands."

"And they love you."

"Yeah, I'm really lucky and I know it. Both of my parents had a hard upbringing and I cut my teeth on the horror stories of their pasts." He paused to look at her. "It's difficult sometimes to reconcile the stories I hear from others about them and their reputations with the reality of the parents I know and love." He smiled. "I've seen grown men wet themselves at the mere mention of my mother's name and all I can think is this is the woman who wiped my nose and played cuddles with me as a kid. You know? And then my dad . . ." He let out a long breath. "I've heard the stories, but I've never seen him lose his temper with me, not even when I set the house on fire as a kid and burned up a significant portion of his ungodly expensive art collection."

She gaped at that. "He didn't kill you?"

Devyn shook his head. "I was sitting with the firefighters, terrified of the ass-whipping I knew was due me. When I finally saw my dad arrive and come running, I just knew he was going to bust me wide open, right? I know you remember that feeling of 'Oh, shit, I'm screwed' from childhood whenever you did something really stupid and believe me, nothing was dumber than setting our house on fire. I wanted to run so bad, but I was too scared to even move. Then he grabbed me up and held me against him until I couldn't breathe. I didn't think he was ever going to let me go. He was so grateful I hadn't been hurt that he never even mentioned what I'd done to the house or his art. It was an accident on my part, but to this day, I feel like shit over it."

"How old were you?"

"Eleven. As punishment for cutting school with a friend, I'd been left at home with my nannies to do homework. I was messing around with my chemistry set when I ignited my dad's desk and the chemicals spread like nothing I'd ever seen."

A muscle worked in his jaw as he shook his head sadly. "It's the only time I ever saw my mom cry. Not because of the house, but because she thought at first when she arrived that I was still inside it. When she found out I was safe, she held me and wept like a baby. Gah, I can still feel her shaking. I think that scared me more than anything else."

Alix tried to imagine her parents being that protective. But honestly, her parents would have killed her dead for something like that. "My parents both had a temper. My dad a lot more so than my mom. But she's always loved me and I know it. It's why I've always been so protective of her."

He scowled at her. "You mean until she ran off when you were little?"

Alix cringed as she realized her slip. *I better be more careful before he kills me.* "It doesn't mean you don't love your mother, Captain. When cruelty is all you know, you make allowances for people's shortcomings. Even bad parents are better than no parents."

He snorted. "My father would definitely argue about that and given what my grandfather did to him, I don't blame him. But I won't pry. I know from my parents how much those memories sting even decades after they've passed. You never really get over a bad childhood."

He pulled a cold pack from the bag and activated it, then pressed it against her cheek. "Keep your cheek iced. I'm going to bed before I pass out." He placed three more packs on her table, then took his leave.

It was only after he was gone that she realized the blood on the packs was from his injuries.

Injuries he'd gotten because of her . . .

She wanted to cry as she thought about the pain she was going to inflict on him and the terror of what his parents might do to her over it. If what he said was true, they wouldn't just lie back and let her get away with hurting their only child.

They would come after her with everything they had and then some.

What am I going to do?

She would save her family. She had no choice. But first, she wanted to thank the man who'd kept her from being raped.

Devyn hissed as he poured an antiseptic over his bleeding knuckles. That one bastard had had a jaw like ragged steel.

"It's what you get for being stupid."

And he was still so hard, he could drive a nail with his erection.

Wasn't alcohol supposed to dull pain? *The fight probably sobered you.*

Oh, goodie. Grabbing a bottle of Tondarion whisky, he went to sit at his desk. He started to get a glass, then decided it wasn't worth the effort. He clicked back the lid and drank straight from the bottle while visions of Alix in his bed tormented him.

Why didn't you take the redhead up on her offer? It would have at least sated you for a few.

Because I'm a fucking idiot.

Yeah, that would be it. He took another swig.

Suddenly there was a hesitant knock on his door. His cock jerked because there was no way it was Sway or Vik being timid or even knocking . . .

Just what I need. More torture.

"Come in," he called, unwilling to get up and move at this point.

The door opened to show him the beautiful face of his worst tormentor. *Damn, I need to be drunker.*

"Did I forget something?" he asked her.

Alix hesitated as she saw him with the bottle in his hand. *If he's still drinking, you should run.* Her father had always been so mean when he drank that it made her skittish around any man who imbibed. But she couldn't. She owed him and, more than that, she wanted to do this. To have one moment with a man who didn't make her skin crawl when he touched her.

What would it be like to sleep with a man she actually desired?

Just once.

Gathering her courage, she crossed the room and knelt in front of his chair.

Devyn frowned as he watched her. She looked up at him from between his knees and his breath caught. He wanted to ask her what she was doing, but the hungry look in her eyes squelched all rational thought.

And when she reached for his fly, he thought this might be another fantasy brought on by his drunken stupor. His heart pounded as he watched her slowly unzip his pants until his cock was free.

Without a word, she lowered her lips to take him deep into her mouth.

He dropped the bottle and ground his teeth as pleasure ripped through his entire body. Cupping her face, he reveled in the sensation of her hot mouth caressing him while he watched her taste him. It was the hottest thing he'd ever seen and it set fire to every molecule of his body.

Alix groaned at the salty taste of him, but it was the gentleness of his hands on her face that surprised her. He was actually caressing her while she pleased him. No one had ever done that to her before. Normally they pulled her hair and thrust against her, not caring if they hurt her or not.

But he brushed her hair back from her face while his fingers played against her scalp, sending chills over her. She looked up to see him watching her. The tenderness in his eyes scorched her.

Smiling, she licked her way down to the base so that she could tease the rest of him.

Devyn growled at the sensation of her tongue licking him. He felt like his entire body was on fire. Unable to stand it, he pulled her up so that he could kiss her.

Alix's head swam at the sensation of his lips on hers. Fierce, yet tender, he explored every inch of her mouth. And it left her breathless. She'd been absolutely right. His kiss was electric as he lifted her up and set her down on his desk.

He pushed her shirt up with a slow, gentle hand. His dark eyes burning, he left her lips to taste her breasts. She cupped his head to her chest as he licked and teased her nipple. She shivered as waves of pleasure racked her body in a way she'd never expected. Each lick sent a tremor through her.

Oh my God, he's incredible . . .

Her blood felt thick as he dipped his hand under her waistband until he was touching the part of her that was white-hot with need.

Devyn growled at how wet she was and at how bad he wanted inside her.

She's your engineer. You shouldn't be doing this.

He knew that deep inside, but she'd come to him. Had he been sober, he might have been able to send her away. But right now . . .

There was no way.

And as he sank his fingers deep inside her, she hissed in his ear. That sound resonated through him.

"Tell me what you want, Alix."

She rubbed herself against him. "I want you, Devyn."

He smiled as she finally used his name. He kissed her before he spoke again. "I want to savor you, but I can't right now. I want you too badly. If you bear with me, I swear I'll make it up to you."

Alix didn't understand that as he stepped back to pull her pants off. Before she could ask him what he meant, he buried himself deep inside her body. Biting her lip, she groaned at how good he felt there. She looked up to see him watching her.

He took her hand in his and tenderly kissed her palm as he thrust against her hips.

She wrapped her legs around his waist and arched her back to draw him even deeper inside her. He lowered his head to taste her breasts as he quickened his strokes.

Devyn's head was spinning at the warmth of her body under his. He had no idea why he wanted her the way he did, why she called out to him, but right now, he was lost to her. He brushed his fingers over her lips, admiring the small Cupid's bow. She wrapped her arms around him and held him close.

And for some reason he couldn't fathom, her embrace soothed a part of him he hadn't even realized was hurting. Her arms made him feel . . .

He wasn't even sure he could explain it.

Closing his eyes, he savored that sensation. His body was pitched on the verge of release. He bit his lip, trying to keep it under control. He'd slighted her enough with the foreplay. He wasn't about to disappoint her in this, too.

He slid his hand down between them until he found her cleft. She jerked the instant he touched her. His breathing ragged, he listened to her body until he found the right rhythm for her.

Alix shivered as Devyn's hand played in time to his strokes. It heightened her pleasure to a level she'd never known before.

"That's it, baby," he breathed in her ear. "Come for me." He drove himself in deep to punctuate those words.

She wasn't sure what he was asking for. All she knew was that she'd never felt anything like this. Her body was completely molten. In the past, she'd been watching the clock, doing any- and everything she could to speed things along so that they'd finish and she could get back to whatever she'd been doing before.

But with Devyn . . .

She never wanted this to end. She loved the way he felt inside her. And then she felt something inside her explode. It came from somewhere deep and shook her entire body. Before she could stop herself, she screamed out.

Devyn laughed in her ear as he moved even faster, increasing the pleasure. Each one of his strong, deep strokes took her even higher.

And then she felt his release. He gasped an

instant before he shook around her. He took her hand into his and laced their fingers together in an act so sweet it branded her heart.

With their bodies still joined, he pulled back to kiss the tip of her nose. He trailed his kisses to her lips, her neck, and then her breasts while she lay there in wonder.

"What was that?"

He frowned. "What was what?"

"What you did to me. I've never felt anything like it . . . It was incredible."

It took Devyn a full minute to understand what she was saying. "You've never had an orgasm before?"

Her scowl matched his. "A woman can have an orgasm?"

Had it not been for the deep sincerity in her eyes, he would have thought she was kidding. He knew he wasn't the first to make love to her, but . . . "You really didn't know a woman could do that?"

She shook her head. "I knew men did. But no. I've never had one before."

His heart broke for her. What kind of selfish bastards had she been with that they hadn't even thought about her needs? Damn it. Had he known that, he'd have taken a lot more time with her.

In the end, he'd been as selfish as all the others who'd used her for nothing more than their own needs. *I am such an asshole.*

"How sheltered have you been?"

"I don't understand the question."

He winced as he realized how insensitive he'd been again. Without her mother and with what was obviously an all-male crew on her father's ship, how would she know anything about female sexuality?

He knew firsthand the kind of morally questionable men poor freighters took on as employees. And that made him wonder if any of them had ever raped her.

Damn it. He was an idiot and he should have sobered up before he touched her.

Well, I'm sober now.

He leaned his forehead against hers and shook his head. "Why did you come to me?"

"I felt guilty."

"For what?"

"For causing your condition and then interrupting your chance to . . . take care of it. Had you not gotten into a fight, you could have stayed until you found someone you wanted to sleep with."

That left him all but speechless.

And insulted.

"You slept with me because you felt obligated?"

"Not entirely." Heat exploded across her face an instant before anger darkened her gaze. "I'm not a whore!" She pushed him back, but he held her fast.

"Shh," he said, keeping her against him to calm her down. "I'm not accusing you of being a whore." Damn, what had her father and his crew done to her? "I just don't want you to think that part of your duties on this ship is to take care of me when I'm horny. Ever."

Alix calmed down as she saw the sincerity in his eyes. Why did he have to be so sweet and handsome?

Why do I have to betray the only decent man I've ever met?

It was so unfair.

"Okay," she whispered. "I just know that men have needs and when you can't get what you want, you take what's available. I won't bother you again."

Devyn wrapped his arms around her, preventing her from retrieving her pants from the floor. "Alix . . . I had the chance on Nera to sleep with the most amazing redhead I've ever seen. She was all over me before I got drunk and believe me, she all but had me naked."

Those words made her ache. "You are such an asshole to tell me that." Then she frowned at his confession, not understanding it. "Why didn't you sleep with her?"

"Because she wasn't *yóu*."

"I'm confused again."

He took her hand into his and led it to his cock, which was already starting to harden again. "Like you said, you're the one who did this to me. I didn't want what was available, Alix. I wanted you."

"Why?"

Devyn was aghast at the fact that she couldn't accept the fact that he was attracted to her because she was hotter than hell. "You're smart. Funny. Fearless, and you come without all the shit and drama most women carry. You don't play head games. You don't tell me you're all right when you're not. You're competent, not whiny . . . and the gods know I've had it with whiny, incompetent women who can't look after themselves." He buried his hand in her hair. "And you have the most beautiful hair and eyes I've ever seen. Best of all you not only get my sarcasm, you dish it back." He grinned at her. "I like a woman with sass."

She moaned as he dipped his head down to kiss her again. His cock hardened even more while he trapped her hand between their bodies.

He pulled back to growl before he jerked his shirt off over his head. Taking her hand, he urged her up and pulled her into his bathroom. She froze as she saw how nice it was. Three times the size of hers, it had gold fixtures and black marble. Everything was so beautiful . . . It was like a dream.

He released her so that he could turn the shower on. While he adjusted the water, she removed her top and bra.

Her breath caught as she watched the play of muscles under his skin. He was absolutely gorgeous. With the exception of several severe scars, his body was perfect.

And when he turned around to smile at her, she shivered. He held his hand out toward her. "Care to join me?"

She took his hand and allowed him to pull her inside where the hot water slid sensually against her skin.

Devyn grabbed the washcloth and soap so that he could quickly bathe himself, then turned to lather her body.

Alix sighed in pleasure as Devyn gently bathed her breasts. He used his hands and the cloth to heighten the pleasure until she was hungry again. And when he nudged her legs apart to bathe the center of her body, she could barely stand. He pressed her back against the wall while his fingers toyed with her. She trembled as his breath caressed her skin. He circled her earlobe before tracing the entire outline of her ear with his tongue.

She came again with an orgasm so fierce it made a mockery of her earlier one. He gave a low, light laugh in her ear as he sank down before her.

His grin was infectious as he looked up at her and captured her gaze. Breathless, she was still recovering when he took her into his mouth.

She let out a delighted squeal.

"Oh . . . my . . ." Her head spun as he gave her three more orgasms.

Only then did he slide himself up her body and enter her again.

Devyn closed his eyes as he savored every inch of her body while he thrust against her. This was what he'd been craving for days. The scent and feel of her was unlike anything he'd ever known.

And when he came, he had his face and hand buried in the wet strands of her long hair.

Alix cradled Devyn against her while the water continued to pelt down on them. "Aren't we wasting resources?"

He laughed. "You're the only one who would think of that right now." Pulling back, he kissed her fiercely.

She moaned at the taste of him.

He finally released her and quickly bathed himself while she watched. She felt suddenly awkward as she tried to cover herself with her hands. Should she leave?

Was she dismissed now that he was done with her?

Just as she started to go, he caught her for another stunning kiss.

He wiped a strand of hair back from her face before he gently nipped her chin. "You look really uncomfortable right now, so I'll leave you to finish." He placed his washcloth in her hand. "I hope you'll stay with me tonight and not go back to your room." He stepped away, then paused. "And that's not an order, Alix. I don't want you there unless you want to be there."

Those words brought a lump to her throat. "I'll stay."

He nipped her lips, then left her alone.

What am I doing? I have to hand him over to the authorities.

And they were going to ruin and then kill him. How would she ever live with herself?

* * *

Devyn frowned as Alix came out of the bathroom with a towel wrapped around her. She twisted one corner of it. He found the uncertainty of her gesture absolutely charming and adorable. "Um . . . I need my nightclothes out of my room."

He pulled the covers back. "No, you don't."

She arched a single questioning brow that charmed him even more. "You want me to sleep naked . . . with you?"

"Not like I haven't seen you."

"What about Sway and Vik?"

"I don't want to sleep naked with them."

Her face turned bright pink. "That's not what I meant."

"I know. It's okay. I promise, I just want to hold you while I sleep. I assure you I don't have enough energy left to do anything else."

Alix hesitated before she crossed the room. She'd never done anything like this before. And the scariest part was how much she wanted to sleep with him like that.

This is wrong.

Even so, she climbed under the covers before she removed her towel.

Devyn wrapped his arms around her and pulled her back against his front. "Thank you for staying."

She wanted to thank him, too, but right now she couldn't speak. She was too overwhelmed by everything that had happened. With his kindness and consideration. How did someone learn to be so nice?

Especially to someone like her, who definitely didn't deserve anything except his scorn and hatred.

And just as she started to doze, his link buzzed. She jumped at the same time he cursed.

Rolling over, he grabbed the earpiece. He inserted it, then tapped it to open the channel. "Yeah, Mom . . . No, I'm not exercising or fighting. I was trying to go to sleep." He let out a tired sigh as he listened to her. "Yeah. I'll call in the morning. Love you, too." He slid a sheepish glance to Alix before he made a kissing sound for his mom.

She bit back a smile as he returned the link to his nightstand. "That's very sweet."

"Humiliating, you mean."

"I find it refreshing that you show her respect. Most men wouldn't."

He laughed out loud. "You say that only because you've never met my mom. You show her respect or she kicks your ass. Trust me, she's small but vicious."

"I'm sure she never kicked yours."

"You'd be surprised. She was loving, but tough at times. My mom doesn't take lip from anyone . . . except maybe Vik. And she has *never* taken it from me. Her basic philosophy is, 'I brought you into this world and I will take you out of it.' " He returned to holding her close.

"I don't think your mom would ever really hurt you."

"Let's just say I have no intention of finding out." He buried his face in her hair and inhaled deeply.

She swallowed as she looked down at his arm draped over her. His skin was so dark compared to hers. His fingers long and lean. Powerful and beautiful. A part of her warmed at the memory of how they'd felt while they pleased her.

And as she absorbed the warmth of his body snuggled next to hers, tenderness for him choked her. She should be sorry over what they'd done tonight, but she couldn't muster that feeling. She'd wanted him, and now she knew exactly how kind Devyn Kell could be.

Even when he was drunk . . .

Alix lay there for hours, listening to him breathe as he slept.

And she hated herself for what she was about to do. *I have no choice.*

Getting up carefully so as not to wake him, she made her way to his computer. With any luck, Vik wouldn't be monitoring it since it was Devyn's. Surely the captain's computer would be immune from the mecha's snooping.

Her heart pounding, she touched the pad to bring it out of sleep mode. The monitor flashed as it came online. She glanced at Devyn to make sure he was still asleep before she searched for old manifests.

She touched the first file that came up to open it.

Instead of a spreadsheet, it was a picture of a young Devyn sitting on the shoulders of a man who looked so similar in features that she was sure it was his father. The only difference was the feral gleam in his father's eyes. It was as if he could look through and see straight into her soul even through the photograph.

He must be truly terrifying in person. As intense and powerful as Devyn was, he had nothing on the man who'd created him. There was no mistaking the ruthless killer that lived inside his father.

She touched back and then went to the next file. It was a list of cargo . . .

That told her nothing. It looked like a million other legal shipping documents. So she moved on.

"What are you doing?"

She jumped at Devyn's low, sharp tone as she quickly closed the file and her search. Luckily, he was still in bed and not making any moves to see what she was looking at. "I—I was trying to pull up the ship's core to make sure everything was holding."

Devyn yawned. "Come back to bed and don't worry about it. Vik'll let us know if something happens. He'll know before it even reaches the sys scan."

She clicked out so that he couldn't find her search and returned to bed.

But as she lay there, she couldn't stop trembling.

That had been too close. Had he gotten up, he'd have seen her search . . .

"Are you all right?"

She nodded. "Fine."

"Why are you shaking?"

"Cold."

He nuzzled her neck and wrapped his arms tight around her as he held her even closer. Every inch of that lean, hard body was pressed against hers. Protective. Sweet. Wicked. "I'll warm you."

I'm so going to burn in oblivion for this . . . But every time she felt guilty about handing him over, all she had to do was see the face of her mother and sister and her conscience was squelched.

She hoped . . .

And yet lying here in his arms, she'd never felt safer.

Cherished.

He doesn't feel like that toward you. He was just a man with an itch and you were a convenient body for him. You don't even know him.

That was hard to say convincingly since he was naked with her. She definitely knew him now . . . his touch and scent were branded in her memory. Rolling over, she stared at the handsome planes of his face. With his eyes closed, he looked almost vulnerable.

Except for his hands. They were still rugged even while the rest of him was relaxed. And as she lay there, watching him, she couldn't help wondering what it would be like to have a man like him in her life. One who would be there for her when she needed him.

One who could love her.

She didn't dare dream of a husband. She was too used and too tired to even go there.

But deep inside, in a place where she was almost

afraid to look, was a tiny kernel of hope that her father's cruelty hadn't slaughtered. That little flickering light ignited and tortured her with images of a home and someone like Devyn who could love her in spite of everything.

You're such a moping fool.

How many times in her life would she be kicked in the teeth by fate before she learned that happy endings and happiness didn't belong to gutter trash like her? It was for free women who were born into nice, normal families.

Yeah, but what if?

Reaching up, she laid her hand against his cheek. His whiskers prickled her palm. And for a minute, she imagined the life she wished she had.

And that unrealistic dream was what sent her off into the most blissful sleep of her life.

Devyn came awake to something pressing hard against his back. At first he thought he was asleep in his pilot's chair, until he heard a light, gentle snore.

Alix.

A slow smile curled his lips as he rolled over to find her knee in his back and her hand in his hair. The low lights highlighted just enough of her bare body to make him instantly hard.

It was so confusing to be attracted to a woman who looked this much like his ex in the face. There was nothing else they shared, except for the way his body reacted. He should be well satisfied after last night and yet . . .

He wanted a bite of her succulent skin.

"Devyn?"

He sighed at the mecha's low voice. No doubt he'd been monitoring his vitals to know when he was awake. "What, Vik?"

"There's something strange that I'm picking up. I think you might want to come up here and look at it."

"Can't you shoot it to my computer in here?"

"I really think you need to come up here and look at it."

That set off the alarms inside him. What was going on? Vik wasn't one to be coy when it was something that threatened them.

Grateful Alix was still asleep, he slid out of bed and quickly dressed, then went to the bridge.

The lights came up immediately.

Devyn went to his chair. "Where's Sway?"

"Asleep."

"Okay, then what's up?"

Vik transferred data to the main computer in front of him. "I think we're tagged." *Tagged* meant that someone had a tracer on them and was able to track them.

"Who?"

"No idea and it's real sophisticated. Something your father would come up with."

Devyn arched a brow at that. When it came to computers and electronics, his father was unrivaled. "Dad wouldn't have bugged me covertly." He knew what devices his father had planted on the ship and in his chronometer. His parents were paranoid as hell, but at least they were openly obnoxious about it. "Can you jam the signal?"

"Let me get back to the part where I said it's like something your father would come up with."

"He also came up with you, Vik."

"Flattery right now might get you shot. I've been trying to isolate it, but it's impressive. I've tried jamming and everything else. Whatever it is, it's beyond my abilities."

That was extremely interesting. And concerning as hell. "Who would have done something like this?"

"Someone wanting to keep tabs on you. Since we don't know who, I think it best we assume they're hostile."

Devyn snorted at a comment so stupid he couldn't believe it'd come out of Vik's mouth. "You think?"

"Oh, sarcasm will definitely get you shot. Especially at this time of the day."

"Sorry, V. You know that's my stress release."

"I suggest you learn to channel that into a new direction that won't end up with you bleeding on the floor."

"Thanks, Vik. Love you, too, man. Just out of curiosity, why couldn't you tell me this in my room?"

He hesitated before he answered. "Because I'm not too sure Alix isn't the source of it."

Devyn's stomach hit the floor as every alarm in his body went into high alert. "What do you mean?"

"I have suspicions where she's concerned."

AI technically weren't capable of being suspicious. But Devyn's father had wired a human central nervous system into Vik, and more than that, he'd crossbred human DNA with some of his wiring. While Vik may not have been born from a mother, he was damn near human in all ways.

All ways.

Which meant that his powers of observation were above reproach. If he was suspicious, Alix was basically guilty of something.

"What's tripped your concerns?"

"Can't put my finger on it and that's pissing me off. Just that I've caught her trying to access some of our records. Shipping manifests and cargo inventory."

"That could be natural curiosity. If I were on a ship and could go to jail for my duties, I'd want to know what we were carrying, too."

"Perhaps. But it feels weird to me."

Devyn would argue if he hadn't had such a bad experience with Clotilde. After that, he'd lost all faith in his ability to judge people. Vik had never liked that bitch and if he'd listened to Vik then, it would have saved him an eternity of grief.

He pushed himself away from his console. "Keep an eye on her and let me know if you see anything concrete."

"I take it that you don't want me to watch her while she's with you."

"Goes without saying."

"Thought so. By the way, she's awake and getting dressed in your room."

Shit. But if she was an enemy, then he shouldn't care what she did.

Something much easier said than done.

This definitely wasn't what he'd wanted to wake up to. Licking Alix for a few hours ... now that had been the plan. "By the way, thanks for ruining my plans for the morning, Vik. Appreciate it."

"Ever my pleasure to irritate you, embryo."

Sighing, Devyn headed for the door.

"Can I ask a question?"

He frowned as he paused in the middle of the bridge. "Sure."

"I understand the physical nature of sex, but why didn't you sleep with your redhead at the station?"

A wave of irritation went through him as he realized he'd been spied on. "Vik—"

"Not my fault. Your heart rate increased, and I peeked only to make sure you were all right. I overheard that tiny bit and then immediately shut down my monitoring."

He would be angry if monitoring his vitals wasn't part of Vik's duties. Besides, there was no real malice in Vik, only an innate curiosity about human relations. "It's complicated. There's sex, which, don't get me wrong, is a good thing. But it's not as good as when you have a connection to someone. That kind of sex is astronomical."

"I don't understand."

Devyn smiled. "Neither do I most days. It's just something about it is more satisfying when you're with someone you know." He looked up at the speaker. "It's one of those things you have to experience to understand, Vik."

"Then I shall never know."

Devyn heard the wistful tone and felt bad for his friend. While curious about human behavior, Vik had always kept himself apart from it. It was almost like the mecha was afraid of the human part of himself. Not that Devyn blamed him for that.

There were times when he was just as afraid of being human.

Wishing he could help the mecha, he made his way to the galley to start breakfast.

As soon as Alix finished dressing, she went to find water and a morning bar. But the moment she walked in, she froze. Something smelled wonderful.

Because of the expense, she very seldom smelled bacon. It was a wonderful, unmistakable scent and it made her stomach rumble as she watched Devyn cooking it.

She scowled at him. "I thought you didn't cook."

"I don't. It doesn't mean I don't know how to, I just hate it passionately."

"Why?"

He turned over two sizzling pieces. "My Aunt Kasen. Love the woman dearly, but she can harp with the best of them and I made the mistake as a kid of asking her how to make these cereal cups she used to give me. Three minutes in, I knew I was screwed." He raised his voice to a falsetto. "No, Devyn, that's not right. Stop that. Stir it this way. Not that way." He let out a disgusted breath. "Two of the worst hours of my life to make a fifteen-minute dish. After that, anytime she caught me near a kitchen she'd start in on me. So I have an automatic sphincter clench any time I reach for a pan."

She laughed at his term. "Then why are you cooking now?"

He leaned down and kissed her senseless. "I'm suffering for you, baby."

Am I dreaming? This couldn't be happening to her. Irn groping her with his cold, dirty hands whenever he caught her alone. Arkley grabbing her when he needed release . . . that was normal.

A man like Devyn Kell cooking for her . . .

Impossible.

Yet as he pulled back to finish making breakfast, she knew she wasn't dreaming. This was real and it was wonderful.

But she didn't understand it. "Why are you being so nice to me?"

Devyn grimaced at her question. "What do you mean?"

"I don't understand why you're treating me this way."

Damn, what had they done to her that she couldn't comprehend a man making her food after he'd slept with her? He turned off the stove and pulled her into his arms. "Sweetie, this is how the people I've been around behave toward each other. Cooking you breakfast after the night you gave me is nothing. You wore me out and I need energy for the day ahead. Now eat up before it gets cold." He let go of her and put the bacon on a plate before he held it out.

Alix took the plate he handed her. As she made her way to the table, Sway walked in and flashed a grin.

"Ah, man, I thought Vik was screwing with me by sending over the scent of real food." He grabbed Devyn into a hug and playfully kissed him on the cheek. "I love you, man. You rule! Thanks for the food. It touches me deep in my tender place."

Devyn bristled under his playful assault. "I don't want to know nothing about your tender place, you freak."

When Sway tried to take the plate from Devyn, Devyn snatched it back. "Get your own plate, *giakon*. I'm hungry."

"You suck." Sway stepped around him to make a plate of his own. He bit into the bacon and moaned. "I always forget how well you cook."

"Yeah, well, you're already married, so cut your eyes away from me."

Sway sat down next to Alix. "You eat bacon?"

"Yes."

He flashed Devyn a grin. "She needs more bacon."

Devyn gave him a droll stare. "You want more bacon, make it yourself."

"I always burn it. Alix, don't you want more bacon?"

She held her hands up in surrender. "I'm so not in the middle of this." But inside, she enjoyed the bantering and play, and she envied them for having grown up like this. She was only now beginning to understand a world where fear wasn't a part of every day. No one yelled at her. No one grabbed her.

And as she thought of the future, her stomach shrank. Once Devyn was gone, what would become of her? She didn't know how to do anything except work on a ship.

Her mother and Tempest didn't even know that much. They had no education or skills at all.

"Are you all right?"

Blinking, she met Devyn's concerned gaze. "Fine."

But she could tell he didn't believe her. Not that he should, since she was lying, and that thought only made her feel that much worse.

Maybe you could trust him.

Yeah, right. Tell him that she'd been sent here by his enemies to arrest him? That wouldn't go over well. She'd kill her if she was him. It would only make sense. While they may have had sex, there was nothing more between them. No loyalty. Not even friendship.

She was his enemy.

And people like Devyn killed their enemies . . .

CHAPTER 4

The next two days passed quickly as Alix tried to catch Vik unaware without alerting him as to what she was doing.

Damn him for being so attentive. Nothing she tried worked. It was like the mecha was everywhere.

And with every day that passed, she grew that much closer to Devyn and Sway. They taught her how to play VR games—something her father had never allowed them to do on board his freighter. While they took mercy on her in the combat and racing games, they were ruthless with each other.

She loved listening to them playfully insult and taunt one another. It made her miss her sister and wish that she didn't have to hurt them.

But even better than the days were the nights she spent with Devyn. He showed her things about her body she'd never known. His mere touch could thrill her like nothing else, and his kisses . . .

She could spend eternity in his arms.

Now she sat on her bed, listening to the whir of the engines as Devyn brought the *Talia* into the docks of Nera VII. They'd invited her to dinner at one of the local pubs and she'd done her best to decline.

Apparently *no* wasn't in Devyn's vocabulary. So she planned to go and eat, then head straight back to carry out her mission.

While she waited for them to dock, she pulled the tie from her ponytail and let the long, thick, heavy hair hang down her back. She would have cut it long ago, but her father refused to spend money on something he deemed a ridiculous waste of credits. So she'd been relegated to what her mother could do with it, which was nothing more than trim it in a straight line.

But one day . . .

One day she was going to have the money to walk into a salon, her and Tempest and her mother, and splurge on haircuts and styles for all three of them.

At least that was the plan, but if her luck didn't turn around soon, that seemed as likely as Devyn falling down on his knees and vowing his everlasting love to her.

With a deep sigh, she ran her hand over the rough material of her taupe pantsuit, wishing she had more suitable clothes. Just once, she'd like to look at least halfway attractive. But it was no use. Her father hadn't believed in paying a slave for her work, and clothes had been bought on a strict need-only basis.

No one's going to be looking at you, anyway, as ugly as you are, and I don't want no bastard children on this ship. Men's clothes'll do for the likes of you. It's all you're worth, anyway. I got other things to spend my money on than your useless ass.

How she loved thinking of her father.

Honestly, she was lucky to have what few things she did. Had her father been any less puritanical, he'd have probably kept her naked.

A knock sounded on her door.

"Come in."

The door slid up to show Devyn, who was dressed all in black. Dang, he looked good enough to lick on for a while. There was an aura of power and danger that clung to him and yet it was neutralized by that devilish grin he wore. "We're heading out. You ready to go?"

She nodded. "How long will we be here?"

"Not too long. As soon as we eat and exchange partial cargoes, we'll leave. You don't have stay around for the latter part. As soon as you're done with the food, you can head on back."

Good. That should give her enough time to start the log scan—she'd accidentally located what she hoped was a back door into Devyn's encrypted files a couple of hours ago. So long as Vik was occupied off the ship, she might stand a chance of breaching it.

But she found it odd that Devyn was so open about his cargo exchanges. Most runners preferred to do that in secret.

He was definitely not a typical runner.

"So where are we eating?"

Devyn didn't hear the question at first. He was too busy noticing the way her pantsuit plunged down between her breasts. Not indecently, but just enough to be enticing. For days now, images of her had haunted him. Not because she was doing anything to attract him. Far from it. Even though they'd made love until he was . . .

Well, he still wasn't sated, but she was completely skittish around him. Yet he couldn't keep his eyes from going to her every time she looked away.

There was something about her that compelled him. She was a beguiling combination of tough innocence. And all he wanted to do was bury his face in the curve of her neck and breathe her in.

To have her lean against him while he ran his hands over her body and made her purr . . .

She glanced about nervously. "Um . . . where are we eating?"

He blinked and forced his thoughts to stay on their conversation and not on having sex with her. "The Runner's Den."

Alix shook her head. Now she understood his lack of secrecy. No doubt everyone in that establishment was a criminal. It was one place his crew wouldn't stand out.

"Why doesn't that surprise me?"

Devyn didn't comment. Instead, he extended his arm to her. "Shall we? I'm hungry enough to eat Sway's foul-smelling boots."

Against her will, her heart pounded in response to his gesture. Before she could stop herself, she tucked her hand into the crook of his elbow where she could feel his muscles flex. She swallowed at the contact, her body warming.

Oblivious to the effect he had on her, Devyn led her out of the ship and into the landing bay, where Sway and Vik stood at one end talking to a group of men.

The men she didn't know tensed visibly when they saw Devyn approach. It was obvious they were on their best behavior—as if they were terrified of him. Unlike Vik and Sway, who never seemed to take him too seriously.

Devyn headed toward them. The fact that he didn't release her arm surprised her. No one had ever publicly claimed her before.

He paused and introduced her to the group of runners who were just leaving. Then he turned to Sway. "Is Taryn here?"

"Beat us here by about half an hour."

"That figures. Competitive little bastard." Devyn inclined his head toward the exit. "Let's go find him and take care of business."

They'd barely taken three steps when a deep voice rang out. "Dad!"

Alix started to ignore it until she saw the look on Devyn's face. A wide grin broke before he opened his arms and someone almost equal to his height ran into them.

Devyn laughed as they embraced, and a huge dog came running up to bark and circle them.

Sway gestured at the two of them and mouthed the word *Omari* to her.

She shook her head and laughed. "I figured as much."

The dog ran at her and looked up, then barked. He had one black ear and the black covered his eyes like a mask, leaving the rest of his coat snow white. He also had a pair of golden eyes that seemed to glow.

She patted his head as she studied Omari. In his late teens, he was absolutely gorgeous with dark brown skin and a riot of curls that hung in perfect chaos to his strong jawline.

Dressed in a long dark green coat that was embellished with heavy embroidery, he had the sleeves shoved back to his elbows. Even so, his right hand was covered with a thick black glove that went all the way up to meet the pushed-back sleeve. His weapons seemed to be knives and daggers that were strapped to various parts of his body.

Definitely not what she'd expected as Devyn's son. Aside from the obvious, there wasn't that big a gap in their ages.

Devyn clapped him on the back and released him. "It's so good to see you, kid. I've missed you."

Omari wiped at his nose. "Yeah, I know. I missed you, too, but I learned a lot of cool things."

Sway snorted. "Such as new ways to annoy me, I'm sure."

Omari let out an evil laugh. "You know it." He sobered as he saw Alix petting his dog. "You must be the new engineer." He held his hand out to her.

"I'm Alix." She hesitated as she touched his gloved hand. It was a lot harder than she'd expected. Stronger.

Omari blushed before he retreated. "Sorry if I accidentally hurt you. I've got a cybernetic arm and leg. Sometimes it's hard to tell how much pressure I'm applying on something."

"You didn't hurt me at all."

The dog ran back to Omari. "This is Manashe. Manny, say hi to the nice lady."

The dog barked, then held up one paw.

Impressed, she shook the dog's "hand." "Nice meeting you, Manashe." He jumped up and licked her cheek.

As she stroked his ears, she looked back and forth between Devyn and Omari, trying to see any resemblance. While they were both extremely handsome, they really had nothing in common.

Omari rubbed his neck as if uncomfortable by her attention. "I'm adopted."

"Which changes nothing." Devyn's tone was sharp.

Omari held his hands up in surrender. "I agree, Dad. I was just explaining to the woman why we don't look anything alike and why you would have been younger than me when I was born. It doesn't mean I don't love you 'cause you know I do." Then he groused under his breath. "Make one snotty comment in anger when you're twelve years old going through puberty and getting grounded, and you pay for it for the rest of your life. Parents ain't got no sense of humor."

Devyn's jaw ticced. "Not about that, I don't. *Ever*." He pulled Omari back into a hug that made the teenager bristle even though he hugged Devyn back while he blushed profusely.

Alix met Vik's gaze and froze. The way he stared at her . . . it was like he knew something.

Omari pulled back and called the dog to him. "Let me put Manny away and I'll see you guys at the restaurant."

Devyn gave him a stern look. "Vik—"

"Watch the embryo. Got it."

Omari rolled his eyes. "Not ten, Dad."

"Yeah, I know. I'd feel better if you were. Watch him, Vik."

Vik moved stiffly, like an old-fashioned robot. "Watch . . . child. Watch . . . child. Does . . . not . . . com . . . pute."

"Don't make me shoot you, asshole. I'd hate to have to call my dad in for repairs."

"Yeah, and it would hurt."

Laughing, Omari headed for the *Talia* with Vik following after him.

They made their way out of the bay and into the long main corridor that ran in a circle around the space station.

Like most stations, shops lined both sides of the corridor. They passed a number of people and aliens, their arms filled with a variety of goods. Others milled about or chatted on their links as they walked past.

Devyn stopped outside a door painted with an encircled freighter—the universal sign of a runner's or smuggler's haven. Alix released his arm, no longer quite so comfortable close to him. Not to mention the clientele would probably be rough and if he needed to fight, she didn't want to be in his way.

Sway opened the door and led them into the dark room as Vik and Omari rejoined them. Loud voices and music mingled in the air, making her ears throb. She'd never cared for these types of places. Too many years of pulling her drunken father out of them while he cursed her for it had left her with bitter memories she wished she could erase.

Banishing the thought, she followed behind Devyn as they made their way through the pub to one of the tables in the back.

She slowed as she saw where they were headed. There were three of the deadliest looking men she'd ever seen gathered around a large round table.

At first glance, one of them had an almost baby face. Portly and tall, he was dressed in black and had a pair of opaque shades covering his eyes. It would be easy for most people to dismiss him as the least harmful of the group.

But that would be stupid and most likely fatal. There was an unmistakable aura of bloodthirst that surrounded him, and it was one she knew well.

The man next to him was absolutely stunning. He had dark blond hair and several days' growth of whiskers on his cheeks. His pewter eyes missed nothing. Dressed in dark brown, he kept one hand on his blaster even though he was leaned back in his chair, looking deceptively at ease.

And as her gaze went to the third one, her breath caught. Lethal and feral were the only words to describe him. He wore his jet-black hair short and had one arm slung over the back of his chair while he drank Tondarion Fire straight out of the bottle.

She could feel the burn of the potent whisky that was so strong, it was banned on most planets.

He sat with a grimace while he listened to some story the baby-faced man was telling him. But when he saw Devyn, his features relaxed and a slow smile spread across his face, making him even more dazzling.

Wow . . . he gave Devyn a good run for his money.

"*Aridos*," he greeted, using the Ritadarion word for *brother*. "Good to see you again." He rose to his feet and held his hand out to Devyn.

Devyn took it and hugged him close. "You're looking surly as ever."

The blond man scoffed as he crossed his arms across his chest. "He *is* surly as ever." He glanced over at Sway. "You sure I can't bribe you to trade jobs with me?"

Sway laughed. "You say that only 'cause you

don't fly with Captain Hothead. If you did, you'd know better. Trust me. He's a bigger PITA than Taryn."

"Yeah, right. You keep saying that 'cause you don't want me to replace you."

Sway stepped back and, in an arrogant gesture, spread his arms out. "*You* could never replace *me*, Sphinx."

"Yeah," Devyn said, laughing. "Thank the gods there's only one Sway. Can you imagine if there was another one?"

They all laughed.

Devyn held a seat out for her. Amazed at the gesture, Alix sat down across from the darkly handsome stranger, who eyed her curiously.

"Who's *your* friend?"

Devyn took a seat at her right and Sway on her left. Omari sat between Sway and Vik.

"She's my new engineer." Devyn inclined his head to the dark-haired man. "Alix, meet another of my childhood friends, Taryn Quiakides."

She scowled at the surname of a man so fierce that he'd once terrified The League into granting immunity to a rogue assassin—something they'd never done before or since.

Even more impressive than that, the man who'd borne that name had gone on to become the Trioson and Andarion emperor. And no one crossed the assassin emperor, who was known to have no mercy or compassion for any enemy.

It wasn't a common name, and she'd only known

of it being used in reference to him. "Related to Emperor Nykyrian Quiakides?"

"My father."

Her stomach hit the floor. This was getting interesting. No wonder Merjack wanted conclusive proof of Devyn's activities. If Devyn was friends with the Quiakides family . . .

He had a lot of political pull.

Titanic political pull. The kind that could get one killed if they didn't follow the exact letter of the law. Holy crap. Going after him was looking less and less promising.

Taryn dipped his head to her. "Nice to meet you, Alix."

"You, too . . ." It was a lame response, but what else could she say? She, a petty slave, was sitting down across from a royal prince at a dive. She had no experience in anything even remotely similar to this.

Was she supposed to curtsy?

"Um, Your Highness," she finished weakly.

Taryn waved her words away. "Don't be so formal. We don't play that shit here. If we're not at court or a public function with my parents, I'm not royal." He swept a gaze around at his men. "God knows my crew certainly doesn't kiss my ass no matter how much I kick theirs."

Sphinx grabbed Taryn's bottle and drank out of it before he responded. "That depends on whether or not you're holding a weapon in your hand."

Devyn laughed. "Yeah, Taryn stinks like the rest of us. More so, most days."

"Fuck you, Devyn." The words were harsh, but Taryn's tone was light.

"You are so not my type, Tar. But I do have—"

Taryn tossed a throwing knife at him.

Devyn caught it without flinching and put it on the table between them. "Testy, testy. What has you in such a foul mood?"

Taryn curled his lip in a look of supreme disgust. "Reen is flying with me. Need I say more?"

Alix frowned. "Reen?"

Omari let out an evil snicker. "His baby sister. They don't really get along."

"Yeah, she's seventeen going on four, and she's been working my last nerve into an apoplexy. I swear if my parents weren't so attached to her, I'd send her headfirst out an airlock."

Devyn shook his head. "Why is she with you?"

"Absolutely don't go there. Little brat's been hanging around my neck like a noose. I tried to leave her at headquarters, but she snuck on board my ship when we headed here to meet you. I'd sell her to a slaver, but I don't want to face my father—never know when those hard-wired assassin reflexes are going to eradicate all sense of paternal instinct." He paused and looked at Vik. "Hey, Vik, any chance you might—"

"Forget it, bonebag. Your father doesn't like mechas."

"Don't take that personally. He doesn't like people, either. Hell, most days he barely tolerates me."

Devyn laughed. "That's so not true."

Vik talked over him to respond to Taryn. "But he won't dismantle *you*. Me, on the other hand . . ."

Taryn *tsk*ed at him. "You're such a coward, mech."

"Absolutely. Would have it no other way."

Leaning closer to Alix, Devyn indicated the blond man next to Taryn. "That's Sphinx, who, besides me, is the best pilot in the universe."

Taryn arched a brow. "I seriously resent that."

Devyn shrugged. "Resent it all you want, but it's the truth." He looked at Alix. "Taryn's skills are much like my father's. Filching and killing."

Sphinx held his hand out to Alix. "Nice meeting you."

"Same."

The other man flipped his long curly hair over his shoulder before he sat forward. "I would be Mered. And I'm *really* good in bed."

Wide-eyed at the unexpected introduction, she glanced around at the other men, who were either rolling their eyes or scoffing.

Taryn let out a long-suffering sigh. "Lack of self-esteem has never been an issue with Mered. Obviously."

Sphinx laughed evilly. "Nah, but lack of hygiene has."

Mered bristled. "You rank bastard. Can't you see I'm trying to get laid?"

"With Devyn's engineer? Give it up, buddy. He'd neuter you if you succeeded."

Mered looked at Devyn. "Dev, help a brother out."

"I ain't your pimp, boy. You better turn those desperate eyes elsewhere. What Alix does with her spare time is her business. But I'm thinking she's got better sense and taste than to waste time on a stink-scab like you."

Mered let out a tired breath. "I'm going to quit while I'm on the ground being viciously kicked by people who are supposed to be my friends . . . but I will remember this." He took a drink of whisky. "Bastards."

Sphinx poked his lips out. "Poor baby. Them mean old people picking on you again and hurting your little feelings?" He reached out sympathetically.

Mered knocked his arm off his shoulder. "You are so not right in the head, you twisted fuck."

Ignoring them, Devyn sat forward in his chair and caught Taryn's attention. "Did you get all the medical supplies I asked for?"

Taryn crossed his arms over his chest. "I got them, but you should know The League enforcers at Paradise City have been scanning cargoes for perillian and antibiotics for the last two weeks. Someone told them a large shipment would be coming in, and that its destination was for the rebel outposters in the mines. They don't know it's you, but they plan to put whoever they find with it under the jail."

Her heart skipped a beat. The last thing she wanted was a run-in with The League. An elite military organization, The League had charters from all the major governments granting it the right to act as judge, jury and executioner against anyone it deemed a threat to intergalactic peace. More than one rumor claimed The League served only itself, and she knew crossing The League would be the last mistake she or Devyn ever made—even with his political pull.

Not even Taryn's father could save them.

Devyn narrowed his eyes at Taryn. That cold, merciless look sent a chill down her spine. "Any idea who leaked?"

Taryn shook his head. "No, but I'd be real careful. You know what a hard-on The League has for you, anyway. They would literally kill to have this on you."

"I'll guard my back."

"And I'll guard the rest of you!"

Taryn let out a foul curse.

Alix turned around at the sound of a sultry female voice. Her mouth opened in stunned surprise. The most beautiful woman she'd ever seen leaned over Devyn and kissed his cheek.

Hair as black as space cascaded from the top of an assassin's skullcap down to the woman's tiny waist. Unbelievably tall and dressed in a skimpy black suit that barely covered the necessary parts of her body, the woman had a figure she would kill for. She wore one blaster strapped to her left hip, and the silver handle of a dagger peeped out of the top of her shiny black thigh-high boots.

Meeting the woman's friendly gaze, she realized the stranger was Andarion—a fierce race of predators who were rumored to eat human meat.

But not even the oddity of Andarion eyes—white irises surrounded by a very thin ring of red—or her long fangs detracted from the beauty of her face.

Devyn kissed her cheek in return. "Someone needs to tie a bell on you. I hate the way you sneak up behind me."

The woman laughed before making her way around the table to hug Sway, then Vik. "Oh, I've missed you guys." She emphasized her words with a tight squeeze to Vik. "So where's Golan?"

Devyn scoffed. "He was arrested and detained. Alix here is our new engineer."

"Hi." She took a seat between Sway and Omari. "I'm Zarina, but you can call me Rina." She cut a hostile glare to her brother. "Not Reen. I really *hate* that."

"Gah, I need to have that tattooed to my forehead." Taryn looked at Sphinx. "You know a good artist at this station?"

Sphinx hit him playfully on the arm. "One day she's going to shoot you and I'm going to laugh my ass off while you bleed from it."

Taryn didn't seem the least bit concerned as he turned his attention back to his younger sister. "Did you lock Strife in the ladies' room again? I swear, Reen, if I have to bail him out one more time because of—"

"Relax, you obnoxious pirate-snot. I only kicked him." She pointed toward the door.

Alix turned to see a gorgeous man drawing near. Like Omari, he had a head full of riotous curls that fell against features that were sharp and virtually perfect, only his hair was dark auburn instead of Omari's dark brown. With a small goatee, he was dressed in a gunmetal-gray battlesuit.

Holding his crotch, he was limping and scowling at Zarina. The mere fact that he could still be hot while doing that . . .

It said it all.

"*You*—" he snarled at Taryn. "Do. Not. Pay. Me. Enough. I want a raise right now or I quit."

Taryn glared at his sister. "It's coming out of *your* trust fund."

"Oh, that's not fair."

"Yes, it is. I can't replace Strife. He's the best damned assassin in the universe. You, on the other hand . . . I've got another sister."

She made a rude noise at him. "Excuse me, Mr. I-Have-a-Twin. You're less unique than I am and I must say Tiernan is by far the nicer of you two."

"Then please, go stay with him. I would sell my soul to be rid of you." He looked over at Sphinx. "Can't you nudge her into submission?"

"Are you kidding? As stubborn as she is? I'd fry my brain trying."

Alix was still stunned over Zarina's appearance. She couldn't believe her brother let her parade around dressed in something so skimpy at her age, and the fact that she was armed . . .

Amazing.

Devyn leaned over and whispered in Alix's ear. Chills went down her arms as his breath tickled her skin. "Can I ask a huge favor from you?"

Please let it start with the words "Get naked in my room."

"Sure."

He pulled his debit card out and handed it to her. "Could you take Rina somewhere else to eat while I do business?"

She wasn't so sure about that. Zarina didn't seem exactly malleable.

In fact, the girl was already glowering at both of them. "Don't tell me." Her next words were spoken in a mocking tone. "We've got business to discuss. Would you mind giving us a few minutes 'cause you're a girl and we're going to play at being men?"

Taryn tipped his bottle to his sister in a mock salute. "Since you already knew our thoughts, why did you disturb us?"

She pierced him with a malevolent glare. "Suck an asteroid berry, you pirate-snot." She glanced at the men around her, all of whom were trying to stifle their laughter at her words.

Realizing they weren't going to interfere on her

behalf, she sniffed in mock hurt. "Fine." She lifted her chin defiantly. "Sit around being inconsiderate asses . . . and you wonder why none of you are married."

Sway cleared his throat meaningfully.

Zarina scoffed at him. "Oh, shush. You don't count. You had an arranged marriage. These losers can't get a girl for more than the three and a half minutes it takes them to embarrass themselves with their feeble gropings that always disappoint."

It was Vik's turn to clear his throat. "On behalf of the mecha population, we don't suffer from certain biological frailties that plague organic life forms."

"Thanks, Vik," Taryn said sarcastically. "Way to defend us, buddy."

"Well, I have been told—"

"Uh-uh-uh." Taryn cut Vik off. "You've done enough damage, mech. Just sit there and be quiet before we organics seek revenge."

Zarina stood. "You know, Alix, men suck. Really. They are the worst. Come with me. I need an estrogen fix before their chromosomal defects contaminate me any further."

Still somewhat confused, Alix followed Zarina out of the pub.

She didn't know what to make of this. Part of her said that she should stay and spy on what the men were doing, but hearsay wasn't proof. She needed hard-core, irrefutable documentation of Devyn's activities, and they didn't strike her as being stupid enough to have that on them in a public forum.

Not even in this place, where illegal activities were happening all over.

Zarina stopped in the hallway, turned around, and glared at the door. Her eyes glittered with malice as she leaned against the outside wall, crossed her arms over her chest, and tapped her fingers against her upper arms. "How can you love and hate someone so much?"

Alix had no idea. She'd never had emotions that conflicting. Hers were basic. She loved her mother and sister, and hated her father. But then, her life had always been one of simplistic survival mode.

Dreams, hopes, future plans . . . those were things that belonged to free citizens. So at her mother's insistence, she'd banished those kinds of thoughts at an early age. It was only now when she had a hope of being free to make her own life that she even began to think about tomorrow as being something better.

Zarina narrowed her eyes before she resumed her tirade. "I swear one day I'm going to kill him." She huffed. "Do you have a brother?"

"No."

"Lucky you. I have four. You want one?"

Alix laughed. "If they all make you want to kill them, then I'll pass. I think I'm all right without one."

"Wise woman. Though to be honest, they're not all total dicks. Jayce and I get along, and I used to be best friends with Adron . . ."

She frowned at the catch in Zarina's tone. "Used to be?"

Her eyes turned dull. "My oldest brother was a League assassin and had a bad run-in with a psycho animal who left him crippled. He'll never be the same again, I'm afraid. Even though he lived through it, a part of him died that night, and I miss the brother I used to have. That being said, I'm grateful to God that I do still have him, even as surly as he is. So I won't complain about him at all. The twins, however—"

"Work your last nerve?"

"Exactly." Letting out a long sigh, she took Alix's arm and pulled her toward a very nice restaurant. "But let's not talk about my brothers. I have something much more interesting to discuss with you."

"And that is?"

"The fact that we need to get Devyn in your bed ASAP."

Where had *that* come from? This was a topic that she definitely didn't feel comfortable talking about with someone so young.

But as Alix tried to talk, she realized something . . .

Zarina didn't listen, and as they walked on, Alix began to panic.

The future Zarina had in mind for her was even more terrifying than the one Merjack wanted.

God help me . . .

CHAPTER 5

"So what gives with you and that new engineer of yours?"

Dev looked up from the box he was storing to find Taryn standing behind him. "I swear I'm going to tie a bell around you, too, if you don't start making noise when you walk."

Taryn grinned. "I blame it on my dad and his hyper-hearing. You either learned to move without a sound or you got busted every time you sneezed wrong—which for me was every minute I was awake."

Devyn laughed. That was certainly true. Nykyrian's hearing had been a serious bitch on them when they'd been kids trying to get away with things. But for all the man's sternness, he'd never once raised a hand or even his voice to any of them.

Then again, Nykyrian was so terrifying, he didn't have to. His glower alone could instantly freeze screaming kids right where they stood.

"And I noticed you didn't answer my question."

Devyn shoved the box into place and moved out of the hold to stand in front of Taryn. He wiped his brow on his sleeve. "There's nothing to say. She's my employee." *Who I'm sleeping with 'cause I'm stupid.*

"Who happens to look just like—"

Devyn held his hand up to cut off that sentence before Taryn finished it. "She's not her so let's not go there." Even though he had to remind himself of that every now and again. It still unnerved him how much the two women looked alike.

But unlike Clotilde, Alix had a conscience.

Taryn tapped him on the chest, right where the vicious scar over his heart was located. "If you say you're okay, I won't push it. But I know what you're not saying. Betrayal like that never goes away. Especially not when it comes from the woman who was supposed to be your better half for the rest of your life."

That was an unfortunate bond they both shared. However, Taryn's fiancée hadn't tried to cut his heart out on her way out the door. She'd only stepped all over it.

"Alix isn't a hired assassin coming after me. She has no higher agenda where I'm concerned." He hated the tightness in his voice when he spoke. Like Taryn had said, some betrayals never healed, and Clotilde's still burned raw inside him.

How he hated that bitch.

He'd known Clotilde was an assassin when they hooked up. What he'd never considered was that after a three-year relationship and just days before they were supposed to get married, she'd take money to kill him. Especially not after everything he'd done for her.

Lethal bitch.

Pushing that thought away, he moved to the next box that was on the ground waiting to be loaded.

"Why isn't Vik loading cargo for you?"

"He's watching Omari, who needs to replace his MVM player. Given the rough crowd here, I didn't want him out on his own. Too many might mistake him for an easy mark, and while he can hold his own, I don't want to take the chance on someone getting in a lucky shot on him. Or even worse, Omari killing someone at his age and having to deal with that crisis." Both he and Taryn had been forced to take a life before they'd turned twenty. It was something a man never got over.

That first kill . . .

He wanted to spare his son that misery if he could.

Taryn narrowed his gaze. "What about Sway?"

"With Claria."

Growling low in his throat, Taryn grabbed the box from his hands.

Devyn cursed as he tried to take it back. "I'm not helpless."

Taryn jerked it out of his reach. "No, but you don't need to strain yourself and you know it. Your heart can't take it."

Devyn felt his jaw starting to tic as his anger

ignited. Yeah, that was Clotilde's gift that kept on giving. It was also the real reason why his parents maintained constant tabs on him. They'd come too close to losing him that night. Had his father not been on his way to Devyn's house, he'd be dead now. His father had saved his life, but the cost for living was a bad heart that seriously limited what he could do.

And he hated being weak.

It could be worse. You could be dead.

Or he could be Adron . . .

True. He had no right to complain about his own physical limitations when his were hidden and unknown to his enemies. While a pain in the ass, his ruptured heart didn't stop him from doing many things.

Still, he hated whenever someone treated him like an invalid.

"You're such a bastard, Taryn."

He grinned. "I know, Reen. Thanks."

Devyn rolled his eyes as Taryn called him by his sister's name. "So how is Adron?" He thought about his old friend a lot. But Adron barely spoke to him anymore. He was isolated in a world of painful bitterness that caused him to shut out everyone who loved him.

Taryn set the box down and sighed. "Same as always. Angry at the world and wanting to kill Jayce."

Their brother Jayce had been the one to save Adron's life, and for that, Adron hated his brother with a passion. The code of the assassin was to die should they ever be crippled by their duties. If another assassin found one seriously comprised, he was supposed to kill him. But Jayce had been unable to kill his own brother.

And even though Adron wanted to die, he refused to hurt his family by killing himself. So he was trapped in a body that wouldn't work while he lived a life of utter misery in constant pain.

"Is Jayce any better?" Devyn asked.

"No. None of us are." His dark eyes flashed. "Which is why I don't want you straining yourself. I already have one hardheaded asshole bent on suicide. I don't need another one."

Devyn held his hands up in surrender. "By all means, get a hernia. Knock yourself out. Gods forbid I stop you. Not like I spent ten years in med school or anything to know when I need to sit down."

Taryn made an obscene gesture before he hefted another box.

But in all seriousness, Devyn understood why Adron hated the world. There were times when he did, too. Nothing like being royally fucked over by someone you loved to suck the will to live right out of you. This was not the life he'd dreamed of when he was a kid.

He'd imagined a world of justice where he'd fight for The League to protect the innocent. A world that included a woman who would stand by his side.

Not one who would smile at his face while she drove a knife through his heart.

Literally.

And babies . . . He'd imagined a lot of kids. Omari would make one hell of an older brother to someone.

You have no right to complain.

True.

It's all good. He had a great son who did honor to both of them, and more than that—*we're all fed and no one's dead.* That had always been his uncle's philosophy. So long as those two things were taken care of, nothing else really mattered.

He saw an image of Alix in his mind and actually flinched. More than anything, she reminded him of those long-buried dreams he'd once shared with Clotilde. Damn her for looking so much like her.

And damn her for being so enticing as to make him want to forget about Clotilde and start over.

Don't . . .

He had a new future to focus on. One that didn't include anything except keeping his crew safe and helping the rebels who opposed The League. That was the only thing he needed to expend his energy on.

"I am *not* interested in Devyn."

You're such a liar.

But it was something Alix had to teach herself to believe.

Zarina made a very undignified sound of disagreement. "Honey, you look at that man like you can already taste him. I know that look. I've had it a time or two myself. Not at Devyn, 'cause . . . ew! That's like fantasizing over one of my brothers, but I know tasty when I see it and I know that man well enough to know that he's not immune to you, either. Devyn is *very* interested."

Yeah, right. Alix was anything but stupid, and she knew that while Devyn was kind to her in bed, he didn't have any deeper feelings for her than that. Dreams were for fools and men only used the women around them. Once done, they moved on.

Unless they owned the woman. Then they used her to their heart's content without any regard for her feelings. That was probably why the Hyshians had chosen to enslave and subjugate their men.

But that was neither here nor there. Devyn was the key to her freedom and that was all he could ever be.

Alix looked away as the waiter brought their dessert. She'd been trying for the last half hour to change the subject, but Zarina wouldn't be swayed. She was an obsessive personality who had a raw determination that only a three-year-old could envy.

"I'm not his type."

Zarina gave her a droll stare. "Do you even know what that is?"

Alix sighed. "No, but I'm rather sure it begins with gorgeous, which is a far cry from me."

"Do you even own a mirror?"

"Yeah. I do." And she'd used it enough to know that she was too curveless, too pale and too fragile. To quote her father, she looked like something a wolf had gobbled up and shit down the wrong side of a mountain.

Zarina rolled her eyes before she dug into her purse. After a few seconds, she pulled out a small photo MVM and scrolled through it. She handed it to Alix. "You were saying?"

Alix's breath caught as she looked down and saw a woman who bore an uncanny resemblance to her. The only difference was the other woman wore a lot of makeup and had short hair.

And her attitude was completely different. Unlike Alix, she stood confident.

No . . .

Defiant.

There was something about the woman in the picture that seemed cold and deadly. Even though she was leaning against a younger Devyn and smiling, there was something about her that wasn't right. She looked too calculating and icy. As if she were only interested in what she could take from the world.

Alix handed the photo back to Zarina. "Who is she?"

"Clotilde Renier."

"She's beautiful."

"And you're a dead ringer for her."

Alix shook her head in denial. "Not quite. I've never looked like that. For one thing, I'm pretty sure I was born in more clothes than she's wearing in that picture." She returned to eating her dessert. "Is she Devyn's girlfriend?"

"She *was* his fiancée."

She paused at the way Zarina had said that. "Was?"

"He killed her."

Alix felt the color fade from her face at the deadly note in Zarina's voice. She'd known Devyn was lethal, but to kill his own fiancée?

He's going to rip you to shreds . . .

"He did what?"

Zarina waved her fear away. "Relax. It was justified."

Only an assassin's daughter could think that. "How is killing your fiancée justified?"

Zarina returned the MVM player to her bag. "She tried to kill him first and almost succeeded. In the beginning of her attack, Devyn refused to fight her, but she gave him no choice. Had he not killed her, she would have killed him."

Alix couldn't breathe as that reality slammed into her. Had Merjack known that? What the hell had he been thinking by sending her in to frame Devyn when he'd killed the woman she resembled?

You are so screwed . . .

And Merjack was a first-rank troll to do something so cruel.

Zarina patted her hand. "Don't look so scared."

If the woman only knew *why* she was so terrified.

"It really is all right. I just wanted you to see what you *could* look like if you wanted to."

"Yeah, well, I think I'd rather look like me and not have Captain Kell go bended and slaughter me during some psychotic episode where he thinks I'm her."

Was Zarina nuts trying to put them together? It was a wonder Devyn had even let her near his ship, never mind his body.

She shook her head. "Alix, you are hopeless."

"Not hopeless. I just know the rules, and men like Captain Kell don't involve themselves with women like me." On many, many levels.

"And renowned dancers don't marry outlawed League assassins. Yet here I am, the daughter of the most unlikely couple in the universe. Second only to maybe Dev's parents." She gave her a hard stare. "I believe in the impossible. It happens every day."

"And I believe in reality."

"Reality is boring."

No, it wasn't. It was dangerous and scary. But Alix didn't try to contradict her as she finished up her ice cream. Honestly, she just wanted to get back and finish this so that she could see her mother and sister again.

Zarina gave her a reprieve while she waved at someone sitting at another table.

Alix frowned as she turned to see two big, burly men not far from them. "What are you doing?"

"Acknowledging my bodyguards."

Now she was completely confused. "I thought Sphinx was your bodyguard?"

"You mean Strife. And no . . . he was tailing me per my brother's orders to keep me out of trouble."

"Isn't that what bodyguards do?"

"No. My bodyguards don't interfere with what I want to do. They just make sure no one bothers me. The appropriately named Strife, on the other hand, is a major buzz kill since he's always terminating whatever fun I find. In turn, I abuse him for it."

"That's really messed up."

"Tell me about it." Zarina pushed her chair back. "I have to go to the ladies' room. I'll be right back."

Alix didn't move as she saw the two men fall in line to follow after Zarina.

Wow. How had she missed them? But then, she didn't normally pay attention to things like that.

Maybe she should.

"What do you think you're doing?"

She jumped at the deep, unfamiliar voice in her ear. "Excuse me?"

Even though the man was at least twenty years older than her, he was unbelievably handsome with sharp features and a lean build. His dark hair fell across a pair of icy hazel eyes. "Merjack put you on orders that didn't include lunching with a spoiled princess and living a life well above your putrid station."

Her blood ran cold at his angry words. How did he know about that? "Who are you?"

He flashed a Ritadarion investigator's shield at her. "Lieutenant Paden Whelms. And I'm your contact until you finish your mission."

She scowled at him as he tucked the badge away. "I don't understand."

He leaned down to snarl at her. "Merjack can't leave his post, nor can he be seen communicating with a slave. But as his agent, I'm able to keep my sights on you. Have you found anything we can use?"

She swallowed in fear at his intense, hostile glare. "N-not yet."

He cursed before he turned that maniacal gaze back on her. There was so much hatred reflected in those eyes that she couldn't fathom it. What had she done to him?

"Don't even think about double-crossing the CMOD, little girl. He eats trash like you for lunch."

"I-I would never. Kell's a very cautious man and I haven't been able to access anything . . . yet. But I will."

"Time's running out." He held a link in her face that showed a photo of her mother and sister. Tears bristled in their lashes as they held each other close. "I expect the files we need at your next stop, which will be at Charisis, day after tomorrow."

She shook her head at him. "We're not going there."

"Yes, you are. I've arranged for a little malfunction that you won't see until you're in space. The only place for the part is on Charisis. You *will* be there, and one way or another, this will end. Trust me."

Funny how those two words gave her chills.

He held the picture up for her one more time. "Their lives are in your hands. Do not fail."

Alix wanted to slap the arrogance off his face. She hated being at his mercy. Most of all, she hated being forced to hurt a man who'd been nothing but kind to her.

Devyn didn't deserve this . . .

With a disdainful curl to his lip, Whelms turned on his heel and left.

She watched him leave as her anger toward him and Merjack mounted. "I'm going to get my family free," she said under her breath. "And then I'm going to kill *both* of you."

That was so long as Devyn didn't kill *her* first.

CHAPTER 6

"Do you ever get the feeling there's something odd about our new engineer?"

Devyn paused while he finished his current log. He looked up to find Sway joining him on the bridge. "I thought you and Claria were . . ." He cleared his throat meaningfully. "Busy."

Sway scratched his chin in an irritated gesture. "She had to take a call that I'm not authorized to hear."

Devyn snorted at the typical government BS and paranoia. "Sorry they interrupted your fun."

"Yeah, me, too. So? What about it?"

He saved his work before he spoke again. "I think she's suspicious of us—not surprising for a woman her age in an all-male crew. I'd be nervous with our sorry asses, too." He glanced back at Sway. "Have you noticed something more?"

"I can't put my finger on it. There's just something about her that doesn't sit right with me."

"Other than the fact that she reminds you of Clotilde, who you always hated?"

"There is that, and I won't be an 'I told you so' where that bitch is concerned, so I won't go there. But no, this is something else. It's like she's hiding something . . . I can feel it."

Devyn shrugged his concern away. "We're all hiding something, *aridos*. My dubious lineage and health, your grandfather's reputation, Omari's abilities and Vik's special programming. If she didn't have something of a similar nature to keep from us, she definitely wouldn't fit in with this crew."

Sway gave him a hard stare. "You're making excuses again. I thought you said you'd never do that for another woman."

Devyn froze at the reminder. Sway was right. He'd made excuse after excuse for Clotilde. Even when every instinct in him had said something wasn't right, he'd dismissed it.

Had he only listened to himself . . .

Was he doing that again?

The thought sobered him. "I'll watch her closely."

Sway inclined his head.

"Here you are. I wondered where you'd gotten off to."

Devyn smiled as he saw Claria join them. Tall and lithe, she was exquisitely beautiful with long black hair she wore in braids that matched Sway's—another Hyshian custom. Damn, for a right to her, he'd have sold himself into slavery, too.

Sway was a lucky man.

She turned her attention to Devyn. "Sway says you've been taking really good care of him for me."

He laughed. "Well, his mom did a great job housebreaking him, so he doesn't require too much work. Not to mention Vik doesn't mind walking him once a day. It's all good."

She rolled her eyes. "You're such a smartass."

"I come by it honestly. You've met my parents. You understand."

Shaking her head, she sobered as she looked at Sway. "By the way, you should know that your Alix is a ghost."

Devyn arched a brow at Sway. "You had Claire look into Alix?"

"No," Claria said quickly. "I took the initiative myself. I want to know who's on crew with my husband."

"And you found nothing?"

Claria shook her head. "She's completely off-grid."

Devyn let that knowledge sink in. "How is that possible?"

"You tell me. I found her birth certificate and nothing else."

This really wasn't a good sign. "What about her parents?"

"Nothing on either one. Only their names on her birth registration."

Devyn felt as if all the oxygen had been sucked out of the room. Ghosts were rare and it usually meant a spy of some sort.

Or one hell of a master criminal.

His father was the king of the untraceable ghosts, so he knew it could mean she wasn't up to anything more than protecting herself. But it could also mean she was here to do who knew what.

She could easily be a danger to all of them.

Claria gave him a hard stare. "I think you should fire her. For everyone's safety."

"I want to know more before I make that call." He picked up his link.

She scowled at him. "What are you doing?"

"Calling my dad. If anyone can find her past, he can." No one escaped one of his father's probes.

Alix watched through the store window as Omari and Vik laughed over something Omari had said while they were looking at MVM players. Even though it was abnormal for a mecha and a human, their friendship made something inside her ache with longing.

She missed her sister so much . . .

Tempest was the only friend she'd ever had, and the two of them had always been a united front against their father and his hostile animosity toward them. If only she could hear Tempest's voice and know that she was all right.

"Are you okay?"

She blinked as Zarina rejoined her. She'd vanished inside a store that Alix had declined entering. An exclusive boutique that specialized in high-end designer wear, Alix had been afraid to browse just in case they charged her for looking at it.

And with her luck, they might.

"I'm fine."

Zarina scowled at her. "You look so sad. Are you homesick?"

No, she was sister-sick, but she couldn't admit that. "Just tired."

Zarina scoffed. "You know, people always say that when it's not true. We barely know each other and you don't want me to pry. I understand." She held a bag out to her. "Here."

Now it was her turn to frown. "What's this?"

"Something I think you'll like."

Alix shook her head. The bag alone probably cost more than she did. "Oh, no, I can't."

"You can and you will."

"Zarina—"

"Ah!" Zarina held her hand up imperiously. "Don't even. I won't hear it. Every woman deserves something to make her feel beautiful and I have a feeling your wardrobe consists mostly of the kind of serviceable clothes you're wearing— which while they're attractive on you, aren't really fun. We all need some fun. Embrace your youth while you have it."

Alix swallowed as her throat tightened. No one had ever been so kind to her. "Thank you."

Zarina hugged her. "You're very welcome. Now let's hit Tadaro's."

"What's Tadaro's?"

Her face a mock mask of pain, Zarina placed her hand over her heart. "Oh, hon, you have been so deprived." She took her hand and pulled her down the corridor into a makeup store.

Alix wasn't so sure about this, either. It all looked so . . .

Girly.

"So what do you prefer?" Zarina stopped next to a perfume display.

She looked at all the various lotions and potions and had no idea. "I've never worn makeup."

Zarina gaped at her. "You're not serious."

She shook her head. Her father would have sooner cut off his arm than allow her to waste money on something so frivolous. Only he could waste money on anything not absolutely necessary.

"Not even lipstick?"

"Nothing."

Zarina put a gentle hand on her shoulder. "You poor child. You've been so deprived." She motioned for a clerk to come help them. "I have a cosmetic emergency here and I need the best of everything to cure it."

"Zarina—"

She made a hissing noise, cutting Alix off as she raised her hand. "Don't even start. No woman over the age of fourteen should walk around bare-faced. Not that you're not beautiful, but . . . we can all use a boost." She turned back to the clerk. "Set my sister up."

Alix literally felt like the only piece of meat at

a kennel as a team of women descended on her to trim her hair, tweeze her brows—something that had to have been invented by a sadist—and make her face over.

"Ow!" She pulled her hand back from the woman who was working on her fingernails. "I didn't know being a woman could be so painful."

Zarina gave her a pitiful stare. "Honey, beauty is pain and that's part of who and what we are."

Yeah, but she really didn't have time for this . . .

She needed to get back to the ship.

How did someone escape Zarina? She felt trapped and overwhelmed.

Someone help me . . .

"Zarina, I really need to get back. I-I have duties to attend to."

"Sit there and be quiet. There's nothing Devyn needs done that can't wait. Besides, you'll be so beautiful when we're through that he won't care. There won't even be any blood left in his brain for him to think with."

"But—"

"No buts. I always win. Give up now before you annoy me."

Alix sighed as she realized that Zarina was a power unto herself. It was better to give in and get it over with than to fight against an omnipotent opponent.

It was not only frustrating. It was impossible.

Please get me out of here soon.

* * *

"Hey, Dad. Where's Alix?"

Devyn looked up from the paperwork he was forging to see Omari and Vik entering the bridge. Manashe ran from where he'd been sleeping at Devyn's feet to attack Omari. "She was off with Rina last I saw."

Omari shivered as he stroked Manashe's ears. "Poor thing. I wonder what Rina's doing to her. Should we send out a search party?"

Devyn laughed. "Might not be a bad idea. I vote we send Taryn in to extract her. He's got nothing to live for."

Vik arched a brow. "Well, at least you didn't pick on me this time."

"Feeling left out?"

"Not where Princess Stubborn's concerned. Happy to be left out, boss. Thanks for the uncharacteristic consideration. You feeling all right, or is there a brain malfunction going on that I need to be aware of before your father removes parts of me I might miss?"

Omari laughed. "You know, I wish I could have seen Vik back in his aviary days. He must have been a riot."

Devyn smiled nostalgically as he remembered Vik's old mecha form. "Not really. He just took up less room and was able to sneak up on me a lot easier. Happiest day of my life when my dad made him human."

"Happy for you, bonebag . . . It cost *me* my girl-friend."

Omari arched a brow as he pulled a treat out of his pocket and fed it to Manashe. "You had a girl-friend?"

Devyn chuckled. "It was a lamp, Vik, not a girl-friend."

Vik sighed wistfully. "I really loved that lamp. She lit up my entire world."

Omari frowned as he met Devyn's gaze. "Is he for real?"

" 'Fraid so. He used to carry it around with him until it stopped working. I think your grandfather screwed up his processors when he pulled him apart."

Vik cuffed Devyn on the back of his head. "Respect your elders, embryo."

Devyn hissed as he rubbed the back of his skull. "I might not know how to repair you, Vik, but I do know how to break you into small pieces."

"As if."

Deciding he was losing this argument, Devyn indicated the bag in Omari's hand with a tilt of his chin. "So what did you get?"

Just as Omari started to speak, the intercom buzzed.

Devyn leaned back and would have ignored it had it not been the station's security. He opened the channel. "Kell speaking."

"Captain Kell, we have a warrant here to search your cargo and review your manifest and logs. We need you front and center. Now."

"On my way." But not at their pace. They could wait until he got there. He didn't answer orders well.

Sighing, he looked at Omari. "Sorry, kid. I'll look at it later."

"No problem. Let me go lock up Manashe so he doesn't get out while they're looking for contraband, and then head over to warn Sway in case they're in his room . . . you know."

"Yeah, I do." Devyn walked off the bridge and to the ramp where the authorities were waiting. As soon as the loading ramp was extended, they barged up so they could bluster in front of him. As if *they* could ever scare him.

Their captain handed him a printout for the warrant. "We want to see your cargo bay and sweep your ship."

It was all he could do not to laugh at them. "Whatever." He stood back as two dozen guards swarmed through his ship. This was going to be highly entertaining.

He pulled the fake manifest and log up on the screen by the door, then stepped aside for the captain to review it. "Just out of curiosity, why are you guys here?"

"We were given a tip that you have illegal contraband on board."

"A tip from whom?"

"A Lieutenant Whelms."

Devyn scowled at a name he'd never heard before. It didn't make sense that someone here would turn him in. Then again, it didn't make sense anyone would turn him in . . . period.

Weird.

He started to argue until his gaze went from the fat officer to the beautiful woman coming up his ramp.

It took a full ten seconds before he recognized her. Alix?

Yeah, it was her, and she was delicious. Someone had lightened her hair a couple of shades, making the blond even more vibrant. Her lips were painted a bright red and whatever they'd done to her eyes made them glow. They were dark and seductive now.

An image of her naked in his bed went through him so fast, he could almost feel her skin against his.

For a moment he couldn't breathe and he actually had a momentary fear that he might be drooling.

She frowned at the officer as she stopped in front of him. "What's going on?"

I want you to get naked . . .

Yeah, that was a bad idea when they were in the middle of a crisis.

Clearing his throat, he diverted his attention back to the enforcers. "We're being searched."

Panic flickered in her eyes, but she caught herself. "Why?"

"Someone reported us for illegal activity."

The officer turned on her. "Who are you and what do you do here?"

Devyn glared at the man and his sharp tone. "She's my engineer."

"She got papers?"

Alix pulled her ID out and handed it to him.

The captain barely glanced at it before he returned it to her and went back to scanning the manifest.

Devyn winked at her. *It's okay,* he mouthed to her behind the officer's back.

No sooner had he done that than six of the enforcers came running back to their captain.

"Sir, we have a problem."

The captain looked absolutely hopeful—like he could already imagine the promotion that would come from busting them. "You found something?"

"Yes, sir. Hyshian Senator Claria Trinaloew is on board and she's . . . she's really angry, sir."

"*Angry* is a mild term for what I feel right now."

Alix turned to see what had to be one of the most beautiful women to have ever lived. Tall, slender and regal, Claria had dark, smooth skin that was flawless. Her dark eyes scanned the men and women in front of her as if she were already savoring their punishment.

The senator cast a chilling, malevolent glare at the enforcers. "I have finite time with my husband and here you and your people dare to interrupt it with this kind of asinine bullshit? How dare you. I want you off this ship immediately. And for those of you incapable of understanding that word, it means now."

They literally ran off the ship.

Except for the enforcer captain. He stood there, trembling. "Forgive us, ma'am. We had no idea you were on board. We were told—"

"I don't want to hear it. Go before I recall my guards and have you up on charges."

He practically left a vapor trail behind him.

Devyn shut down the logs before he turned and smiled at her. "Thanks, Claire."

She gave him a peeved grimace. "Why can't you guys do something safe and sane for once like run bunnies or slippers or something?"

"It wouldn't be any fun."

She rolled her eyes. "I can't believe I let Sway travel with you. I must be insane."

"Yeah, but you love me."

"Not today I don't. You better watch your back, Kell. I might not be here the next time they want to search you." She looked at Alix and her gaze narrowed. "You must be the new engineer."

Alix hesitated as an absolute chill went down her spine. She sensed that Sway's wife didn't think much of her . . .

Did Claria know she was a slave?

"I am."

The senator cocked her head as she swept her gaze slowly over Alix's body in a less than complimentary way. With that one look, she made Alix feel less than nothing. "What ship were you on before this one?"

You worthless worm who is unfit to breathe the

same air I do . . . Claria didn't say the words per se, but her tone conveyed them loud and clear.

Devyn growled. "Claria—"

She held her hand up to silence Devyn in an imperious gesture. "Don't take that tone with me, Kell."

Devyn went ramrod stiff and an air came over him that was truly frightening. "I'm not your bitch, Claire. You don't *ever* talk to me like that." He cut a sideways look at Alix. "She's a member of my crew. You have an issue with her, you take it up with *me*."

Out of nowhere, Sway appeared. Before Alix could blink, he was between Devyn and Claria. He grabbed Devyn by his shirt and shoved him back. "You don't take that tone with my *wife*."

Devyn broke out of the hold and returned Sway's shove with one of his own. "You want to start some shit, boy? Let's go outside."

"Oh, good. I'm just in time for another round of Grand Testosterone Overdose. Ooooh, Alix, Claire . . . anyone got popcorn? Or maybe I should get Taryn? Then we could insult *his* manhood and watch him pop a gasket, too." Zarina's humor succeeded in breaking the tension as the men stepped away from each other.

Devyn turned that hostile stare toward Zarina. "What are you doing here?"

"I love you, too, Pookie Bear." She held a bag up. "Alix forgot this."

Claria watched them closely before she turned

her attention back to Devyn. "I still want to know something about her, Devyn. And considering the fact that your son is on board this vessel, you should, too."

So that was what was going on . . .

Claria was suspicious of her. Great. Just great. That was all she needed. Not that the woman shouldn't be suspicious, since she was here to ruin them.

But still . . .

Alix lifted her chin with a pride she really didn't feel right now. "The *Starfire*. It was a freighter owned by my father, who died two weeks ago. He was a pathetic alcoholic who seldom did his paperwork. We lived off-grid because he was a League conspiracist who woke up one day from a four-day bender with a tattoo on his arm that looked like a bar code of some sort. He swore it'd been put there by a League soldier and that they were getting ready to round all of us up and enslave us. I personally think our gunner did it to screw with him, but my father didn't listen. What else would you like to know?"

She wouldn't have thought it possible, but Claria managed to look even more haughty. "Where did you go to school?"

"I didn't. Again, my father didn't believe in leaving a trail to locate us by and he didn't believe in educating women." Actually, that wasn't true. He didn't believe in educating property, but to him women *were* property, so . . .

"Then how do you know how to read?"

Devyn took a step forward. "Claire—"

"It's all right." Alix refused to blink as she met the senator's penetrating glare that she was sure the woman used to intimidate people a lot more important than her. "I taught myself because I got tired of being called stupid. I used the voice search online to find the texts I needed and I went through them until I could speak and read in six languages, including Universal. I don't have any degrees and I don't have any formal training. I don't have any savings or money. Nothing but a sack full of worn-out clothes to call my own." She swallowed. "And it's obvious you don't think I'm good enough to be on this ship with your husband. I get it and it's okay. My father never thought I was good enough to be on his ship, either."

With those words spoken, she stepped past Claria and headed to her room so that the woman couldn't see just how hurt she really was.

Devyn glared at Claria. "That was cruel."

Claria refused to back down or apologize. "You don't know anything about her."

"And I told you I'd find out. You didn't have to humiliate her like that."

She looked at Zarina. "Would you help me out here?"

Zarina held her hands up in surrender. "No offense, but I'm on his side in this. I've just spent the afternoon with the woman and I really like her. She's very sweet and unassuming."

Claria curled her lip at them. "You're both fools, and I'm not about to leave my kitty with you."

Devyn sucked his breath in sharply at the term "kitty"—a derogatory Hyshian term for *property*. Had she even realized what a slip that was?

By Sway's demeanor, it was obvious he'd caught it.

Claria snapped her head toward her husband and in a tone that was a serious mistake said, "Collect your things. I'm taking you home with me."

Sway froze. "I'm not going."

She closed the distance between them and whispered in his ear, but her fury was so great that Devyn easily heard her words.

"You will do as you are told and you will not argue with me. Now move!"

Devyn motioned for Zarina to follow him so that they could give Sway and Claire privacy. He knew his friend well enough to guess there was about to be one hell of a battle over this, and it would go worse on Sway if there were witnesses to it. Sway might fight to the death to defend his wife, but not even she could order him around like that.

Sway hated orders as much as he did. Probably more so, given the way Sway had been raised. It was why he didn't stay with Claria's family—something customary for husbands who had no children. May the gods help her female relatives if they thought they could get away with what she was trying.

On their planet, Sway would be beaten hourly for his insubordination.

As soon as they'd closed the blast door and were moving down the hallway, Zarina arched a brow. "What hostile parasite is tunneling through *her* sphincter?"

"No idea, but that wasn't a wise use of her authority. Sway hates to be questioned even more than she does."

"Should we have left them alone?"

"Definitely. He won't hurt her and he might be able to defuse her temper if her authority over him isn't being questioned before witnesses."

Zarina shook her head. "I can't imagine being owned by someone. It has to be horrible."

"I can tell you from my League stint, it sucks. I hated being under someone else's control."

She passed a puzzled glance at him. "I still don't know why you did that."

He sighed as he remembered the stupidity of his youth. "I didn't want to be locked inside a hospital, under the control of admins and bureaucratic bullshit. Your brothers joined and seemed happy with it, so I thought I'd give it a try."

She scoffed at him. "My brothers were and are assassins, Dev. *Big* difference."

"I realize that . . . now."

She patted him lightly on the arm. "You know, there are times when 'You a fool' just doesn't cover it."

"Thanks, Rina."

"No problem. So, you gonna let me travel with you now?"

"Hell no."

She poked out her lip in a becoming pout that never failed to bend her brothers or father to her whims. "C'mon, Dev, be the sweetie I know you can be. I'd be a great addition to your crew."

Luckily, he was immune to her pitiful look. "Hell. No," he repeated more forcefully. "Your father would kill me, and mine would probably help."

She sighed. "You suck."

The door opened.

Sway came through it, but there was no sign of Claria. His face a mixture of anger and agony, he glared at them. "That didn't go well."

Zarina arched her brows as he stopped by her side. "What happened?"

"I'm not a woman, Reen."

She passed a confused look between the two of them. "What does that mean?"

He didn't respond as he pushed past her.

She looked at Devyn.

"Give him enough time to find some Tondarion Fire and take a few shots of it. Then ask him that question. Until he's loaded, he's not about to share his feelings with anyone."

She rolled her eyes. "I'm so glad I'm not a man." She handed him the bag she'd brought for Alix. "Speaking of, let me go find my brother and drive him to a bottle, too. Maybe then he'll loosen the knot in his butt and be human again." She kissed Devyn's cheek. "Stay safe."

"You, too. And whatever you do, don't poison Taryn. We'd all miss him if he were dead." He saw her to the door before he went to find Alix.

Alix looked at herself in the mirror, wanting to die. She'd scrubbed all the makeup off and it still didn't help.

You're ugly and pathetic . . .

Why couldn't she get her father's voice out of her head? *You're just a worthless slave. Not fit to be with your betters.*

Sometimes she could forget that, but all it took was one look from someone like Claria and she felt just as puny as when her father stepped on her.

A knock sounded on her door.

Shaking her hair loose from the knot she'd put it in to keep it out of her face while she washed, she crossed the floor and opened it.

Devyn froze when he saw Alix. Her face was pink as if she'd scrubbed it raw. But it was the hurt in her eyes that brought an ache to his chest. He'd never seen anyone look more miserable.

She drew a ragged breath. "I was just about to run the checks, Captain. Sorry I kept you waiting."

He caught her before she stepped past him and pulled her to a stop. She locked her eyes on the floor.

Cupping her chin, he made her meet his gaze. "Are you all right?"

Alix swallowed as she saw the sincere caring in his eyes. No one other than her mother and sister had ever cared about how anything made her feel. She didn't know why, but it touched her. "I'm always all right."

"Claria didn't mean to hurt you. She's just overprotective when it comes to Sway."

The thing was, this apology should have been coming from Claria, not him. But then, the senator would never deign to apologize to someone as low as she was.

"It's fine." She tried to move past him, but again he blocked her way.

When he didn't speak, she arched a brow. "Is there something else?"

"No one can make you feel low unless you allow them to. You're not stupid, Alix." He brushed his hand lightly across her cheek. "And you're very beautiful. I just thought you should know that." Dropping his hand, he handed her the bag she'd forgotten.

Without another word, he turned and left her there.

Alix stared after him as her heart pounded. She didn't know why he'd told her that, but it cheered her immensely.

If only things were different . . .

He's too good a man for you to betray.

But what choice did she have? They would kill her sister and mother if she didn't.

Sighing, she glanced down at the bag and noticed

a small notecard. She fished it out, expecting it to be from Zarina.

It wasn't.

Tick-tock. Don't be stupid.
Remember, I'm watching you.
~PW

Anger burned through her that Whelms would be so stupid as to put that where Devyn or someone else might have seen it. But more than that was the fear of how he'd gotten the note inside her bag . . .

Could he see her right now?

Of course not.

If she could only convince herself of that. But for all she knew, he could have tapped into the ship's feed . . .

No, if he'd done that, he'd be able to get the evidence he needed without her.

And still her panic mounted.

Terrified, she tore up the note and made sure to drop it in the garbage chute on her way to her post.

She had two days to their next stop. Two days to find the evidence to convict Devyn Kell or Inspector Whelms would kill her.

CHAPTER 7

"Alix? We have a problem. Could you please come to the bridge?"

She'd just hung up the dress Zarina had bought for her—a gorgeous black number that was so soft it should be sinful. She knew she'd never wear it.

But Tempest might one day.

Provided we survive this.

"Coming, Vik." She pressed the button to shut the closet door and headed out. No doubt this was Whelmis's "present" that the others had found.

As she entered the bridge, she saw Devyn and Vik standing over a panel, discussing a leak in their fuel line.

How weird for Vik to be here after launch.

But that thought vanished as she ground her teeth at the sight of their leak. *Thanks a lot, you idiot.* A leak like that could get them killed.

She donned an innocent stare as she faced the men and pretended not to know what had been done to their ship. "What's going on?"

Devyn pointed to the red area on the ship's

schematics. "We popped a seal and are leaking fuel all over the place."

She had to force herself not to react to Whelms's stupidity as she saw his other gift. "And our hydraulics, too."

Devyn turned with a glower. "What?"

She pointed to the diagram. "You have no hyperdrive right now, and limited stabilizer control. You won't be pulling any of your piloting stunts until we get it fixed." And if they came across any unexpected debris in space, they'd be hard-pressed to avoid it, which could also get them killed.

Yeah, Whelms wasn't the brightest bulb on the string.

Devyn's brow was furrowed with bewilderment. "How did it clear launch prelim?"

She hoped he couldn't detect her lie. "Maybe something snapped while we were launching."

He cursed. "Can you fix it?"

"I can try."

Devyn's gaze went to Omari, who was napping in his chair, and she saw the fear that flickered in his dark eyes. That protective instinct touched her. Unlike her father, Devyn would die to protect his child. "We need to be fully operational. Immediately."

"Will do, Captain." She headed for the door only to have Vik follow after her.

She frowned at him. "You need something?"

"I'm along to give you a hand should you need one."

Great. Just what she needed. Something else to make her nervous. "Shouldn't you be at your post?"

"I was, but the leak was interfering with my link, and so I came out to tell Devyn what was happening and to see if he could repair it."

"I find it odd that you know so little about ship maintenance."

"Because I'm a mecha?"

She nodded.

"It's no different than you not being a doctor. Just because you're human doesn't mean you have an innate ability to do surgery on your own kind or even treat a mild illness, never mind something major."

"True, but I can't upload a program and learn something extremely complicated in a few minutes, either."

He pressed the controls for the lift. "Nor can you be hacked for schematics, diagrams and system vulnerabilities."

She paused at that. "What?"

He stepped inside and pressed the button for the lower deck. "I have no autonomous working knowledge of the ship because Devyn's father is afraid someone could hack one of my databases and use it against Dev. In fact, I have no knowledge of Devyn's weaknesses, medical history or anything that could be used against him. Omari, either, for that matter."

Now that surprised her. "Really?"

He nodded.

"Then how do you run the ship's security?"

"I have to be plugged into the ship to see it. Everything goes to a temporary cache while I'm there. Once I'm detached from my post, all data is wiped."

So that was the real reason why he was so scarce when they flew. It made complete sense now. "His father is that paranoid?"

"No. His father is *that* good. Syn understands computers and mechanics on a scary level. There are times when I wonder if he's more mecha than I am. He knows exactly how to breach a secured and encrypted network and learn things about people that would astound you. I've never seen anyone like him. He can control the entire universe with a few well-placed keystrokes."

Her stomach hit the ground as she considered him doing a background scan on her.

Don't panic. There's no way he could breach a government's system. Merjack had assured her that they'd wiped out all traces of her past.

She was a ghost now, and not even a filch could find her history.

Devyn picked up his link while he continued to scan the ship for other problems. He checked the ID and saw his parents' number. Putting it in his ear, he clicked it on. "Hi, Mom."

"It's the other parental unit. Not as pretty or as fierce as your mother, but loving nonetheless."

He smiled at his father's deep voice in his ear. "Sorry, Dad. It's that time of day. I just assumed you were Mom wanting to tuck me in."

His father laughed. "Yeah, and she'll want to burp you, too, I'm sure."

"Probably. So did you find anything on our ghost?"

His father hesitated before he answered. "Is she around to overhear anything?"

"No."

"Good, 'cause there's definitely something weird about her situation."

Devyn checked his chronometer. Less than two hours since he'd asked for the search and he already had an answer . . . that might be a record even for his father.

And to think Claria's "experts" had found nothing after days of searching.

"Enlighten me."

"Her father, Tyson Gerran, was a typical freighter, in debt out his ass to over half a dozen creditors. He came from the lower ranks of the Kronobian desert and is the son of a nomadic branch of the Boudins. *His* father sold him into the military when he was seventeen and was conscripted to the crew of the *Silver Eagle*."

"A League ship?"

"No. Strictly local military. His record's peaceful and mild. Nothing out of the ordinary, one way or the other. He did his fifteen years of service and earned his freedom. He then went back to his father and sold that bastard, along with his mother and younger siblings, into slavery and used the money he made for a down payment on his own ship."

Devyn sucked his breath in over treachery so raw he could barely understand it. "Damn, that's cold. But what has that to do with Alix?"

"In short, she's a slave. Just like her mother, Doria, and her fifteen-year-old sister, Tempest. All owned by her father, who marked his daughters as such the moment they were born . . . until a few weeks ago when he was executed as a smuggler."

Devyn went cold as each revelation hit him like a physical blow. Just how many lies had she told him?

Alix had a living sister?

A mother?

And she was a slave . . .

"He was executed by whom?"

"The Rits."

Devyn's heart stopped beating at his father's tone. His father was a Ritadarion . . . one who wasn't a friend of that government since he and Devyn's mother had brought down their ruling house several years before Devyn was born.

This was getting fuglier by the minute. "You don't think it's a coincidence."

His father scoffed. "Do you?"

"Not really. I don't believe in them."

"I knew I raised you right."

That he did, and right now, every instinct Devyn

had was on high alert. "Did you find out anything else?"

"Just that she was scheduled to be auctioned off, along with her mother and sister. The Rit gov called it off literally right before they were hauled to the block."

"Why?"

"That, there's no record of. It only shows the canceled auction."

Devyn let out a slow breath. Wasn't *that* interesting? "So who owns them?"

"The Rit gov. Holding them for her father's debt, which he owes them for the cost of his trial and execution. You gotta love the Rits and their sense of irony."

Sonofabitch . . .

That only left Devyn with one conclusion over all of this. "She's a spy."

His father made a sound of agreement. "I'd lay money that Merjack is using her to get intel on you that he can use to fry you."

"Kill her, baby! Don't let that bitch hurt you."

Devyn grinned at his mother's bloodthirsty order that she yelled out from across the room. Gods love that woman, she had a hair-trigger on her temper that was unrivaled. He was the only person she reined it in for. "Tell Mom not to worry."

"Easier said than done. She's already suited up and ready to meet you at your next stop so that she can kill Alix herself. I've had to disarm her three times since I started the search—which is why it took me so long to find it all. You're making my life a living hell, buddy. Don't get hurt or I'll never live it down."

"I'm on top of it."

His father gave a sarcastic laugh. "In all seriousness, I don't know what game they're playing. But you know how much Merjack would love to have a piece of us. You stay out of Rit territory whatever you do."

"Don't worry. A wise man once taught me that an enemy known is better than one unknown, and as long as you know who and what you're dealing with you can handle it."

"Yeah, but what I'm willing to face myself and what I'm willing to let my son face are two entirely different things. You walk with caution every step of the way."

"I will, Dad. I promise. Love you guys. I'll talk to you later."

"Launch the bitch out of an airlock now before it's too late!"

He shook his head at his mother's angry tone.

His father sighed. "We love you, too. You need *anything*, call."

"Devyn, baby?" His mother must have snatched the link from his father. Her voice was now fully in his ear and it was low and lethal. "You kill her, you hear me? You don't take a chance with your safety. I want her heart handed to me. Don't you *dare* let your compassion rule you. You take her out before she hurts you or Omari."

"That's your maternal advice?"

"Absolutely. If she so much as breaks one strand of hair on your head, I will rip her into so many pieces, she'll be begging me to kill her. No one touches my babies."

Devyn had to bite back a laugh at a threat he knew she'd more than deliver on. As his father had said, his mother was tiny, but fierce. "All right, Mom. I have to go now. I can't kill her while I'm talking to you."

"This isn't a joke, Devyn," she snapped at him.

He glanced over to Omari, who was now snoring while Manashe slept at his booted feet. "Believe me, I know. I'm going to handle it. I'm not about to endanger Omari any more than you'd endanger me."

"Good. Love you, precious."

"Love you, too."

"And?"

He cringed. The one thing he hated about talking to his mom . . . The one grueling, awful thing she insisted on . . .

He made a kissing noise at her.

She kissed him back. "Good night, baby. Sleep in peace . . . after you kill that bitch."

" 'Night, Mom." He hung up and ran his hand through his hair as he debated what he should do.

Confront or wait?

If he confronted Alix, she'd only lie again. At

this point, he'd lost track of how many of them had come out of her.

But if he waited . . . he might be able to turn the tables on Merjack. The man hated his parents. Even though Merjack's father had almost killed Devyn's— had ruined Syn's life for the first half of it—Merjack still wanted blood from them.

And for what?

Because Merjack's father and grandfather had committed murder, and Devyn's father had uncovered the evidence and brought them to justice for it?

Obviously sanity ran shallow in their gene pool.

But that didn't matter to him right now. Ousting the traitor among them did.

And now that he thought about it . . . Fuck mercy and screw deceit. It wasn't in his genetic code to play head games. Devyn Kell might be a lot of things, but a coward wasn't one of them.

It was time to face the devil in his midst and make her squeal. He might have been blindsided by Clotilde.

But this time, that advantage was with him.

"So Devyn threw away his entire military career to save Omari?"

Nodding, Vik helped her repair the hydraulics— that was the one thing she could take care of without a spare part. She was rerouting the lurine coils to compensate for it. Should they be attacked, it would give them the boost and stability they needed without tearing up the engines.

Vik held the line higher so that she could get to the screw. "He loves that boy more than anything."

She frowned at his low tone. "But don't you find the concept of love unusual?"

"Not at all. Love I understand completely. It's hatred that puzzles me. I don't comprehend finding pleasure in cruelty."

She paused to look at him. "You know, Vik, you're amazingly human at times."

"I know. But I wonder if the feelings I have are real or just electrical stimulations in my cortex that simulate human emotion. I wish I knew if they were real or imagined."

Alix smiled at him. "And that makes you completely human, sweetie. We all have those doubts."

"Truly?"

"Every day. In fact, my mother always says that emotions are what the gods gave us to distract us from the pain of life. They are what make life bearable and what keeps us going no matter how hard it gets."

"And what happened to your mother?"

She jerked around to find Devyn standing behind them. When had he arrived? She didn't understand why he got so angry at Zarina when he was every bit as silent when he moved.

Bracing herself for the deceit, she dropped her gaze back to her work. "She died."

"When?"

Vik scowled at him. "Are you all right, Devyn? I sense an elevation in your heart rate."

"I'm good. Why don't you go plug in and check on things for me? I want to see if anything else has malfunctioned."

There was no missing the accusation in his tone. Somehow he was on to her. She knew it.

Vik handed her the wrench in his hands and left them alone.

Alix swallowed as a cold chill went down her spine. Something wasn't right.

How does he know? What had clued him in on her treachery?

More than just her feelings picked up on his hostility. She could see it in the depths of those dark eyes. See it in the way he had his jaw clenched.

He definitely knows.

"Is there a problem, Captain?"

He moved closer to her with the gait of a ferocious predator. The air around him sizzled with his restrained fury, making her feel trapped. Suffocated. If she weren't on his ship, she'd run for it. But there was nowhere to hide that he wouldn't find her.

"I'm curious."

She tried to act nonchalant against the frigidity of his tone. "About?"

"You."

You're so busted.

Don't panic. You don't know that for sure. It's your nervous paranoia. There's no way he could know anything.

Yeah, right. Sweat beaded up on her skin as she

felt the air between them thicken with his growing fury and her fear. She was way too aware of how massive he was.

How dangerous.

"Tell me about your mother, Alix. How did she die?"

She licked her lips as a bead of sweat trickled down her back. "I don't like to talk about my mother."

Devyn wanted to strangle her. So much for playing it cool. He'd had all good intentions, until he saw her talking so comfortably with Vik. Charming the mecha. As soon as he'd neared them, his temper had ignited.

Damn, I'm just like my mother. Suicidal the moment my temper kicks in.

His father would have kept his cool and played her right into a confession. Unfortunately, he'd rather beat the truth out of her.

A veil came down over her face as she confronted him. "You know, don't you?"

Lie. Give her a dose of what she gave you. But it wasn't in him to play those games. He was a soldier, not a politician. "Yeah, I know everything about your mother *and* your sister."

Alix wanted to cry as she heard the anger in his voice. Fear seized her. She threatened his crew.

His son.

It would only stand to reason that he'd want her blood. "So what are you going to do with me?"

"That depends."

"On?"

"Whether or not you help me."

His words caught her off guard. What could he possibly want with her? "I don't understand. Help you do what?"

"Merjack sent you after me, didn't he?"

She nodded. There was no point in protecting him or even lying. Not now.

"Then I want you to help me take him down. Hard."

She scoffed at his offer. As if . . . "I can't do that. He'll kill . . ." She bit her lip to keep from saying anything more.

"Your mother?"

She winced and nodded. "And my sister. I can't let them die or be raped—which is his other threat should I not cooperate."

His nostrils flared as those dark eyes singed her. "You should have told me."

"I don't even know you, Devyn. Not really. Why should I trust you with anything?"

"Because I took an oath to help people. To protect them from The League and any corrupt government."

"Yeah, and I know people better than to believe that for even an instant. Altruism is dead. People use and they take until you're nothing but a bleeding corpse on the ground at their feet."

Devyn ground his teeth at what she described. She was right—the world was harsh. But not everyone was an animal. "Lucky for you, it isn't. If it were, you'd have been launched into space right about now."

He saw the doubt in her eyes. "You're really not going to kill me?"

Part of him felt like a heel for scaring her, but she needed that fear. Because in the end, if it came down to her or Omari or Sway or Vik, she would lose. No questions asked. "That depends on you."

"I definitely vote you don't kill me."

He would find that funnier if he weren't so pissed off. "So what did you do to my ship?"

Alix held her hands up. *Tell him nothing* . . . But at this point, he knew everything. All lying would do was get her into more trouble. "Look, you took an oath and so did I. Since the day Tempest was born, I've been the only one who's protected her from what my father and the other men in our crew would do to her. Right now, she's alone and she's in danger. Her and my mother. Swear to me on Omari's life that you'll help them and I'll tell you everything."

"You just said that you don't trust people. What difference would my oath make?"

"You love your son. I know you do." She blinked back the tears that swelled in her eyes. "I have no one in this world, Devyn. No one. I'm the only one I and my family can depend on. If anything happens to them because of me . . ." Her words broke off in a sob as all the weeks of abuse, humiliation and terror combined inside her.

"Alix! Don't let them take me, please!" The sight

of Tempest's face as she reached for her was branded in her heart. Merjack's men had torn them apart. Still, her sister's screams had echoed and they were seared inside her now.

That memory finally succeeded in breaking her as her tears flowed.

Devyn tensed as she started crying. His first reaction was anger over being manipulated. It was something Clotilde had always defaulted to. But her grief wasn't feigned. Her sobs came from deep inside and they wrenched at his gut.

Before he could stop himself, he pulled her into his arms. "It's all right, Alix. It's all right."

"No, it's not." She pulled away from him. "I'm so tired of this. Tired of being the one who has to come up with solutions. And I don't know what to do now." She looked at him and he saw the desperate sincerity in her eyes. "You think lying to you has been easy? It hasn't. I don't like using people and I hate lying. You're a good man. The only one I've ever met. But I can't let them kill my family any more than you could save me if it meant seeing Omari abused and murdered." She brushed angrily at her tears. "I want Merjack's head in a way you can't imagine. If you swear to me that you'll help me get it, then I will trust you."

Devyn pulled her back into his arms and kissed her wet cheek. Closing his eyes, he inhaled the scent of her and debated the sanity of trusting her. Clotilde had carved out his heart.

How could he open himself up to Alix after this?

And yet, he understood her motivation. He would have done the same himself.

"Let me tell you a story, Alix." He pulled back to show her the ship around them. "This ship . . . the *Talia*? It's named after my father's older sister."

He swallowed as he saw the image of his aunt's battered childhood face staring at him from the sole photograph his father had of her. "She killed herself when she was fourteen because she couldn't stand living the horror of her life for another day. With her death, she both condemned and freed my father from his monster of a father. I never knew the pain of her life or his. But I named this ship after her to remind me of all the children out there like her and Omari . . . the children like you and your sister who are silent in their pain. They have no voice and no hope."

He gave her a hard stare. "But *I* hear them. Every time I think of my parents. Every time I see Omari, I hear the sobs that are kept inside for fear of it making their lives worse, and I will not stand by and see your sister torn apart by an animal. You help me nail him and I swear to you, I will lay Merjack down at your feet and hold him there while you take your revenge."

Alix bit her lip as she heard words she'd never thought to hear. Did he really mean them?

She swallowed. "I'm going to trust you, but know that it's not in my nature. If you betray me—"

"I won't betray you."

She reached up to cup his prickly cheek in her hand. Trusting was so hard . . .

I will believe in you, Devyn.

"I didn't do anything to your ship. Merjack's agent, Lieutenant Whelms, did it. He wants me to have you land on the Charisis station for repairs. I'm supposed to have evidence then that he can use to arrest you."

"And if you couldn't get the evidence?"

"He wanted me to fabricate it."

His jaw ticced under her hand. "Frame me?"

"According to Merjack, bring you to justice."

He growled low in his throat as he pulled away. "That sleazy bastard. You do realize that if they did arrest me, that means the entire crew would go down, including you."

"They offered me immunity to testify against you."

"And you believed them?"

"No. I'm not that stupid. I'm sure somehow I'll end up being sold again. It's what I am, right? Worthless property."

He saw the humiliation in her eyes as she said that, and while he might be mad at her for what she'd done, he didn't want her to hear those haunting voices. "You're not worthless, Alix. But right now, I have to say that I don't like you as much as I did before I found all of this out. I don't appreciate being toyed with or betrayed."

Alix wrapped her arms around herself as those

words hit her like a hammer. He'd killed the last woman who'd dared to do that.

But at least he wasn't killing her.

Yet.

"So what are we going to do?"

His eyes glittered with malice. "We're going to set our own trap."

CHAPTER 8

"I think we should kill her."

Devyn gave Sway a hard stare as they sat around the council table to brainstorm a plan of action.

"What?" Sway actually managed to look innocent in a cold-blooded, ruthless sort of way. "She's ruined my entire day. Made me fight with my wife and now you tell me she's a spy sent to put us all under the jail. What part of 'kill your enemies before they kill you' did you sleep through? Your dad was an assassin, same as my mom. Don't puss on me now, boy. You know what they'd do if they were here. Hell, your own mother would tear her up, spit her out in pieces, and not blink."

"He's right," Alix agreed. "None of you have any reason to help me. Why should you care?" She clicked the vid wall and a picture of a teenage girl was there. One who bore a scary resemblance to Alix except that her sister held an almost angelic quality to her features.

"That's my baby sister, Tempest Elenari Gerran.

Her birthday was day before yesterday. She turned sixteen in jail with my mother. I may be out of line, but I'll bet when you guys turned sixteen, you had a celebration for it with presents and friends wishing you well."

She clicked to the next photo of a frail-looking woman around the age of Devyn's mom. Her blond hair laced with gray was pulled back from her wan face. Defeat and despair haunted her pale gray eyes. Unlike her daughters who still held fire in their gazes, she'd been broken by the harshness of her life.

Alix met Sway's hostility without flinching. "You won't just be killing me. You'll be killing them, too. Tempest is a prime sexual age and a virgin. Any idea what's the first thing her new owner will do to her when she's sold?" She looked down at the table before she added, "I don't want her to ever know the horror that was my sixteenth birthday."

Devyn's stomach churned at the thought.

A tic started in Sway's jaw. "How many days do we have to get them free?"

"I was given three weeks to bring you in, but Whelms said he wanted something on Devyn day after tomorrow."

Devyn let out an aggravated breath. "The *Talia*'s still running under capacity. I've contacted Taryn. He and Starla are headed in to provide support for us in the event we run into something unpleasant while we're en route."

Sway scoffed at his euphemism. "Unpleasant . . .

like League battle cruisers out to hang a crew of idiots?"

Omari snorted. "We're not all idiots, Sway. Just you. Remember you could have gone home with Claire and chose to stay with us."

"Muzzle it, punk. I'm not in the mood." Sway turned back to Devyn. "Starla's coming, huh? You okay with that?"

"Not really. But there's not much I can do about it."

Alix frowned at the unfamiliar name. By the look on Devyn's face, she could tell there was history between them. "Who's Starla?

Sway smirked before he answered. "The sole daughter of Darling Cruel and third in command of The Sentella."

Alix gaped at the names. Darling Cruel was an aristocrat with hefty political ties even Taryn would envy. He ran The Sentella which was the most important organization that opposed League authority. But since they didn't outwardly break any laws, The League couldn't shut them down.

"How do you know the Cruels?"

Devyn flashed a grin at her. "Haven't you learned by now? We all grew up with Starla and we all want to choke her. She's balls to the wall, in your face, and has more testosterone than all of us guys put together."

That confused her even more. "If you can't stand each other, why's she coming?"

"We're family and it's a fight. She'd never want to be left out."

"Neither would I."

Alix jumped as a new voice was added to their group. She jerked around in her chair to face the unexpected newcomer.

Holy . . .

He was gorgeous on an inhuman level. Tall and lethal, he had the coldest gray eyes she'd ever seen. Dressed all in black, his hair was pulled back into a loose ponytail. The collar of his jacket rode high with silver buttons that fell in a line from the collar to his waist. There was an air of imperial grace and one of feral brutality.

He made the hair on the back of her neck rise.

Devyn didn't appear so intimidated as he let out a sound of utter disgust. "What are you doing here, Nero?"

He pulled up a chair beside Omari and leaned back as if he owned the ship. "Your dad called and sent me in with a replacement part. He doesn't want you down for even a second. I'm also here to, and I quote your father, 'Fuck up anyone who comes at you.'" Nero held his hand out and a bottle of water shot from the cooler in the middle of the table into his hand.

Her eyes widened as she finally understood how he'd come to be on the ship and in their room without opening a door. "You're Trisani?" The Trisani were an almost mythical race of people whose psychic abilities were the stuff of legends. And male Trisani were even more rare since their powers were so strong they normally killed the males before they left puberty.

Nero took a drink of water before he spoke again. "Nice to meet you, Alix."

"How do you know my name?"

"As you noted, I'm Trisani." He winked at her.

Omari snorted. "Yeah, be careful what thoughts are in your head. He can pluck them out without even trying."

Nero passed him a droll stare. "And I'll be so thrilled when you finally get laid and stop the . . . oh wait, you're male. You'll never stop those thoughts. Damn, I need eye bleach."

Devyn laughed. "So where's my part?

"I've already installed it. It doesn't do me any good to bring it here and then leave it on the floor."

Sway let out a low, appreciative whistle. "Man, I would kill for those powers."

And therein was the problem. Many people had.

Nero rubbed his thumb along his jaw. "So what are we plotting?"

"Suicide." Devyn leaned back in his chair. "Glad you could join us for it."

Nero rolled his eyes before he looked over at Omari. "How are your studies coming, sport?"

"I'm not dead yet. It's all good."

"Good. That whole spontaneous combustion thing can be a real buzzkill. Ruins your clothes, too.

Take it from someone who knows." Nero turned his attention back to Devyn. "So are we killing Merjack?"

Alix was puzzled by the man's ADD and the speed with which he'd gone from one topic to the next.

But Devyn wasn't quite as bloodthirsty as Nero. Or maybe the correct term would be stupid. "Unless we can come up with a reason we can sell it to The League and get a warrant for assassination, we can't."

Nero curled his lip. "Gah, you are your mother's son." He spat the words out as if they were nauseating to him. "Trust me, Dev. I know over two hundred ways to kill someone and all but two of them will look like accidents."

Alix shook her head as she met Devyn's bemused frown. "You run with the most bloodthirsty people."

Nero blinked at her as if she were dull-witted. "It's what happens when assassins spawn. They tend to bequeath their warring ways straight to their children." He turned back to Devyn. "I'm telling you right now I could make him pop an aneurysm and no one would know."

Alix grimaced at him. "Doesn't that kind of murder bother you at all?"

His gaze turned brittle. "Given everything people have done to me in my life, little girl, especially in my childhood when I was helpless against them, humanity is lucky I'm not on a perpetual killing spree. As for the Merjacks . . . I owe them a debt that no amount of violence on my part will settle. So, no. Nothing about killing him would bother me."

"But this isn't your fight," Devyn said, drawing Nero's icy stare away from her. "It's mine. It's my family he's after and *I* will be the one who settles this."

Nero scoffed at his bravado. "Don't be stupid, Devyn."

"I'm not. This is a blood feud. The man doesn't want me, he wants to hurt my parents. *I* will end this."

Nero shook his head. "Aneurysm's quicker. I'm just saying."

Devyn was unamused by his persistence. "Merjack needs to suffer for what he's done to Alix's family. If he dies, they're still slaves. Legally owned. And they will be sold to the highest bidder . . . after they've been raped. We have to get them emancipated and then deal with him."

Nero let out a sound of supreme disgust. "I still don't understand why I can't kill them and you buy her and her people. Not like you don't have the money, Dev. The handful of people who could outbid you are your own family and they wouldn't dare. Even if they did, they would never hurt her or her family."

Devyn wanted to choke him for the obstinacy. "Scalera, it's not that simple. A, the government doesn't have to sell them. They can choose to keep them as slaves and there's nothing I can do about that. B, because they're government-owned slaves, the Rits could just kill them for no reason. Disposal of property . . . which is vintage for those bastards."

"That's a good point."

Alix looked at Nero. "Can't you teleport them to safety? Like you just did with the part?"

"No. The part wasn't organic or all that heavy. It doesn't move and drain my powers or fight against me. I can do quick pops in and out with people, but to pull two women out of there for the distance I'd have to travel . . . it'd burn my brain cells out and leave me a vegetable."

Sway laughed. "That would be different from your normal state, how?"

Omari ignored his barb as he sat forward. "Maybe we could find something Merjack wants and exchange it for them?"

"That would be your father, pup," Nero said as he rolled his water bottle back and forth in front of him. "You want to make that transaction?"

"Uh . . . not today. He hasn't pissed me off."

Devyn stroked his chin as he considered their options. "There has to be dirt on him. His family was too corrupt for him to be the only innocent one."

"Dirt is always good," Nero agreed. "What are you thinking?"

"I'm not sure. Let me get my father on this and see what he can find out about Merjack's past. There has to be something he's hiding. Something we can use."

Alix wished she could believe in that. "And what if we're wrong? What if there is no dirt on Merjack?"

"Oh, I can answer this one." Omari raised his hand like he was in a classroom, then dropped it to his side. "We all die."

Nero snorted. "I just love teenage angst. By the way, chip, there are worse things in life than dying."

"Like what?"

Alix answered before Nero could. "Living as a slave."

Nero passed a look to her that said he understood exactly what she meant, and it made her wonder if he shared a past so similar to hers that he would know.

Devyn's throat tightened at the pain he heard in Alix's voice. He wanted to comfort her, but this wasn't the time for it. "All right, guys and lady. We have a day and a half to get everything in place. Merjack wants evidence and we want Merjack. Let's hope the best team wins."

Omari cleared his throat. "Otherwise, we're screwed."

Alix buzzed Devyn's quarters. She probably shouldn't be here, but she wanted to talk to him alone and thank him for a kindness she'd never expected, especially after she'd lied to him.

His door opened.

Devyn sat at the desk across from her where he

was working at his computer. "What can I do for you?"

She was hesitant as she stepped inside and the door slid shut. "I just wanted to say thank you for not launching me out an airlock and for helping me and my family. It was something I never expected."

"It's all right. Helping people is what we do."

"Yeah, but unlike the others, I have no way to pay you for it."

He froze as if she'd just insulted him. "You think I'm getting paid for what I do?"

"Of course. It's why you run. It pays a lot more than freighting."

He curled his lip. "I have never and I will never take a single credit for what I do. We run humanitarian missions to those who have nothing. What we do is out of compassion, not for profit."

Alix was as baffled by his indignation as she was his words. "I don't understand. How can you afford a ship like this if you don't get paid?"

"I'm loaded, Alix. In the filthiest sense of that word."

"I don't understand." His father was a retired filch and his mother a tracer. While more lucrative than what her father had done, those weren't exactly professions that made people wealthy.

"In addition to owning a part of The Sentella, my father owns Precision Shipping."

Alix gaped. Precision Shipping was the number-one freight company in the universe. They had contracts with everyone. Literally.

"And my mother is the co-owner of the Dagan Investment Group."

That stunned her even more. DIG was the largest charity organization in existence. They funded schools, co-ops, hospitals . . . you name it.

His gaze bored into hers. "The only person on this ship who gets paid for what they do is you, Alix. The rest of us live off our trust funds and we use those funds for our humanitarian missions. I do what I do because I can't stand to see innocent people bullied by a corrupt government. I don't want to see a baby starve and die because some fat politician wants to work its parents into the ground for a mineral most of them can't even pronounce."

She felt ill at his words and at the way she'd misjudged him. "I am so sorry, Devyn. I had no idea. I can't believe I almost got you killed."

"Well, you're not the first person to misjudge me. I doubt you'll be the last."

Yes, but she felt terrible as she moved closer to him. "I don't understand then. If you're not gouging people, why is The League after you?"

"Simple. I was a League soldier who tore down my commanding officer and half my unit. Taryn's father, Emperor Quiakides, got me off the charges, but it doesn't mean The League isn't still after me. After all, running through a League blockade when they've cut off supplies to a civilian population is considered treason. They catch someone doing that and it's over."

"Why did you tear down your unit?"

"They wanted me to leave Omari to die."

She was aghast at that. "Vik told me that you'd left The League to save Omari, but I didn't know you'd attacked them when you did it. I thought he was being metaphorical when he said you'd ruined your career for him." Horrified, she shook her head. "How could they ask you to leave your own son?"

"He wasn't my son then. He was just a wounded kid, crying for his mother who was lying dead in the ditch next to him, the victim of a League attack. I was raised that you don't hurt kids. No matter what they do, they should be cherished."

She stared at him in wonder. "Do you have a single vice?"

He laughed as he leaned back. "More than my share."

"Such as?"

The humor fled his features. "I killed the woman I was supposed to marry."

"While she was trying to kill you."

"Yeah, but most men wouldn't have done it. I have a hair-trigger temper that explodes. And while I have a code, I will kill anyone who threatens me or my family."

"Except for Merjack."

"Merjack lives only because I want it to stop. I take him out and his son comes for us, et cetera. My goal is to break the chain and make sure that when I'm done with Merjack, he won't ever have the guts or the ability to come after my family again."

"And if you can't?"

"'Can't' isn't in my vocabulary. I will take him down. Hard. And this will end the feud once and for all."

A tremor of respect mixed with desire ran down her spine. She loved whenever he was fierce, especially when it was protecting the ones he loved and it made her wish that she'd been born to a different time and station.

But those were stupid dreams. He was the son of a rich shipper and she was a worthless slave.

Disheartened, she dropped her gaze to the picture frame on Devyn's desk. A smile played at the edges of her lips as she saw a beautiful woman with dark auburn hair. "Your mother?"

He nodded as the screen flashed to a couple. "That's my dad with her."

"You look just like him."

"That's what they tell me, but I don't see it. Except for our eyes."

The next picture was of him and Zarina when Zarina was a little girl, then a bunch of pictures flashed with him and two blond males.

"Zarina's brothers, Adron and Jayce," he explained.

"Your family is huge."

"Tell me about it. I had no privacy growing up. Adron was always staying over at the house because he wanted space." He laughed. "The boy lived in a palace ten times the size of our house, which don't get me wrong, was pretty big, but still . . ."

Then she saw Taryn and his twin, along with several photos of Omari growing up.

She touched one photo of him holding Manashe when Manashe was a puppy. "Omari is gorgeous, isn't he?"

"Yeah. I couldn't be prouder or love him more if he'd been born to me."

Alix smiled at the pride in his voice as she leaned down to kiss him.

He arched a brow at her actions. "You're getting frisky again?"

"I get frisky every time you're near me. I really can't thank you enough for what you're trying to do."

His eyes darkened as she opened his shirt. "You don't have to do this to thank me."

"I'm not." She was doing this because she wanted to feel safe again and the only place where she'd ever found that was in his arms.

Devyn stood up and started for the bed.

Her gaze dropped back to the photos and when another picture flashed, her smile and desire died instantly. She reached out and froze the scroll.

No . . .

It couldn't be.

Yet there was no mistaking that face. It was a younger version of the man, but it was him. Definitely.

She looked at Devyn in total shock and horror. "Why do you have a photo of Lieutenant Whelms?"

He scowled. "That's my half brother, Paden."

"Yes. Paden Whelms. He's the man who wants me to hand you over to him on Charisis."

CHAPTER 9

Devyn sat in stunned silence. His brother wanted him dead . . . No, not dead.

Convicted.

Why?

He just couldn't believe it. He'd never done anything to his brother. Hell, he hadn't even met Paden. Only heard stories about him from his father.

"Are you all right?"

He was completely stunned as he met Alix's concerned frown. "Not really . . . Are you sure about this?"

She nodded. "Believe me, he left an impression. That man"—she pointed at the picture of Paden—"wants your head on a platter. I saw his ID and everything. If Paden Whelms is your brother's name, then he's the one I'm supposed to deliver you to."

Last he'd heard, his brother's name was Paden Belask, but it was too similar to not believe her. After all, people changed their names, and while he'd never known the name Whelms, it didn't mean it wasn't the same person. "It doesn't make any sense. I've never met him."

"You don't know your own brother?"

He shook his head. "My father had him with his first wife. After their divorce, Paden had no use for him, and I was born after he was grown. Honestly, I wouldn't know him if he was standing in front of me."

"Then why do you have a photo of him?"

"In case I ever ran across him by accident. I just wanted to know what my half-brother looked like."

Alix was baffled by all of this. "But that doesn't explain why he would be after you."

"The only thing I can figure is that he wants to use me to hurt my father."

She cocked her head. "Has your father done anything to him?"

"No. In fact, it's just the opposite. He's taken care of Paden his whole life. That little bastard has his own trust fund from my father. Paden, on the other hand, hates his guts and won't have anything to do with him."

"Why?"

"In my opinion, it's because he's a selfish idiot. But honestly, I don't know. It's not really something my father talks about with me. I only have the one picture, and that just to remind me that I do have a brother out there. I kept thinking one day we'd meet, but not because he was coming after me to arrest me."

"Are you going to tell your father?"

Devyn considered it, but knew he couldn't. "Nothing good could come of that. Paden's hurt him enough by rejecting him. To hear this . . . it would kill my father."

She didn't know about that, but she took him at his word. "Well, I can tell you this—your brother's not a nice man."

"No shit? I would have thought he was a sweetheart of a guy."

His sarcasm amused her. Strange how he could make her smile no matter how dire the moment. "So what are you planning to do?"

"No offense, but I'm not going to confide that in you. I'm still not sure I can trust you."

Those words hurt, but she understood them. He had no reason to trust her, especially given what he'd learned about her today. "All right. I'll go back to my room, then, and sulk."

Devyn didn't speak as she left him. Part of him wanted to go after her, but why? Had his father not uncovered her deception, she'd still be after him.

To protect her family.

Yeah, but—

You would do the same and you know it.

He wanted to argue that he wouldn't, but in the end he knew the truth.

And right now, he had another enemy to investigate.

* * *

Alix made her way to the galley to restock the water in her room. She paused as she found Omari in there, feeding Manashe. But that wasn't what stunned her.

It was when he held his hand out and opened the door to the cooling unit without touching it. More than that, a bottle of soda lifted itself up and . . .

Slammed to the floor.

Omari cursed. "I'm never going to get the hang of this. It kills me that Nero makes it look so easy."

Manashe barked in her direction, which made Omari look straight at her. The startled look on his face probably mirrored the same one on hers.

"You're Trisani, too?"

A tic worked in his jaw as he went to the soda and picked it up with his cyber arm. She could see the panic in his eyes.

"It's all right, Omari. I won't tell anyone your secret. Does your father know about it?"

"Yeah." He returned the soda to the cooler. "It's why I stay with Dad instead of at home with my grandparents. It's harder for the Chillers to find me."

Chillers—a term for those who were trained to hunt, enslave and kill the Trisani. They were a part of The League that was second only to the assassins when it came to brutality.

"Did your father know that when he saved you?"

"No. I didn't even know it when he saved me. My powers didn't manifest until I hit puberty. I had no idea why my family was so transitory. My mom always said that my birth dad's job kept us on the move. It wasn't until I was older and looking back on it that I started piecing together why half of our moves were in the middle of the night, and that my mom was human while my dad wasn't."

They'd been running from those out to enslave them. Poor kid. She couldn't imagine how hard that must have been for him.

"You miss your parents, don't you?"

He shrugged as he fed Manashe a treat. "Not too much. My real dad was an angry asshole who hated the entire universe. He was eaten alive with resentment. But I do miss my mom . . . and my brother and sister. My mom was the kind of woman who could make the worst day better. No matter how bad things seemed, she could find something good in it."

"I'm sorry, Omari."

"It's all right. I'm really lucky Dad threw his military career away for me, and I never forget that. It may have cost me an arm and a leg, but it was worth it. I really couldn't ask for a better family than what I have now. I know Dad doesn't like living out here in space all the time. Like my mom, he makes the most of it with our humanitarian runs, but I see the way he looks at pictures of home and I know how much he misses it."

Her heart went out to both of them. "Doesn't he visit?"

"Not really. He won't stay stationary for more

than a few hours because he doesn't want the Chillers to find me. By the way, don't tell Dad you know about my powers. He wigs whenever someone finds out."

"I won't. And you can trust me, Omari."

"Believe me, this is the one crew that gets trust. There's nothing we wouldn't do for each other."

Alix moved to grab water out of the cooling unit for her room. "Thanks, sweetie."

He gave her a devilish grin. "You know, you're really nothing like Clotilde. But it is weird to hear your voice coming out of her face."

His words made her pause. "You knew her?"

"Yeah." He pulled a box of sweets out of the cabinet beside her. "She was a nasty piece of work. She'd be all nice to me whenever Dad was around and then the moment he left, she'd go psycho. Her head would spin around and she'd turn into this insulting, domineering bitch."

"Did you ever tell him that?"

"No. He loved her and she treated him all right. I figured it wasn't my place to ruin what he had with her."

"I don't think your dad would want his happiness bought at the expense of yours."

"I know that now, but as a kid . . . I was stupid."

"No." She gave him a smile. "You were decent. Most kids wouldn't be that caring or altruistic."

"I wouldn't say it was entirely selfless. There was still a part of me back then that kept waiting for Dad to abandon me, and so I didn't want to say anything against her in case it made him leave."

"Except for that one comment about him not being your real father?"

He laughed. "Yeah, that was really harsh. Right before he met Clotilde, I told him he wasn't my real dad and that I didn't have to listen to him. That he had no right to tell me what to do."

She patted him on the arm. "We've all said similar things to our parents."

"Yeah, but he looked so hurt when I did it. Like I'd kneed him in the crotch. I don't ever want to make him look like that again."

"I'm sure you won't. You can see it in his eyes how much you mean to him and how proud he is of you."

"Thanks. By the way, just so you know, Dad never looked at Clotilde the way he looks at you."

"Excuse me?"

He opened the box of candy and grabbed a handful of sugared squares. "I'm not stupid, Alix. I'm pretty sure you two have been together. There's . . . something different about my dad when he looks at you. It's like he sees you. Not what he wants you to be, but what you really are. He never did that with Clotilde. What he saw in her was a fantasy."

"That's not making me feel better."

He laughed. "I'm sorry. I don't mean fantasy like he wanted to strip her clothes off and ride her around the room. He saw the life he wanted for himself, but she wasn't the one."

"And what life is that?"

"He wants what my grandparents have. A partner who will stand at his back while all hell rains down on him."

"You know, Omari, the sad thing is I think that's what we all want."

Too bad it was a myth made up by dreamers and idiots.

Devyn sat alone. He'd made sure he had Vik banned from his room as he worked. What he was doing . . . He wanted no reports going back to his father.

It was time to get down to business, and he wanted no witnesses. What no one knew, and what he'd never admit to, was that he had every one of his father's skills when it came to hacking.

And he wanted to get to the bottom of what was going on. So, in the solitude of his private chambers, he used the tracing signal the Rits had on the back chip embedded in Alix's arm to locate the source of it . . .

It wasn't from Ritadaria. It led back to a transmitter using a subspace frequency that was only a few ticks from them.

The bastard was using it to trace their location.

"That's all right." Devyn was going to use it to trace Paden. Narrowing his gaze, he broke through until he was able to grab audio from it.

Great. Paden was having sex. Not what he wanted to listen to.

Turning the volume down, he took advantage of that distraction to breach Paden's computer. Since his brother was preoccupied, he wouldn't notice that someone else was poking around his files.

Within a few seconds, he had located Paden's simple encrypted orders that had come straight from Merjack himself. *Get Kell at any cost.*

Sickening, really. But what else had he expected after what Alix had told him? It still pained him that the brother he'd never known would hate him and his father so much as to try and destroy them both.

What a fucking bastard. Little did Paden know that if he succeeded, he'd have to contend with Devyn's mother. May the gods help him then. There would be no mercy for him.

But that was all right. Paden didn't know just how deadly and determined Devyn was. And those orders gave him the fingerprint he needed to trace the file back to its originator.

Merjack.

He lost track of time as he searched through Merjack's records. The frustrating part was that everything looked aboveboard.

Everything.

"Come on, you bastard. I know there has to be something . . ."

His link buzzed.

He picked it up and answered without looking at the ID.

"We have a problem, buddy."

It took him a second to catch the voice over the static. "Sphinx?"

"Yeah. Guess where Taryn is?"

"Some woman's bed."

"You wish . . . No. He's in jail."

Devyn's eyebrows shot up at that highly unexpected answer. "What?"

"I think our ship is bugged and someone knew we were coming to help you guys out. It's a bullshit charge they're holding Taryn on, but it's enough to detain us until his father's admins get here. Meanwhile, Starla's being detained over a ship malfunction that has her locked down by the authorities who won't allow her to launch until it's repaired. Now, one of us having misfortune . . . possible. Both? I don't think so. This is bad shit, my brother. Bad shit."

He couldn't agree more. "Are you guys all right?"

"Other than being stuck with Zarina, yeah. Taryn wants me to head out to you in a fighter so that you have at least one of us at your back."

"No." He glanced around, wondering if someone was listening in on them right now. If they were, he wasn't about to give them anything they could use. "I don't need any more supplies. We're doing good on groceries."

"You conniving little bastard. I gotcha. We can still send someone else in."

"That's all right. We don't eat that much. We're

really careful with the garbage, and I have more than one compactor on board to take care of it."

"I get it. But you need us . . . you have Nero get word out, preferably in time for us to actually help you, and as soon as we can, we'll rendezvous."

"Yeah, takeout works. It's been awhile, but I could use some."

Sphinx laughed. "All right. Watch your back."

"You, too." Devyn clicked off the link and ground his teeth in anger.

This was getting fugly.

He switched his console on to record Paden's current porn channel before he went to inform his crew that they might be bugged, too. Which made sense. What better evidence than to have them in their own voices chatting about illegal activities. And as he walked, worry set in. What had he said to Alix? Had he admitted to doing anything illegal?

Dammit, he was always so careful about that. But had he fucked up?

He was sure he had. The only question was, who had heard it and had they recorded it?

Your luck . . . you know they did.

I am such an idiot.

He knew it was always a possibility and yet . . . in the comfort of his own ship, it was easy to forget that anyone could theoretically access their audio. Because of the complexities of it, most people didn't.

But they could . . .

Disgusted with his carelessness, he found Sway on the bridge, sexing with his wife over the audio. Great. Everyone was having sex tonight *but* him.

Well, if anyone was listening in on their equipment, Sway's foreplay should screw with their heads. He cleared his throat just as Claria verbally licked a part of Sway's anatomy that Devyn didn't even want to think about.

Sway sat up straight and threw the mute on. "What the hell are you doing here?"

"My ship, and last time I checked, I was captain. Sorry for the coitus interruptus. While I'm glad you two have made up, we have a situation. I need you to say good-bye to the wife, throw on the autopilot, grab Vik and Nero, and meet me in the command room." Without waiting for confirmation, he reversed direction and went to find Alix and Omari.

They were in the galley, talking with the door open. He paused as he heard his name.

"I think your father's wonderful, but I'm not stupid, Omari. I know what happens to slaves like me. All I want is to save my sister and my mother if possible. What happens to me isn't important. I just don't want Tempest to get hurt any worse."

"We're not going to let you get hurt, either."

"I know you have the best intentions. But I don't believe in dreams. Only reality, and it's a very harsh thing."

Manashe stuck his head up as he finally caught a whiff of Devyn. Sitting up, he wagged his tail, alerting Omari that they weren't alone.

Devyn walked forward to pet the dog's head. He motioned for them to remain quiet before he led them to the conference room. The others were already there and seated.

Vik scowled. "What's going on?"

Devyn didn't answer as he picked the loudest, most offensive music he had to blast over the intercom.

Alix and Nero flinched and covered their ears.

"What the hell is this shit?" Nero growled.

Devyn picked up the pad from the table and disconnected it from the computer so that his words wouldn't enter their possibly compromised network. He wrote on it.

Taryn has been arrested. Starla is being detained. We have reason to believe we're being spied on. Everything we say is compromised.

He passed the pad around the group, one by one, so that they could read it.

Sway switched to military sign language, but Devyn stopped him. He motioned to the vidcams.

Vik rolled his eyes before he plugged into the network slot in the wall. "For shit's sake . . . there." The music stopped instantly. "I have the room secured."

Devyn looked at him skeptically. "Are you sure?"

"Absolutely."

"Could my father access us?"

"Probably."

Devyn held up his pad. "Then we use this . . . Just in case."

That paranoid or that bad? Nero's voice exploded in his head.

He looked at Nero and shot his thoughts back at him. *That bad.*

Nero nodded. *Anything I can do?*

Get out of my head and let me think while I write.

Nero held his hands up in surrender before he crossed his arms and waited for Devyn to write out what was going on. Once he was finished, he passed the pad around for everyone.

I know we're heading into a trap. I want Omari off the ship immediately. Nero, can you launch an escape pod and take him?

"Oh, hell no!" Omari snarled as soon as he saw it. "Forget it."

"Don't you dare argue with me. I'm your father."

"And I'm your son. A grown man. It's time you realized I can pull my own boots on, you know? I don't need you to wipe the drool off my chin anymore. If this was Grandpa who was in danger, would you walk away and leave him?"

Devyn ground his teeth as his anger warred with his common sense.

But in the end, he knew Omari was right.

All the way around. He wouldn't be able to walk away and leave his father in danger, and Omari, in spite of Devyn's denial, was a man. At his age, he'd been in the middle of his medical residency with people's lives dependent on his skills. And he didn't even want to think about what his parents had been into at Omari's age.

The kid was grown.

Sway snatched the pad from him and wrote on it quickly. *We're in this to the end.* Then he added one additional word. *Asshole.*

Devyn laughed. "I hate you."

Sway blew him a sarcastic kiss.

Devyn went back to writing. *Fine, then. Let's at least try to control the situation.*

"How, genius?" Vik asked.

I don't know. I was hoping one of you did.

Sway gave him an obscene gesture.

Vik unplugged from the wall. "You know, Captain Obvious, that part we need is only available on Charisis. I think we should stop there and procure another one."

Devyn mouthed the words, *What are you doing?*

Go with it, Vik mouthed back. *I have a plan.*

Sway added in a stilted voice, "If that's the only place we can go . . ."

"Good, then." Vik cut him off before Sway gave away their plan with his really bad acting. "You organics should get some rest. Let the mecha handle everything."

"All right, Vik." Sway used that same choppy speech. "See everyone in the morning."

Alix didn't move as the room cleared. Her thoughts were on her family.

Without thinking, she reached for Devyn as he

walked past her. "I'm so sorry," she said, her voice tight. "I wish I could go back and—"

"And do what? What could you do differently? Besides, had it not been you they sent for me, it'd have been someone else."

She looked around the room nervously while the warmth of his hand seeped into her skin. "You think he can hear us?"

"Probably."

"Do you think we stand a chance?"

"There's always a chance. In this case, not a good one. But there's always something."

Alix sighed. She'd really screwed up this time. The phrase *No good deed goes unpunished* rang through her mind. All she'd wanted to do was give her family a chance. A better life than what she'd had.

A taste of freedom.

And now she'd risked causing everyone aboard this ship the chance of losing their own lives.

How could she have been so selfish? Looking into Devyn's eyes cut her to the core. He was the only man who had ever treated her decent, and because of that, his entire crew and ship were in grave danger.

He couldn't die.

Not because of her.

Not because of the lies she'd told to help her family.

A whirl of emotions played through her. How

did this get so complicated? "I'm sorry." She peered up at him, hoping he didn't hate her.

He should hate her. He should detest being in the very room with her. Like her father always had. But the way he looked at her . . .

Devyn growled inwardly as her gaze met his. He could almost believe she actually was sorry. The softness of her face, the way she was so tough yet feminine. She'd done so much to endanger them, and yet . . .

He couldn't hate her.

Alix laced her fingers through his. Dainty long fingers intertwined with his, and the sight of them made him possessive. He wanted her. He wanted her with everything inside him.

Right here.

Right now.

Pulling her to him, he melded her body to his.

"I'm sorry," she repeated, the words so sincere he almost believed her. A tear welled in the corner of her eye and it damn near tore through him. What had she been through?

Well, she was worth something. She was worth more than she could ever imagine, and he was about to show her just what she meant to him.

He lowered his mouth to hers and kissed her slowly. Tiny moans escaped her as their lips met with a passion that almost brought him to his knees.

Alix truly was sorry, but with Devyn's mouth

on hers the only thing she was sorry for at the moment was that he wasn't inside her.

Imminent danger radiated through her. It haunted every member of the crew. They could all be dead in a matter of minutes, and the only thing she could think about was Devyn and the way he made her feel.

Special.

Wanted.

Important.

In his arms, she wasn't a convenient body to ease an itch he had. She was a human being with feelings that seemed to matter to him.

God, she didn't deserve his attention, yet she had it. The hardness of his chest pressed against hers as his lips commanded hers. The tip of his tongue tangled with hers and all she could do was revel in the taste of him.

Devyn moaned into her mouth as Alix's hands moved over his chest and down. If the ship was in danger and it was the end, he'd have one last pleasure.

Alix.

He groaned as she pressed her thighs closer. Damn, he was so hard, he could burst. Sucking in air, Devyn ground his teeth at the feel of her hips brushing against his cock. He fingered her long, soft hair, drawing her face closer to his, tasting her.

Sampling her.

Alix groaned deep in her throat. The feel of

Devyn's erection against her body reminded her of what pleasure was. He was the only man to ever give her an orgasm, and the reminder of it played heavy in her mind with the feel of him brushing against her.

The man was pure heaven. Maybe not a piece of it she could claim forever, but didn't she deserve one tiny morsel?

All while kissing her senseless, Devyn slid his strong hands down her body to pause at the heat between her legs. She was wet instantly. He rubbed lightly—just enough to make her body ache for more. She sighed into his mouth as his kisses grew more possessive. In all her years, she'd never dreamed it could be this way.

What had she done? What was she doing now? Maybe her father was right after all. She was just a stain on humanity. Not worthy of anyone's love. With all she'd done to Devyn, with the danger she'd put him and his family in, he still touched her as if she were royalty.

The weight of her guilt was too much.

Pulling back from his touch, "I-I can't."

Devyn scowled at her. "Why not?" He appeared insulted as she pulled away from him. "Did I do something wrong?"

She could weep. After all she'd done, he was worried he'd done something to offend her.

"No, it's not you." Alix stepped back from him. It was too hard to think when he was so close.

Whenever Devyn was near, she wanted him to be on top of her, inside her.

She moved to the table, sitting on the edge. She had to get her composure if she was going to get through this.

"What is it, then?"

"How can you bear to look at me?"

Devyn was puzzled. "What do you mean?"

"I . . . This is all my fault. All of it."

"I won't argue with that."

Alix sighed. "We could all die any second. For all I know, they're listening to us right now."

"Yeah."

She wanted to punch him for taking this so well. He should be throwing insults at her, making her feel like the scum she was. Instead, he was agreeing with her?

She sank down, resting her hands on the table and feeling like total crap.

"I don't deserve your kindness. None of it." The truth was harder to admit than she'd realized. It was certainly stinging as it came out.

Devyn deserved someone to love him and his son. He was such a good man.

The kind of good man who could blast someone into smithereens if they looked at him wrong, but nevertheless—a thoroughly good guy.

And good guys didn't want filth like her.

He walked over to her, feathering a single finger down her cheek. "Baby, deserving has nothing to do with it." With the most delicate of lips, Devyn dipped down and kissed her with such tenderness she wanted to weep. Warmth splayed over her entire body, and at that moment, she became putty in his hands.

Devyn couldn't believe how little she thought of herself. She was the most amazing woman he'd ever met and then some. She deserved more than she could ever imagine. She deserved to be loved for who and what she was—amazing.

Slowly, Devyn undid the buttons on her shirt and slid it from her shoulders. The sight of her standing vulnerable in front of him caused a protectiveness to build in him so strong, it was scary. No one would ever hurt her again.

Not while he drew a single breath.

Alix couldn't believe the intensity with which Devyn looked at her. His lips captured hers again before trailing to her neck. He took her nipple in between his fingers and toyed with it. She threw her head back and closed her eyes, enjoying the way his hands felt on her body. She sucked in a sharp breath as he moved from one breast to the other.

With his other hand on the small of her back, he laid her back onto the table, all the while kissing and fondling her.

His cock, hard through his pants, teased her as he rested it between her thighs. The material separating them was driving her insane.

Devyn hissed as Alix grabbed his cock through his pants. How it ached to be free and in between her warm, welcoming embrace, but this wasn't about him. This was about making sure she felt what it was like to be cared for. For once in her life—and if this really was their last moment, he wanted to make sure she experienced love. It was the least he could do.

He continued rubbing her until she made tiny moans into his mouth. He pulled back from her for only a short time—just long enough to free himself and her from the material separating them.

Once he did, he allowed his gaze to trail over her body.

Delicious.

Never had he seen such a beautiful sight.

He claimed his position on top of her and prayed they lived to make it through this moment. Everything else be damned, he would have it.

Alix reveled in the way Devyn looked at her. Maybe he did care for her more than she'd thought. Maybe he didn't hate her for what she'd done.

Dare she even hope for that?

He reached down to her sides and took both of her hands into his. Once on top of her, he moved both hands above her head and entered her.

She gasped at the way he filled her, perfectly, completely. He was so hard she feared she might break in two. The pleasure from it overshadowed the thought. Stroke by stroke, he slid himself deep inside her until she writhed in pleasure.

He nibbled her ear, whispering into it with each stroke. "You're amazing. So beautiful."

Alix closed her eyes and prayed this wasn't a dream. His body worshiped hers. There wasn't another word to describe the way he touched her. She wanted to free her hands and pleasure him. She could've if she'd wanted to, but he held them there with just enough strength.

She tugged once.

"No," he breathed, shaking his head. "This is for you."

Those words made her want him all the more. She spread her legs further as he dove deeper inside her. Pressure built with each caress. He trailed kisses down her neck, over her mouth, each time murmuring sweet things to her.

If she was going to die, let it be now. Let it be while she was dreaming and loved. For once. Was it too much to ask that this be real?

Then, when she could stand it no longer, she splintered around him, screaming out his name.

Devyn smiled in satisfaction as his name rolled from her lips. He wanted to join her, but not yet. Not until she came over and over again. This would be her moment. He wasn't some selfish bastard who only took and never gave in return.

He rolled them over until he was on his back and let her take the reins.

Alix just looked at him, bewildered. She'd never been on top of a man and wasn't sure she knew what to do. All the selfish assholes on her father's ship had never let her be in control.

"Are you okay?"

Still trying to catch her breath, Alix nodded. She just hoped she didn't disappoint him.

Noting her hesitation, Devyn reached up and grabbed her hips, guiding her down on top of him. As she descended, he groaned. She was still so pliant, so wet on top of him, and the way she rolled her eyes back almost made him come right then and there.

Alix bit her lips. Within a few strokes, she began to enjoy riding him. She could take him in fully and the crazy thing was he watched her each time. His heavy-lidded eyes let her know she was doing everything just right.

Reaching up to her, Devyn cupped her neck and moved her hair from her face before pulling her down for another kiss. His other hand reached around to take her nipple between his fingers again.

It was all too much. Within seconds, pressure built and she screamed out his name.

Again.

Devyn soon joined her and she collapsed on top of him.

She lay quiet in his arms, wanting it to last forever. And he held her as if it could . . .

But that was what happened to other people.

Not slaves.

And definitely not her.

That choice had never been given to her, and it was something she'd just have to accept. At the end of all of this, if they lived, she'd have to leave him.

The mere thought of being separated from him ripped through her like nothing ever had.

This is all we have. This one moment.

Hang on to it.

But it wasn't enough. He made her selfish and she wanted to live this dream forever.

Devyn wanted to savor the look of her lying on top of him forever. No woman had ever felt better in his arms. And the greatest pleasure had been watching her explode as she looked down at him.

He wanted to see it again.

With that thought in mind, he withdrew from her to dress. He handed her her clothes and savored the sight of her dressing next to him.

Once they finished, he lifted her up in his arms as if she were a bride.

Alix scowled at him as he made her feel tiny and petite. Weightless.

Most of all, he made her feel treasured.

"Where are you taking me?"

He grinned at her. "You read my mind, love. Next I'm taking you on my bed. Then probably the floor and bathroom. And wherever else meets my fancy."

"Fancy?" What a strange word for him to use. It was so out of character.

"My Aunt Tessa's favorite word. I don't use it much, but it seemed to fit."

They made their way to his room, where he immediately placed her on the bed and removed her clothes so fast it was like they teleported off.

Even after having had two orgasms, Alix still had a hungry look in her eyes. "Come here," she commanded.

"I think I've created a monster." But he was loving every minute of it.

"Where you're concerned, Captain, I don't think I can ever get enough."

That admission made him instantly hard again. *What is wrong with me? I'm becoming hopelessly addicted.*

The sad thing was, he didn't want a cure. Especially not if it meant giving her up.

Alix loved being in his bed. The scent of him, masculine and powerful, lingered on his sheets. She wanted to bury her nose in it and inhale the warm delightful smell for days. The silky softness of the sheets moved over her naked body and made her feel feminine.

Desired.

Things only Devyn had ever made her feel. And there in his bed, he made love to her until she was breathless and spent.

When she was sure her body would never work again, he pulled back to look down at her. "All this has made me need a shower." He smiled, then got up and walked into the bathroom.

She growled at the sight of his perfect butt as he left the room.

A few seconds later, the water came on, and it wasn't long before he came back holding out his hand for her to join him.

In an instant they were in the shower, water pouring over their bodies and kissing so heavily, Alix wondered if she'd die from the mere pleasure of being around him.

But what a way to go. She could imagine no better death than drowning in his kisses.

He tangled his fingers through her wet hair and lifted her up and against the shower wall. Before she knew it, he slid himself into her. Slick from the shower and hard as a nail.

"Do you know what you do to me?"

Devyn looked at her with a gaze so intense, it was a wonder she didn't break under the weight of it. Then he drove himself into her over and over until they both came.

They spent the rest of the shower bathing each other. It was amazing how tender Devyn was as he washed her hair. Taking extra time to condition and rinse it.

It was pure heaven.

Caring.

He even massaged her shoulders as the water's warm rivulets moved over their bodies. This was it. She could die happy now.

They finished up the shower and made their way back to the room.

As he dressed, he raked another hungry look over her body that made her shiver. "I could still eat you up, but I've spent way too much time already being distracted. I've got an enemy to trace."

And she had duties to attend. So she kissed him and watched as he left her alone in his room.

She finished pulling her clothes on and froze as she realized what they were in for.

Merjack and Whelms wouldn't be satisfied until Devyn was dead. They were like madmen who couldn't be won with reason or intellect.

Devyn was going to die.

And most likely so would she.

CHAPTER 10

Devyn stood outside the galley, watching Alix and Omari attempt to cook something together. Manashe ran between them, looking for dropped scraps while they laughed and worked. Alix's eyes twinkled in a way that made her entire face glow.

And Omari . . .

He was open and happy—something Devyn hadn't seen in a long time. They had music playing in the background and every now and again, Omari would spin her around to the beat of it.

"W-w-wait!" Alix said excitedly as she dipped a spoon into the pot. "You have to try this." She held it up for him with her hand cradled under it to catch any spills.

Omari opened his mouth and let her feed him. He moaned as he savored it. "Oh, my God. Who made it taste like that? You or me?"

"Definitely one of us. We did good, I think, and I'm happy to let you have the credit for it."

He grabbed another spoon to eat more and some of it dripped on his chin.

Smiling, Alix picked up a napkin and cleaned it off—like a mother would.

Something inside Devyn clenched as he watched that. The one thing he'd always wanted to give Omari . . .

But his son was too old for a mother, and when he looked at Alix, he saw a lot more than just her kindness.

He saw a future that he wanted her to be a part of.

You are out of your effing mind.

Yeah, he was, and it was the most unlikely of sources who made him that way. A slip of a woman who was a strange mixture of competence and insecurity. More than that, he could still smell her sweet scent. Feel her touch on his skin.

What had she done to him? And in such a short time, too.

He'd never been the kind of man to let his emotions rule him. Even with Clotilde, it'd taken a year before he'd felt like this toward her.

Yet with Alix . . .

He wanted to be with her. To hold and protect her. She awoke something deep inside him that he hadn't even realized was asleep.

And as she turned to catch sight of him and smile, his body erupted again—even after their hours of play. It was like every nerve ending inside him was attuned to her.

Like every part of him begged for her.

Omari turned and grinned. "Hey, Dad, you've got to taste what we just did. It's actually good."

Manashe barked his agreement.

Moving to join them, he allowed Alix to grab a new spoon and feed him like she'd done Omari. The moment the sauce hit his tastebuds, he groaned. "That *is* good. What did you two do?"

They laughed.

Alix lifted her chin in pride. "No idea. We just added spices until it didn't suck anymore."

Her laughter was infectious and before he even realized what he was doing, he dipped his head down to capture her lips.

Alix's head spun at the unexpected taste of Devyn as she brought her hand up to cup his face while his tongue danced with hers. Never in her life had she thought to feel like this. To feel safe on a ship with a crew who could make her laugh and have fun—even while her life was threatened . . . while everything fell apart . . .

This isn't happening.

It's a dream.

"Um, should I leave you two alone?"

Devyn pulled back as Omari's voice broke through his lust. "Sorry, Slim."

"Don't apologize to me. So long as you don't try to kiss me like that, it's all good."

Devyn pulled him into a headlock. "You're such a smartass."

Omari laughed as he spun out of the hold. "I learned it from the best."

Alix stood back as Nero and Sway joined them and they all sat down to eat. While they chatted and joked, a strange feeling came over her. Like a dream fog. This peaceful moment was so surreal and hard to accept.

Her entire life had been a study in insults and degradation. Yet with Devyn and his "family" . . . she had found a place she wanted to belong to.

And all too soon the moment was over, and Vik notified them that they were coming into Charisis.

She met Devyn's stare and her heart slid into her stomach. A feeling of bad foreboding hit her hard. "I'll get everything cleaned up while you land us."

"I'll help you, Alix," Omari offered. "Only fair since I started the mess."

Devyn inclined his head to them before he and the others went to the bridge.

True to his word, Omari helped her clean the table. "Don't be so sad, Alix. It'll be all right."

She paused as she picked up Devyn's plate. "You said that you kept waiting for your dad to leave you when you were younger. How long did it take before you lost that feeling?"

Omari's face was haunted. "I lost it the night Clotilde almost killed him."

What a weird thing to say. How could something like that take away his fear? If anything, she would think it would worsen it. "I don't understand."

A muscle worked in his jaw. "I was with my grandfather that night. We'd gone to a game together to give Dad time alone with Clo. When Dad called, I saw the look on my grandfather's face and I knew it was bad. I can't even describe it. It was like staring into the face of hell. One second we were driving normal through traffic and in the next, I saw a side of my grandfather that I hope I never see again. He got me home so fast, I still think we broke some kind of land-speed record."

Omari fell silent as that night replayed through his mind. His grandfather was still in prime shape, and while he knew the man was a lot older, he definitely didn't look it. Syn was in better shape than most men half his age.

"I was told to stay outside, but I didn't listen." He'd followed his grandfather up to find Clotilde lying dead in the foyer.

Terrified and sick, he'd stared at her open eyes, transfixed by the horror of her death. Blood had been splattered all over the white walls and across the marble-topped table, showing him exactly how brutal their fight had been. Pictures and paintings had been knocked from the walls and shattered. There were burn marks from blaster shots through furniture, on the walls, floor and ceiling.

The large arrangement of flowers that had always stood in the center of the foyer table had

been knocked to the floor where the vase had broken, and the flowers lay floating in her blood.

*"Stay with me, Devyn. Goddammit, boy, don't
you dare die on me! You hear me? Stay with me!"*

Those words had pulled him away from her
gruesome death pose and toward the living room,
where his grandfather was kneeling beside his father, trying to staunch the flow of blood that poured
out of his chest. He could see the trail marked by
the blood his father had left as he crawled from the
foyer to the coffee table to get his link so that he
could call them.

And in that one instant, he'd been taken back to
the day his family had been slaughtered by The
League. And he'd heard his own mother telling
him to survive no matter what.

"Devyn! Look at me!"

Instead, his father had seen him as he entered the
room. Omari's first instinct had been to run away
and hide like he'd tried to do when his mother had
been killed. But as he met his father's gaze, he knew
he couldn't.

Omari shook his head as those memories burned.
"My dad was on the floor, coughing up blood. His
skin was already turning blue." Tears gathered in
his eyes as he looked at Alix. "He was dying. I knew
it. Even though my grandfather is one of the best
surgeons in the universe, I didn't think he could
save him. But when I looked into my dad's eyes, I
saw a raw fire ignite." A single tear slid down his

cheek and he brushed it away. "He reached out for me and I took his hand. His grip was so weak that I thought he was going to say good-bye to me . . ."

Even so, his father had pulled him close enough so that he could whisper in his ear. *"Don't worry, kid. I won't leave you alone."*

It'd been the same promise his father had made to him when he'd saved him from The League.

"He fought his way back from the brink of death to keep me safe. To keep the promise that he'd made to me. And I knew then that he'd never abandon me. Not even death would keep him away. My father might be a lot of things, but he's not a liar or a coward."

She couldn't agree more, and the fact that he hadn't killed her for her pact with Merjack made him a true hero.

And there was no way she was going to allow him to be hurt.

She hoped.

Alix froze when she saw Devyn meeting them at the door to de-ship. This wasn't the man who made jokes with Sway or who loved his son.

This was the captain she'd glimpsed on her arrival. Cold-blooded and lethal.

He handed her a chip of files he'd fabricated.

Her throat went dry as his hand lingered on hers. This was his life she held . . .

"As we planned."

She nodded.

Devyn watched as she left. He exchanged a nod with Nero before he pulled his blaster out and shot Omari where he stood. Devyn quickly caught him before he hit the ground.

Sway gaped. "No, you didn't."

Devyn handed his son to Nero. "Get him out of here."

"He's going to be pissed at both of us."

"I know. But I can't take the chance. He can't control his powers when he's emotionally compromised and I'm not going to chance him giving himself brain damage to help me."

"All right. I'll keep him occupied." He flashed himself out with Omari in his arms.

Sway shook his head. "Damn. You planning to shoot me next?"

Devyn holstered his blaster. "Depends. You going to piss me off?"

"Not intentionally."

"Then I might let you stay conscious."

Vik cocked his head as he tried to compute everything that was happening. "So what is this plan that you have?"

"You'll see."

Alix shook all over as she went to meet Whelms.

Devyn's half-brother. What could make someone turn on their family so viciously? Especially on someone as decent as Devyn.

He deserves a father like I got stuck with. That

would teach him to appreciate a father who loved him.

As promised, he was waiting for her in a small café where he sat checking email on a small hand-held device. His features turned to stone as he saw her approach.

Steeling her spine, she moved to stand at his table and noticed that he didn't invite her to sit.

Because you're not good enough.

"You have evidence for me?"

She held out the chip.

He looked at it suspiciously before he took it from her hand and plugged it into his portable. And still he left her standing.

Disgusted on every level, she saw the smug satisfaction gleaming in his eyes. "Is it everything you need?"

He turned his device off. "Is this real or fabricated?"

"Fabricated. He's actually not breaking any laws. His ship is licensed through his father's company and he runs freight for him."

Your father's company that keeps you fed, too, you sleaze.

"I told you, that doesn't matter to Merjack."

"I would think it should matter to you."

He grimaced at her. "To me? Why?"

Because you're his brother. Not that they favored each other overmuch. The only thing she could see that was similar was the deadly gleam in their eyes. Other than that . . .

Paden was a loser asshole.

"Isn't part of your job to upkeep the laws? I would think framing an innocent man would go against your grain."

His eyes turned brittle. "Don't lecture me on the law or my duties, slave. After all, I'm not the one who framed him. You are."

"Because you gave me no choice."

He raked her with a sneer. "Whatever lie lets you sleep at night, little girl." He tucked his portable into his pocket. "And now your services are no longer needed."

"What about my family?"

"That's up to Merjack." He stood up and jerked his chin in her direction as he addressed the table of men next to his. "Arrest this vagrant."

Alix gaped at his order as the men stood to carry it out. "What?"

"You're a runaway slave. We're taking you in."

No! The lying bastards . . .

What am I going to do? If they arrested her as a slave, she would have no rights whatsoever. No way to help her family. No say over her own body or future.

And as they reached for her, her panic set in with steely talons. Before she could rethink her actions, she grabbed Paden's drink and threw it in the face of the first agent to reach her. She kicked him into the other and ran for everything she was worth.

She made it through the door and ran down the

hallway until she saw Devyn, who was headed her way with Sway one step behind.

He caught her in his arms. "What the hell?"

"They're going to arrest me."

"For what?"

"Being a runaway slave."

Devyn's jaw went slack. Runaway slaves weren't simply arrested. They were publicly tortured as a warning to others who might think about leaving their masters.

Taking her hand, he started to run only to see a group of enforcers cutting off their escape.

"Release the slave," their captain ordered.

Devyn turned to run back toward the café. His blood went cold as he faced his half-brother. Alix had been right. There was no mistaking Paden's features.

And as they faced off, Paden raised a blaster and aimed it straight at Devyn's head. "Surrender the slave or surrender your own freedom."

His breathing labored, he met Sway's stern glare. The penalty for knowingly aiding a runaway slave was to become one. Either he gave her up to them . . .

Or both he and Sway would become slaves, too.

And as he looked at Sway, he knew he only had one choice . . .

CHAPTER 11

Alix's heart slid into her stomach as she saw the cold, harsh look on Devyn's face. The lack of pity in Sway's eyes. Honestly, she didn't blame them for turning her over to her enemies.

She'd been willing to do that to them. Her ruthlessness deserved nothing more than their combined scorn.

But it still hurt deep inside to know what they were relegating her to. What Devyn, after everything they'd shared, would do to her by his inaction.

If the Rits really treated her as a runaway slave, she'd be stripped naked and beaten before a live broadcast as punishment. The price of the broadcast, her punishers, and the enforcers who brought her in, as well as her reward, would be something she'd have to pay back, thus guaranteeing she'd never be free in her lifetime.

It's what you deserve.

Soul sick over it, she tried to let go of Devyn's hand. But he refused to release her as he passed a subtle nod to Sway.

To her complete stupefaction, he slid his blaster out of its holster faster than she could blink and opened fire on the Rits. He pulled her back toward the docking bay as Sway covered their retreat.

"What are you doing?"

"Fucking up my life again, I'm sure." He fired more rounds behind them.

"You can't do this."

He snorted. "Little late for that now. I don't think an 'Oops, my bad, my weapon accidentally misfired two dozen rounds' will work to get me out of this." He cursed as his link started buzzing.

Firing another round, he answered it. "Hi, Mom . . . Yes, I know my heart rate's dangerously elevated." He ducked a blast that almost pinned his head to the wall. "That sound? I'm being shot at, Ma. Gotta go now. Love you much. Hugs and kisses." He tapped his ear to close the channel. "Where the hell's Sway?"

Before she could respond, Vik came out of nowhere. He ran past them to find and shield Sway while she and Devyn ran for the ship.

Four enforcers were already there, waiting. Devyn finally let go of her. At a dead run, he went for them. They shot at him while he dodged the blasts. Amazed at his skill, she watched as he fell to his knees and skidded between them, shooting as he slid.

Two went down and the other two dodged for cover.

Devyn jumped to his feet as he reached the ship

and popped the controls to extend the ramp. He shot at the two enforcers to keep them pinned down. "Alix! Move it."

She ran as fast as she could into the ship, where Nero was waiting.

"Get the ship ready to launch," Nero ordered between clenched teeth. He flashed out, hopefully to help Devyn with the others.

She headed for the bridge to fire the engines and start the preliminaries. As she worked, she looked out to see Devyn, Sway, Vik and Nero fighting off the enforcers.

For her.

Tears swam in her eyes. For the first time in her life she felt like she had a family. One that was willing to die for her.

"Alix?"

She jerked around at the sound of Omari's voice. He leaned against the doorframe as if he were ill. "Are you all right?" she asked.

He shook his head as if he were trying to clear his vision. "Dad shot me."

"What?"

He brushed a shaking hand through his hair. "Dad stunned me right after you left . . . What's going on? Where is everybody?"

She pointed at the monitor. "Ironically, getting shot at themselves. We need to get the ship launched as soon as they're safely inside it."

That motivated him. He practically flew into Devyn's chair to start the flight prep. "Ah, damn, my head hurts. I swear I'm going to kill him for this."

"I'm sure he did it to keep you out of trouble."

"Yeah, but damn . . . I'm seeing stars . . . Oh wait, I am seeing stars. I'm looking at the course trajectory. Heh."

Alix rolled her eyes as she scanned the core system and mechanics to make sure the *Talia* was ready to roll. She heard the motor of the ramp. Devyn and the others must be inside.

A few seconds later, they were on the bridge.

"Jump up, Baby Judy. Jump up." Devyn nudged Omari aside.

He slid out of the chair and sat on the floor, hissing as he cradled his head in his hands. "Next time, just knock me unconscious. This stunning crap hurts."

"Sorry." Devyn fired the lifters.

The ship rose and slammed into the ceiling.

Sway sneered as he buckled himself to his chair. "We're not cleared for launch."

"No shit." Devyn turned to Nero. "Can you get the door?"

"Already on it." A weird yellow glow emanated from his body as he stared intently at the bay doors. "I swear you are your father's son."

Alix strapped herself in as Devyn gunned the engines and flew toward the closed blast doors. Cringing, she expected to slam into them and disintegrate.

Devyn didn't back off the speed even a little. He

shoved the throttles forward with a gleam in his eye that said he was barely one half-step from insanity.

We're going to die. We're going to die.

Alix braced herself for the impact.

Just as they reached the doors, they snapped open and the *Talia* flew straight out.

Nero staggered back, cursing as he put his hand to his head. "That's some painful mojo. Thanks for the migraine, Dev. Appreciate it."

Devyn gave him a fierce, droll stare. "You were told to take Omari out of this. Had you done what I asked, you wouldn't have a headache now."

"Yeah. That lasted a few seconds until I heard their plans for Ms. Gerran there. I knew you'd never let them take her so I had no choice except to come back and save your rank ass. Besides, I know Fido, and Fido would be out of it for a few while I rescued you guys."

Omari glared at the Trisani. "I'm not a dog, Nero."

Nero ignored him. "By the way, you guys seriously screwed up just now."

"We know," they said in unison.

Nero locked gazes with Devyn. "Yeah, well, what you don't know is how grateful your girl is to you. I just thought you should know that you guys are a hero to her . . . and she thinks we're all idiots."

Alix gave him a peeved glare. "Thanks for outing me."

He winked at her. "Anytime, cupcake. Now I'm taking my psychic ass to bed. That door spanked me. Get me up when The League comes to arrest us."

Sway's head snapped from his console to Nero. "Is that a premonition?"

He gave Sway a *duh* stare. "I don't need to be psychic to know they're coming. You guys just cold-cocked them—they tend to take that kind of thing personally." He vanished.

Devyn met her gaze. "We need to get that tracer out of your arm immediately."

Before she could respond, a man flashed up on the screen in front of them.

Alix froze at a face she was sure belonged to Devyn's father. His hair was longer, worn to his shoulders, and he had a small goatee. But those dark eyes, black hair and features were unmistakable.

"What did you do?" His accusatory voice was thick with a Ritadarion accent.

Devyn cleared his throat. "This isn't time for a lecture, Dad. I'm kind of busy."

"Yes, you are. I located your bug with Vik and he's deactivated it. Now you need to get the chip out of the woman. Immediately."

"That's what I was about to do." Devyn frowned. "Where's Mom?"

"Don't ask questions you don't want answers to." Then he switched topics. "Right now, Merjack has called out everyone for your arrest. There's a three-million credit bounty on your heads . . . each . . . for you to be delivered to him. The good news is he wants you alive. The bad news—"

"For that amount of money everyone will be after us."

He nodded. "Land that damn ship before you're blasted out of the sky."

"Dad—"

"Don't give me no lip, boy. You haven't had to really run from the authorities. Take it from an expert. Get the chip out of her now and set down. I have another unmarked runner for you at Trinaro and a crew willing to cover you. Get to it."

A tic worked in Devyn's jaw as he held a look that said he wanted to argue but knew it was useless. "All right. I'll change out."

Relief shined bright in his father's eyes. "And Devyn?"

"Yeah?"

"I love you." His gaze went to Omari and then Sway. "I love all of you. Don't make me regret teaching you loons how to fly." He cut the transmission.

Devyn swung around in his chair to issue orders to them. "Omari, take the helm. Vik, scan and let us know if someone starts after us. Sway, check the guns and make sure we're ready for anything." He motioned for Alix to follow him.

He led her down the hallway to the infirmary.

And as soon as the door closed, she grabbed him

and kissed him passionately. She still couldn't believe what he'd done for her. What he'd risked.

"Thank you, Devyn."

Devyn held her close as he breathed her in. "I'm the biggest idiot ever born."

"No. You're a hero. You could have let them take me and you didn't." She tightened her arms around him. "I can't believe you did that for a nothing like me."

"You're not nothing, Alix, and I'm only this stupid for people I care about."

Those words hit her like a blow. Dare she believe it? "What?"

Devyn hesitated as he stared into those blue eyes that seared every part of him. *Tell her you love her.*

I don't even know her.

It didn't matter to his heart. To the confusing feelings inside him. Whether he'd meant to or not, he'd made a giant commitment to her tonight. Hell, he may have just consigned himself to slavery.

He kissed her lips, then forced himself to step back. "We have to get you detagged."

She left him to lie down on the examining table so that he could pull her tracer out.

"Do you know where it is?"

She pointed to a scar on her arm. "I should probably tell you that they messed up when they put it in. It's embedded in the bone."

Devyn grimaced. "How old were you when they did it?"

"Three."

That made him curse. No one under the age of sixteen was supposed to be tagged. The risks were too great. But obviously her father had never wanted a daughter.

Only property.

"I'll have to break the bone."

"Whatever it takes." She met his gaze. "I trust you, Devyn."

He didn't know why, but those words made his chest ache. Kissing her cheek, he stepped away and prepped the room for surgery.

Alix lay in silence as she struggled with her fear. Not for herself. She didn't really care what happened to her. It was the ones helping her who mattered.

And most of all . . . "What do you think they're doing to my family?"

Devyn paused beside her to look down at her as she watched him closely. "Nothing."

"Don't patronize me. I'm not stupid. I saw the way Whelms turned on me. I've now put my mom and sister in the line of fire."

"Listen to me, Alix. I have a friend who's watching over them from inside the jail. If anyone comes near them, they won't live long enough to regret it."

"What?"

He smiled. "I come from a family of assassins, and not all of them are tied to The League. Believe me, no one's going to hurt them. We'll make sure they're not caught in the crossfire." He put the mask over her face.

Alix inhaled the anesthesia as her thoughts drifted. She wanted to believe him, she did.

But Merjack was trickier than that.

And while Devyn might know how outlaws and assassins lived, he didn't know anything about slaves.

Please, please don't let them rape my sister.

"How bad is it?"

Nero grimaced at the loudness of Syn's voice in his ear while his head felt as if it were about to explode. He should never have answered the link while he was "napping." But he'd known his old friend was beside himself with worry and had stupidly thought to make him feel better. "You wouldn't be asking me that if you didn't already know."

Syn cursed. "I don't understand this. Why would he risk everything for her?"

"You know that answer, too. He loves her."

"Yeah, and the last woman he loved almost killed him."

"This isn't your fight, Syn. It's Devyn's."

He could sense the turmoil, anger and fear that Syn's stoic voice hid.

"Tell me about her. Do we need to execute her?"

That comment would be harsh coming from anyone else, but Nero understood his friend and what had made him that cold-blooded. And the truth was, Nero would be every bit as harsh about his child, too.

"She loves him."

"So did Clotilde."

"No. Clo loved herself, which I tried to tell him and he didn't listen. Alix is entirely different. She barely thinks of herself as human."

"So what do we do?"

"Keep them safe."

Syn paused before he spoke again. "Can you do it?"

"Not right now, asshole. My head is killing me. I've got to recharge my powers or I'm going to be more worthless than tits on a boar hog."

"Fine. But are you sure about her feelings for Devyn?"

"I know you didn't just ask me something that stupid. If I thought for one minute she'd betray him, you better believe I would have left her to the Rits."

"All right. You recharge. The gods know you're going to need every ounce of your powers to protect my boys. Merjack is pulling out everything to come after the lot of you."

And he knew the one thing Syn wasn't saying. Merjack's grudge against Nero made a mockery of the hard-on he had for Syn. Syn had only brought down the bastard's family.

In his case, it wasn't something he'd done to Merjack's father and grandfather.

It was personal.

Devyn removed the mask from Alix's face and let her breathe normally again. He'd removed her chip and destroyed it. Then he'd knitted her bone back and sealed the wound. Whoever had implanted the chip had been clumsy and stupid.

But then, everyone in her life had been that way toward her. That was something he was grateful he couldn't understand. He'd always been a priority to his parents. Even when they yelled at him and punished him, it'd never been done maliciously. Never done with anything other than love and their wanting him to be safe and a better person.

He brushed the hair back from her pale face. "I wish I could take it all away from you."

But right now, both of their lives were in jeopardy.

"Dev?" Sway's voice came out of the intercom. "We need you. Now."

"On my way. Can you come watch over Alix while I take the helm?"

The door opened for Sway. "Done. We have a shitload of fighters out there with your name on them. Go give them hell."

Devyn inclined his head to him. "Thank you, by the way."

"For what?"

"Being my friend. You didn't have to help her back there."

Sway scoffed. "I wasn't helping her. I was helping you, buddy. I still think you're an idiot. But I know what I'd do to keep Claria safe and I know that you'd be there with me to the bitter end." He held his hand out. "Brothers forever."

Devyn took his hand and pulled him into a quick man-hug. "Watch her."

"Get the assholes off our backs."

Nodding, he ran for the bridge, where he saw Omari and Manashe already strapped in.

He slid into his seat as the warning alarms started blaring through the ship.

"Attention, *Talia* crew, you are all ordered into League custody, effective immediately. Prepare to be boarded."

"Board this." Devyn opened fire on them.

Vik cursed through the intercom as he released the controls so that Devyn could fly manually. "Oh, that's not smart."

"And I'm not about to let them board us, Vik. Remember, we have contraband they're looking for and no real manifest for it. The League gets on this ship, and helping a runaway slave is the least of our crimes."

"Oh, yeah."

Omari let out a hiss. "There's more of them coming in. Dang, Dad, looks like the entire West Fleet Armada has been sent after us."

Devyn banked hard left as the other ships returned his fire. Several shots landed on the hull, dimming their lights and shaking the entire ship. His stomach lurched as they lost gravity.

"They're targeting our directionals," Vik warned.

He banked again, trying to flee the range of their ion cannons. Something much easier said than done as three more cruisers came out of hyperdrive.

One of them materialized directly in front of them.

"Shit!" Devyn hit the retros and swerved to miss the newest addition, but it was too late. Their sides struck.

Hard.

The sound of the collision, breaking titanium and circuitry, echoed loudly as their lights failed.

"Shields are down to one percent." Vik's voice belied the pain he was in. He must have taken a hit along with the ship.

Devyn tapped orders to the ship. "Status?"

"Screwed."

"Vik! Dammit, answer the question."

"We need our engineer to lock down the core, which was ruptured. Oh, wait, she's still unconscious. Our hydros aren't leaking, they're flowing. We're losing life support, and unless Nero can do some major mojo, you'd better surrender before they blast us again."

Nero flashed onto the bridge. "I can't touch this. If I were at full strength, maybe. But right now . . ." He shook his head.

Devyn took a deep breath as he stared at the ships out there. Ships with crews who were determined to kill all of them.

But it all came down to one simple thing. "I don't believe in surrender."

Vik cursed. "Devyn. They are going to kill us."

"Balls to the wall." He slammed up the three throttles and pushed the ship as hard as he could.

They careened forward as he flew through debris and blasts.

The sudden acceleration knocked Nero to the floor. Without fear or comment, Omari joined him at the helm, manning the guns to destroy anything that got in their way. His Trisani powers helped him to aim and see the traps coming before they arrived.

"The engines are failing," Vik shouted.

Devyn ground his teeth in raw determination. "Keep her together for fifty more seconds."

"Why?"

"Because then we'll be in the gravitational pull of that M-class planet over there."

Omari frowned at him. "We're crashing?"

"Yeah," Devyn said ominously. "We're crashing."

He just hoped their wounded ship didn't disintegrate on impact.

CHAPTER 12

Omari pointed to the monitor in front of Devyn's face. Not that he hadn't already seen it, but the boy was rightfully concerned. "They're falling in behind us."

"I know." He'd have to be blind to miss the number that was so massive it looked like a blob moving toward them.

Devyn glanced up at the intercom. "Vik? Any more shields you can give the rear?"

"Generator is dead and gone."

"They're firing," Nero's voice was calm, but the underlying panic was hard to miss.

Devyn cursed as he banked and the rear engine sputtered, then failed. The ship shuddered around them.

The League commander hailed them again. "This is your last chance, Kell. Surrender your crew or lose them."

Devyn looked around at the faces that were dependent on him for their freedom and, more importantly, their lives. He was the only hope they had.

She turned sixteen in jail . . .

He looked at Omari and made his decision.

Devyn kicked the thrusters with everything they had. The ship lurched forward and tilted. But that motion finally propelled them into the planet's gravitational pull. He let out a relieved breath.

No matter what, they couldn't be taken. None of them.

The League ships diverted immediately. Their battle starships were too big to land and the fighters were space-class three, which meant they didn't have the coating they needed to land. Any attempt to enter the atmosphere would have them breaking up.

The *Talia*, though . . .

She was a tough lady. But at the moment, she was limping and wounded. Even though she was designed to land anywhere, he wasn't sure she'd make it in her current condition.

Devyn opened the channel to let Sway and Vik know what was coming. "Batten down. It's going to be a rough landing."

Sway buzzed him back. "Dev, are you trying to say we're about to crash?"

"Yeah, we're crashing."

Sway had one last surly comeback to that. "Asshole."

Shaking his head, Devyn prepared himself as best he could. The atmospheric friction against the hull made it feel like they were traveling through steel. Without the dampeners, the sound was excruciating.

Sparks flew from the damaged circuits as Manashe whined in response to the sound. Nero fastened himself in.

Was that a precaution, or did he know something they didn't?

With no time to think about that, Devyn did the best he could with what he had. But by the time they broke through into the planet's normal atmosphere, he could barely steer.

"Let's try for someplace soft," Omari suggested.

Devyn snorted. "How about I try to avoid the mountains?"

"Even better idea."

But there was no way to avoid slamming into the trees. Everything seemed to slow down as they popped, spun and tumbled through them until Devyn lost all sense of orientation. Right now, they could be flying upside down for all he knew.

Finally they landed with a harsh jolt in the middle of the woods.

Devyn cursed as his body's full pain hit him. The wound in his side tore even more, but he knew he didn't have time to worry about it. He looked to Omari. "How you doing, kid?"

"Not dead yet."

He nodded. "Nero?"

His tone was dry and sarcastic. "You haven't helped the migraine."

Manashe barked.

"That helped even less."

Devyn ignored him. "Vik?"

Silence answered him.

Devyn's heart stopped as raw panic set in. Had the mecha been hurt in the crash?

Or worse . . . killed?

"Vik!"

Again nothing.

Nero looked up from where he was cradling his head in his hands. "Communications might be out."

Maybe.

"Sway?" Devyn tried.

And again there was no answer. Without waiting on the others, Devyn bolted from his chair and ignored the protest of his body.

Please don't be dead. His mind tortured him with images of what he might find.

He went to check on Alix and Sway first. His heart pounded as fear took hold of him.

Damn, when had the ship gotten so big? It seemed like it was growing while he ran.

Finally, he found them in the infirmary right where he'd left them. Alix was strapped down on her table, but Sway . . .

He was on the floor a few feet away. And he wasn't moving at all. Not even a twitch.

Terror consumed him as he ran to him. He pulled him over to see the gaping wound in the center of his chest.

No!

Devyn's entire body shook as he saw the extent of the damage done to Sway. There were contusions on his head and arms. A severe gash above his eye, and he was covered in blood.

Sway coughed as he stared at him. "I slipped."

Devyn wanted to curse him for his condition, but it wasn't Sway's fault.

It was his.

He'd done this to his best friend, and from the looks of it, Sway wasn't going to survive. "You never could walk in a straight line, you lumbering asshole."

Sway laughed, then grimaced and groaned. "I'm dying, aren't I?"

"Not on my watch."

Devyn looked up as Nero joined them. With raw determination gleaming in his eyes, Nero knelt on the floor and placed his hand over Sway's chest. It was obvious how much pain the action cost Nero, but he didn't say anything while he healed him. He merely winced.

Amazed, Devyn gaped as Sway's color returned to normal. Nero's, on the other hand . . .

He looked like he was ready to barf.

Nero let go of Sway and leaned back.

"Are you okay?"

Nero slowly shook his head. "Headache, worse. I really don't feel good."

"You really don't look good."

And sure enough, he hurled.

Devyn started to check on him, but Nero held his hand up for him not to approach. "Go to Alix. I don't need a mother."

"Maybe not, but you look like you need a doctor."

Nero flipped him off. "I just need to recharge. There's not a damn thing you can do to help me right now."

Holding his hands up in surrender, Devyn went to check on Alix, who was still unconscious from her minor surgery. Her pale hair was spread out, making her look like a vulnerable angel as he unstrapped her from the table.

He took a moment to lay his fingers to her warm cheek, grateful that she was alive and unhurt.

Alix blinked open her eyes to find Devyn standing over her with a stern frown. She scowled herself in response to it as her head throbbed and she remembered his removing her chip. Was it done already?

She looked around to see the room in ruins. Boxes were scattered throughout the room from where they had fallen out of cabinets that were now dented and hanging open. Glass had shattered and medicine bottles were strewn everywhere.

More than that, they were at a strange tilt. "What happened?"

"We crashed."

No kidding. She'd already deduced that much. "Where?"

"Not real sure. Didn't have time to pull up anything more than the fact that it can sustain our life forms without life support."

That was definitely important, but it wasn't the only thing to know. "So we're walking into death?"

"Gods, I hope not. I don't have on the right boots for it. These are only good for a mild ass-whipping."

Alix was unamused by his attempt at humor. She hurt too much and their situation was far too dire.

Omari popped his head in the door. "The League is sending in scouts for us. We need to get out of here . . . ten minutes ago."

Devyn nodded. Taking Alix's hand, he led her to Vik's station on the upper bridge to find the mecha pinned down by debris and wreckage. He skirted around it, trying to find Vik's seat. Something much easier said than done.

Alix helped him dig around until he found Vik on his back, still strapped to his chair. The mecha seemed to have lost some of his fluids, but otherwise he didn't look to be in too bad of a shape. Especially given the fact that a large crossbeam had come free and was now draped over him.

"Vik? You all right?"

He opened his eyes to pin a glare on Devyn that would have shriveled a lesser man. "Not really. And for the record, I hate your father for giving me human emotions and sensitivities. I liked it better when I couldn't feel pain."

"Believe me, I know the feeling." He, Sway and

Nero moved the beam while Alix unstrapped him from the chair and pulled him out from under the wreckage.

As soon as he was free, Vik glared at Devyn. "Whoever gave you your pilot's license should be shot."

"Thanks, V. Love you, too."

"Then why did you almost get me killed? No offense, but I'd rather you hate me, since you seem to abuse your enemies a lot less than you do your friends."

Alix had to stifle a laugh at his surly tone.

Nero stepped forward. "No offense, people, we're on a time crunch. We gotta go."

Devyn nodded before he led them through the smoldering ship, which could ignite at any moment. But getting off was going to be a problem.

The crash had pushed the door in, jamming it.

Devyn let out an irritated sigh as he stepped back from trying to shoulder it open. "Anyone got a can opener?"

Nero gave him a droll stare. "You guys aren't going to be happy until you fry out my brain, are you?"

Omari moved forward. "Let me do it."

Nero rolled his eyes. "You're an embryo."

But Omari refused to back down. "I can do this."

"Omari—"

"I got it, Dad. Trust me."

Devyn looked skeptical.

Sway passed a deadpan stare to Alix. "Where have you seen that face recently?"

"I'm pretty sure it was when Devyn's father said the same thing to him."

"Yeah, scary, isn't it?"

Shaking his head, Devyn backed off. "Fine. Get a headache, too. What do I care?"

Nero moved to stand behind Omari so that he could coach him. "Close your eyes and concentrate. See the door and what you want it to do. Breathe slowly, and if it starts to feel like your brain is melting, stop. Because it is."

"No melting brain. Got it." Omari closed his eyes and took a deep breath.

The metal in the door started creaking almost instantly. Alix could see the muscles working in Omari's face and arms as he physically strained to do his mental magic.

Vik pointed to the device in his ear that must have been allowing him to still monitor their enemies' communication. *They're almost here*, he mouthed to Devyn.

Nero cursed, then threw his arm out and blasted the door with his own telekinesis. The door went flying as blood started pouring from Nero's nose.

He wiped at it angrily.

Alix was worried about him. "You all right?"

He tilted his head back to slow some of the flow. "Yeah. What's a little brain damage, anyway? Not like anyone would notice."

Omari glared indignantly at him. "I could have done it without your help, you know."

"Yeah, but we're about to have company."

Devyn grabbed Omari by the arm and shoved him through the door. As soon as they were outside, they could hear the sound of approaching engines. Vik had been right—The League operatives were practically on top of them.

Omari paled. "We are so screwed."

Sway chucked him on the arm. "Only if they catch us."

His gut twisting, Devyn looked at Vik as he weighed their options. But at this point, it was like choosing between a slow, agonizing death and a slower agonizing death. "Can you still pick them up?"

"They're being told to bring you and Alix in alive. The rest of us are expendable."

Omari gaped. "I don't feel expendable."

Devyn ignored his outburst. "Well, then, if it's a fight they want . . . Sway, you and Vik take Alix and Omari toward the town that's supposed to be five ticks north of here. We'll rendezvous at whatever landing bay they have."

Alix didn't like the sound of that. She knew he had something planned, and knowing Devyn, it would be scary. "What about you and Nero?"

"Don't worry about us."

Yeah, right. The man was insane and Nero wasn't much better.

So Alix stood her ground. "I don't think we should split up."

The look on his face was hard and sincere. "I'm a trained soldier, Alix, and Nero is a survivalist. Believe me, they won't be able to touch us. But I need you guys out of harm's way, otherwise we won't stand a chance." He leaned down to whisper in her ear words that sent a shiver over her. "Please, for my sanity, get to safety. I damn near lost Sway today. Don't make me lose you, too."

Alix pulled him close and kissed him. It wasn't until she stepped back from his kiss that she looked down and saw something red on her hand from when she'd touched his side.

Blood.

Devyn's. Her heart lurched, but before she could ask about it, a streak of color sizzled past her cheek. So close she could feel the heat of it.

"Run!" Sway shouted. "We'll meet at the rendezvous."

Devyn slid his weapon out and started firing at the enforcers. "Go!" he ordered her.

"Not without you." Alix grabbed his arm and pulled him after the others.

Devyn would have protested, but at this point, they were being swarmed, and there was no time to argue with anyone.

Hell, they barely had time to run.

Taking her hand, he cut through the underbrush, wishing they had on thermal-shielded suits that would keep their pursuers from using infrared to pick up their body heat. As it was, right now they were moving targets, and he had no idea if the others had already been apprehended or not.

But more than that, he felt the pressure on his wrist that warned him he was pushing himself too hard. It was his warning sensor that monitored his body.

Shit.

Alix slowed down as she noticed that Devyn was falling behind. She doubled back to his side. "We have to hurry."

He shook his head. "You go on. I'll cover you."

"Don't be—"

"Alix!" he snapped. "Don't argue with me. I can't keep up with you."

"Of course you can."

He glared at her. "No, I can't. I have a severe heart condition."

She frowned at his words and the note of panic in his voice. "I don't understand."

"When Clotilde attacked me, she sliced through my heart. Because I'm half Rit and half human, there's no donor. Rit anatomy is very different from a human's. One of the biggest is that they have a six-chamber heart. What I have inside me is a mechanical heart my father made, but it won't take this kind of abuse. I can't keep running or it will explode and kill me."

She winced as she realized what this meant. He was going to be taken.

And he was willing to sacrifice himself for her.

But looking up into those dark brown eyes that haunted her, she knew she couldn't leave him to his enemies. "Then I'll stay with you."

"Don't be ridiculous."

She eyed him. "You wouldn't be here but for me." She was the one who'd put all of them in harm's way. "I won't leave you."

Devyn wanted to tell her what kind of fool he thought she was, but as he stared at her, he realized something.

I love her.

In spite of the lies. The deceit and aggravation. In spite of everything, this woman meant the world to him. And he didn't want to see her hurt.

"I don't want to lose you, Alix."

"Then you understand how I feel about you."

He pulled her lips to his for a quick kiss. "All right. We'll do this together, then."

She inclined her head to him. "Together."

But then he realized exactly how many enforcers had been sent after them. It was actually ridiculous to go to this kind of effort for a runner. There were far worse criminals in the universe.

Hell, he was related to most of them.

The attention would have been flattering had he been in a better mood. As it was . . .

He wanted to kick their asses into oblivion.

Alix led him to a small dip in the woods where they had some degree of protection from their pursuers. "I think I have an idea. Can you fly one of their airbees?"

"Yeah."

She nodded and he could see her calculating something in her head. "How much charge do you have in your blaster?"

"Three-quarters."

She smiled. "All right, then. Let's play dead."

Devyn wasn't sure about her plan as she had him lie down on the grass. She lay by his side. He had an idea of what she wanted, but he'd rather blast his way out.

Trust her. Something much easier said than done, but in the end, he listened.

Within seconds, the probers were there to check on them. Devyn waited until the first one got off his airbee and came over. The moment he touched Devyn, Devyn grabbed his arm and pulled him forward. His partner shot, searing the blast across the man's chest.

He screamed as he went down. Devyn pulled his blaster out and shot the other one. He grabbed the link from the one who'd fallen closest to him and put it in his ear so that he could keep tabs on the others.

"They're headed this way."

Alix nodded as she slid onto the seat of the airbee. Devyn got on in front of her. Wrapping her arms around his lean waist, she slid closer to him and held tight while she tried to ignore how good he felt in her arms.

Devyn kicked the thrusters into high gear. They rose up and shot forward at a speed that was terrifying. While she'd seen airbees before, she'd never actually ridden one.

This was scary.

And as the enforcers realized that there were two of them on it, they gave chase.

"Hold on tight," Devyn warned.

Alix buried her face against his shoulder and locked herself around him with both her knees and her arms.

Devyn shot through the brush, hoping to shake the enforcers off them. But that was no easy feat. Especially given the fact that with two peole, they were at a severe speed disadvantage. Airbees were designed for a single rider, and while Alix didn't weigh that much, it was enough to be deadly to them.

Through the link, he could hear that they were setting up a trap for them.

He shot left, away from the trap, deeper into the woods. The little bastards weren't making this easy for him.

Why should they?

'Cause I don't want to die . . .

And as the enforcers closed in, he began to see a dismal end to their chase.

Until Alix drew his blaster from his holster and opened fire on them.

To his shock, she was an amazing shot as she took them down one by one.

"Girl, you've been holding out on me."

She laughed in his ear. "I was my father's gunner."

"I can tell."

Laughing, Devyn headed for the town. It didn't take long to reach it, but as they pulled in, he realized it was crawling with their enemies. Everywhere he looked, he saw a uniformed officer, either local or League.

Damn, who would have thought . . .

He abandoned the stolen bee in a full lot, so that hopefully it wouldn't be found for awhile.

Alix glanced around nervously. "You think the others have been caught?"

"No. Nothing's been said through their link. They're still hunting all of us."

Alix let out a breath in relief. "Where do you think they are?"

"Hopefully somewhere waiting on us."

They skirted around a group of enforcers who were questioning the locals.

"There they are!"

Devyn let fly an expletive that made her blush before he pulled her down an alley. The guards fired shots that narrowly missed them.

He turned to the right and ran down an even tighter alley that turned sharply to the left. Alix ran in front of him until she got to a fence that cut her off.

Devyn picked her up. "Climb."

She moved as fast as she could until she was on the other side. He landed beside her. Leaning back against the fence, he clutched at his chest as if his heart was hurting.

"They're calling in reinforcements."

Her stomach sank.

Devyn pulled her toward a building on her left where he quickly picked the lock and let her in. They ran down the hallway to a small lobby.

"Freeze!"

She turned and gasped.

It was Whelms, and his blaster was aimed straight for Devyn's head.

CHAPTER 13

Devyn whipped around, drawing his blaster at whatever fool thought to stop them. But the moment his gaze focused, he couldn't breathe as he stared into the one face he'd always wanted to meet.

His older brother.

Time seemed suspended as they stared at each other, locked in momentary disbelief.

The loss of this one single person had haunted his father in ways he couldn't even begin to understand. Every year on the anniversary of Paden's birthday, his father lit a candle and prayed for him. Most of all, he wished him well, even though Paden wasn't there to hear it. He also had a gift delivered to Paden wherever he was living.

One that was always returned unopened.

And still his father tried, refusing to give up on his child. It was one of many things Devyn admired about his father. But it was also a source of anger for him.

Because with every present returned, he watched

a part of his father die. Every time, year after year, his father reached out only to have Paden bitch-slap him for the effort.

At twelve, he'd been angry enough to ask his father, "Am I not enough son for you that you have to try and claim one who hates you?"

His father had pulled him into a fierce, crushing hug. "*You* are the greatest son any man could ever have and you're better than any I ever deserved. My love for Paden doesn't take anything away from how I feel about you, and it never will. But you have to understand that I grew up without a father, and it's a pain I'm glad you don't know.

"Paden was brought into this world against his will, and I don't want him to ever think his father doesn't love him. Yes, it hurts to be kicked when he refuses to talk to me, but I've been hit a lot harder in my life and if he wants nothing to do with me, that's all right. It will never change the part of me that loves him. The part of me that taught him how to tie his shoes and brush his teeth—just like I taught you."

He had brushed the hair back from Devyn's head and kissed his brow. "At least this way he knows someone out here still loves him. Sometimes that's all we have in this world. When everything else falls down around us, just knowing that there's another person who will miss us when we're gone is enough to see us through our darkest moments. Never underestimate how powerful that knowl-edge can be."

It was only after Devyn had adopted Omari that he fully understood what his father had meant that day. Blood didn't make a family.

Caring did.

And now he was face to face with the son his father still grieved over.

Paden's gaze narrowed dangerously. His finger tightened on the trigger.

Just as Devyn thought he'd be shot, Paden aimed the blaster over his shoulder and shot the enforcer behind him.

Confused, Devyn didn't react as Paden grabbed him by the shirt and shoved him through a door. He pulled Alix in behind him and motioned for them to be quiet as he locked the door. The room was someone's small office, complete with a desk, office chair, two padded chairs in front and a computer.

Devyn exchanged a puzzled frown with Alix while Paden closed the curtains to block their presence from anyone outside.

Paden's eyes were blazing as he neared Alix. "Why couldn't you have just done what you were fucking told?" He growled low in his throat. "You've screwed all of us now. Good job. Really. It's what I get for thinking a slave would obey me without thinking on her own."

She shook her head. "What are you talking about?"

He raked Alix with a fierce sneer. "I was going to use your fabricated evidence to convict Merjack.

I've been trying to bring that bastard down forever, but he's too clever. He's always hiding everything he does and he leaves no trace for us to find. His hatred for Kell was his only weakness. Now . . . dammit. You've ruined everything."

Devyn was stunned by Paden's tirade as he pieced together what he hoped was the truth of his brother's motivations. "You're not trying to kill me yourself?"

It was Paden's turn to look baffled. "Why would I do that?"

"Oh, I don't know . . ." he said in a voice dripping with sarcasm, "our history and your hatred of my father?"

Paden's face blanched. "You know who I am?"

"My older brother."

He expected Paden to deny it, but he didn't. Instead, he shook his head in disbelief. "I didn't think Syn would talk about me to you."

"Why not? He loves you. He always has."

"Bullshit. He's not even my father."

Devyn was disgusted by his brother's betrayal and his continued rejection of a father who only wanted to love him. "How can you say that about someone who loves you so much? Honestly, I think he's an idiot for not cutting you loose after the way you've treated him. But—"

Paden pulled out his blaster and held it to his head. "You know nothing about me. I'm not his son."

Devyn disarmed him so fast, Paden couldn't do

anything but gape. He tightened his grip on the weapon, tempted to beat him with it. "I'm not your bitch, boy. Don't hold a gun to my head unless you're shooting it. It won't go well for you. And you better be glad our father loves you because right now that's the only thing saving your life."

Paden scoffed as he continued to stare at him in complete disbelief. "You really don't know, do you?"

"Know what?"

"Syn isn't my biological father."

Devyn narrowed his gaze at the last thing he expected to hear. "What?"

"My mother had an affair with another doctor at the hospital where he worked. We're not really related."

It couldn't be. Surely his father wouldn't keep chasing after a kid who wasn't his? Why would he abuse himself for someone who . . . "Does my dad know?"

"Of course he does."

Devyn was absolutely stunned. That just made everything worse in his opinion. The fact that his father would still care for someone he really owed nothing to at all . . . "You're an even bigger bastard than I thought. Has your real father ever done anything for you?"

He saw the shame in Paden's eyes.

"Yeah, and you spit on the one who took care of you even though he didn't have to. You are disgusting."

"I may be disgusting, but right now I'm the only chance you have of getting out of this."

Devyn gave him a dry stare. "Need I remind you that you're the reason I'm in this mess? I was—"

"Breaking the law."

"Prove it," Devyn taunted. That was the one thing he shared with Merjack. When it came to electronically covering his tracks . . . not even his father could match his skills.

Alix moved to stand between them. "Gentlemen, can you please focus for a minute? We have a most dire situation here and while I understand your mutual distrust and anger, we have something greater to think about right now."

Paden snorted. "You don't know the half of it."

"Then please enlighten us."

He raked her with a sneer. "I don't answer to a pathetic slave. Ever."

Devyn slugged him hard. "You better pick a better tone for her. I don't like that one. You will give her the respect due a human being or I will give you the beating you deserve for being a callous asshole. Your choice."

Paden spat blood on the floor as he cupped his swelling jaw and eyed Devyn like he could kill him. "You bastard!"

Devyn was less than intimidated. "According to what you just divulged, you're the only bastard in this room. My mother never cheated on my dad, and I'm pretty sure neither did Alix's."

Paden started for him, but Alix came between

them. "Please, can we focus on what's important? Like our lives?" Then she raked her own scathing glare over Paden. "And while I might be a worthless slave, you've just helped me evade custody, which makes you an accessory as much as Devyn. One word, and I own *you* for that kindness."

Devyn scowled at him as he realized how right Alix was. "Why *did* you help us?"

"Because I'm not the heartless bastard you think. I loved Syn as much as any son could. When I found out he wasn't my father, I was just a stupid kid, and I blamed him for it. Then when I learned his family history and who he really was, I was grateful to the gods that I didn't share his DNA. I was mortified at the thought of someone learning that a man like him had been married to my mother." He paused to glare heatedly at Devyn. "Don't give me that look. I notice you don't share his name, either."

That made him seethe and had always been a source of extreme aggravation for him. "Devyn *Wade* Kell. I do have his name and I'm proud to call him father. Regardless of his past or his family, he's the greatest man I've ever known. And I couldn't give two shits that my grandfather was Idirian Wade. Unlike my father, I personally don't care who knows it. I only go by Kell because that's the name my parents gave me as a child, since they feared assholes like you abusing me over it before I was old enough to defend myself. Personally, like the father I love, I don't believe in running from anything. As Uncle Digger always says, Wades don't run.

Sometimes we want to. Sometimes we ought to. But Wades don't run."

Paden raked him with a look of supreme disgust. "You're no better than me."

"I never said I was. You're the only one in this room who seems to have an inferiority complex. Alix and I are fine with our places in the world."

Paden looked away as the truth behind those words tore through him. Because of his mother's hatred of his father, he'd felt unclean and unworthy the whole of his life. Like he needed to prove himself to his mother, who hated him for what his father had done.

It wasn't his fault. He wasn't the one she'd driven away. All he'd ever wanted from her was her love and approval.

But even on her deathbed she'd cursed him. *You're as worthless and pathetic as your father. I should have killed you as an infant. Now leave and let me die in peace. I don't want to carry your despicable face into eternity with me.*

The only person who'd ever loved him was the man he'd spurned in an effort to earn his mother's love.

It's me or him, and if you choose him, you'll be spit on by the whole universe. They'll never see you as anything more than the pathetic waste that you are. Go on and be the son of a worthless thief. Then everyone will know exactly how disgusting you are.

It was why he'd never married. He didn't want a

woman to turn on him the way his mother had turned on Syn.

But none of that mattered right now.

The slave was right. By saving them, he'd just put his own head on the chopping block, and if she opened her mouth, he'd lose everything.

Even his own freedom.

Paden let out a frustrated sigh. "I don't know how to get us out of this now. The original plan was to have Merjack abuse his power to hang you," he said to Devyn, "and then use your unjust incarceration to bring him down. But now you've blown it all to hell."

Alix frowned. "What about my family?"

He gave a short, bitter laugh at her as if she were an idiot. "You didn't really think Merjack would ever free any of you, did you? He'd intended to sell the lot of you as soon as he had the evidence he needed to convict Kell. Well, except for your sister. He intended to keep her for himself."

"And you were okay with that?"

"No, I despise slavery, but I can't fix it by myself. All I can do is make sure Merjack gets caught. At least that was the plan until you two screwed it up by not following orders. Why couldn't you just listen to me and do what I told you to?"

Alix was aghast at his anger toward her given what he would have relegated her to. How dare he! "Well, you'll have to forgive me if the idea of your political gain pales in comparison to me and my family spending the rest of our lives as slaves. Sorry if your promotion seems a little stupid to me."

He curled his lip as if she disgusted him, then he turned his attention to Devyn. "How can you stand her mouthiness?"

Devyn passed a proud look to her that warmed her through and through. "I think she's adorable and her mouth is one of the things I find most enjoyable. In more ways than one."

Before Paden could respond, Devyn turned serious as he pressed the link deeper in his ear. "They're starting to search the buildings. There's still no word on Omari and the others. Maybe, just maybe, that's a good thing."

Paden gave him a droll stare. "I wouldn't count on it. Not with your luck."

Devyn cursed as he heard the next bit of news from their "friends." News that made him sick to his stomach. "Yeah. It just turned. The League has brought in a group of assassins to help search for us." Unlike enforcers, assassins were highly trained. Nothing escaped their attention and they took mercy on no one. They were also a jumpy crew, and the last thing he wanted was to have Omari hurt because he was resisting arrest. "I don't see a way out of this." He pierced his brother with a stern glower. "I have one favor to ask you."

"And that is?"

"Get Alix and the others to Gouran."

Paden looked at him as if he were insane. "Why Gouran?"

"My godfather is Emperor Quiakides. He'll make sure they and you are safe from The League and Merjack."

"What about you?"

"I'm turning myself in."

Alix shook her head. "Are you out of your mind? You can't do that."

Her concern touched him, but it changed nothing. Least of all his mind. He brushed the hair back from her face as he cherished the look of worry in her dark blue eyes. "Trust me, Alix. This is the only way. By now the *Talia* has detonated and they won't find anything there except melted-down scraps. As Paden said, they have nothing on me except the fabricated files you gave him, which we can prove are bullshit. Gouran doesn't recognize slavery, so you'll be free the moment you step one foot on their soil, and Uncle Nyk isn't about to let Sway, Omari, Nero, Vik or Manashe get hurt. All of you will be safe."

"What about my mother and sister?"

"See what Nyk can do to free them. He'll pull out all the stops. I promise." He pulled her against him and held her close. "Trust me, Alix. I'll get them out."

She wrapped her arms around him and he savored her touch. She really did mean everything to him.

Paden rolled his eyes. "Do you know how many holes this plan has in it?"

"You have a better one?"

"Not really."

He stepped back and released Alix to his brother. "Then get her out of here and meet up with the others." He paused. "By the way, I'm trusting you . . . brother." He held his hand out to Paden. "Don't let me down."

Paden took his hand in his. "May the gods walk with you."

"And you. Remember, you're watching over the most important things in the world to me."

Devyn met Alix's terrified gaze and wanted to reassure her. "Don't be afraid. I will get your family out of this. I promise."

"Your promises are the only ones I've ever been able to count on, and it's not just them I'm terrified for. Don't do anything stupid, Devyn. I don't want your life to be the price you pay for their freedom."

Smiling, Devyn kissed her hand. He inhaled the scent of her skin before he lifted his head and claimed her lips. "I will protect you."

She nodded even as images of him danced in her head. "Be safe."

"You, too." He looked at Paden. "I'll leave first. Once they have me, get the others out of here."

"Will do."

Devyn took one more look at Alix, hoping this wasn't the last time he saw her. She was disheveled by everything they'd been through and still she was the most beautiful woman in the world to him.

His wounds were throbbing, but not even that pain could override the desire he had for her.

Part of him wanted to forget the others and run with her, but he loved Omari and his crew just as much.

This was the only way to save all of them. His life for theirs.

It was a bargain, really.

His heart heavy, he turned and left the room, then headed down to where the largest group of soldiers were waiting outside the building. The moment they saw him, they swarmed.

It took every ounce of will he possessed not to fight them as they cuffed his hands behind his back. This was for the others.

Yeah, but subjugation sucked.

Just don't let Paden betray me.

He was putting a lot of trust in someone who could easily stab him in the back and kill the ones he was trying so desperately to save.

But at this point, he had no choice.

Alix eyed Paden warily. He hadn't been exactly friendly or trustworthy in all of this, and she still wasn't sure Devyn's plan was sane. *Please be all right.* She wouldn't be able to live with herself if she'd just consigned him to death to save her family. "Were you lying to him?"

Paden gave her a hard stare. "Not about you I wasn't." Then he added dryly, "I know you think I'm a worthless bastard and I really don't care."

But she caught a tremor under his voice. One that told her something he wasn't saying. "You love your brother."

Paden looked away, but she caught the look of shame in his eyes as if the very idea of it embarrassed him. "My feelings for him and my father are none of your business. Now move, slave. If it comes down to you or me, I won't be as stupid as Devyn."

His words offended her, but she found it strange that he claimed them as family now that Devyn wasn't here to hear it.

Before she could really delve into that, he grabbed her by the arm and hauled her from the room.

"Where are you supposed to rendezvous?" he asked her as they made their way to the rear of the building, where they had the least chance of being seen and apprehended.

"The landing bay."

He scowled at her. "The landing bay? Are you insane? That place will be crawling with enforcers."

"Well, that was the game plan."

He let out a sound of supreme disgust. "Fine."

Alix jerked her arm free. "You're hurting me."

"Like I care." But he didn't retake her arm as he led her carefully toward the bay.

Alix wasn't too sure about this as they entered the bay through a side door. She had a bad feeling in her stomach that she couldn't shake.

They hadn't gone far when she understood why. Behind them, she heard a deep, scary voice.

"Surrender in the name of The League."

CHAPTER 14

Alix's gaze went straight to two of the deadliest-looking men she'd ever seen. Dressed in black League uniforms, there was no mistaking their occupation.

They were assassins.

One had white-blond hair that was braided down his back—the customary fashion for an assassin. His sleeves bore the deep burgundy mark of a dagger topped by a crown. That denoted him as the baddest of the bad.

A Command Assassin of the First Order.

And beside him was what appeared to be an Andarion with short black hair worn in a series of spiral curls. There was no mistaking his fangs as he tongued one of them as if he were sizing them up for dinner. Either he was newly trained or something had happened to his long hair.

Both of them wore opaque shades—a wardrobe choice designed to unnerve those around them. And boy, did it ever work. It also kept people from knowing who the assassins were looking at.

Or, more to the point, targeting.

Though right now, the blasters aimed at them gave her a good idea that the targets du jour was her and Paden.

The dark-haired assassin came forward to disarm Paden and pat her down. It took all of her restraint not to protest or fight, but confronting a trained assassin wasn't exactly an award-winning act of intelligence.

The assassin handed Paden's ID to the blond, who flipped it open and frowned. He looked back at Paden and studied his features. "You don't look like Syn."

Paden scowled. "Excuse me."

The Andarion sniffed at him. "I say we kill him just to be sure."

The blond screwed his face up. "I don't know. Might ruin Syn's day, which would then ruin ours, and I can do without another bitch session." He paused as he looked back down at the ID. "Bugger it, let the bastard pass. We can always kill him later."

What in the known worlds?

But as she watched them, Alix had a strange suspicion about who these two men were. "Do your people know our people?"

The blond flashed a grin that took the badass right out of him. No wonder assassins didn't laugh or joke, especially not when they were as good-looking as these two. He lowered his blaster and held his hand out to her. "Commander Jayce Quia-kides. Nice to meet you."

She arched her brow at a name she recognized. "Zarina and Taryn's brother?"

"On the days when I claim them." Jayce indicated the assassin beside him. "This is Captain DJ Hauk."

She tried not to react to the name. *DJ* just didn't fit with his lethal aura. It was the name someone gave a child, not a killer. "DJ?"

He passed an angry glare at Jayce. "It's actually Darion. I was named after my uncle. No one calls me DJ anymore except for a certain group of derelicts and my parents."

Jayce let out an evil laugh. "It could be worse. His father's named Dancer."

DJ didn't appear the least bit amused by that. "Don't go there, Jay. I'm only one kill away from becoming a Command Assassin. Be a damn shame for that kill to be you."

Jayce snorted. "You ain't that good, punk. Now let's get them inside with the others."

Alix hesitated, unsure about this even if they were friends with Devyn and his family. "Are we in custody?"

DJ nodded. "Yeah, the protective kind. Where's Devyn?"

"Turning himself in."

They both gaped at her.

"What?" Jayce asked in a ferocious tone.

"I tried to talk him out of it, but I don't think I need to tell you how stubborn he is."

Jayce sent a peeved glare to DJ. "No, you don't. Obstinance runs thick through his gene pool."

DJ snorted. "Yeah, 'cause it so passed straight through yours. You have met your sister, right?"

Jayce shoved him.

Paden stepped forward to break up their good-natured fight. "Look, if you guys have her, I want to go back and check on Devyn."

Jayce cocked his head. "No offense, but I don't know how trustworthy you are." He turned to Darion. "Go with, and if he begins to look suspicious—"

"Kill him before I make the call to let you know. Got it, boss."

"Good man."

DJ grabbed Paden by the arm and hauled him out.

As soon as they were gone, Jayce led her into a League shuttle where Omari, Nero, Sway, Vik and Manashe were lounging around as if completely comfortable with their surroundings and oblivious to any danger.

Omari looked up as she entered and left Manashe's side to hug her close.

She squeezed him tight, grateful that this wasn't a trick of some kind. "I'm so glad to see you guys."

"You, too." Omari released her and stepped back. "Where's Dad?"

She hated to be the one to answer that. "He turned himself in to buy us time to get out of this."

Every male there cursed. And inwardly, so did she.

"That was about stupid," Nero sneered. "Where was his head?"

"Obviously up his sphincter." Vik's tone was snide and dry.

Alix tried to explain it. "He didn't know Jayce and Darion were here. He was just trying to save us."

"It was still stupid," Vik and Nero said simultaneously.

She had to give them that, and it wasn't worth arguing a point she actually agreed with. "I know. I tried everything to talk him out of it, but he wouldn't listen."

"It's all right." Jayce drew near. "I sent DJ over. He'll keep an eye on him."

Nero rolled his eyes. "You have the pot watching the kettle? I swear, Jayce, you must have gotten brain damage when Adron shoved you down the stairs when you were a toddler."

"It'll be all right," she assured them. "Devyn said that once they realize the evidence was fabricated, they'll let him go."

Sway looked ill at the news. "Alix, we had to make it real to sell it for this plan."

"I don't understand."

"He didn't fake that evidence. It's all true. Devyn just sent himself to prison to keep all of us safe."

* * *

Paden arrived just as they were loading Devyn into the shuttle for transport to Ritadaria. He caught the look of fury on Devyn's face when he saw Paden, and he instantly understood the source of it.

As soon as he could, he mouthed the words to his brother, *They're safe. Promise.*

Still, the skepticism burned him. Not that he blamed Devyn for it. He wouldn't trust him either.

"Good job, Lieutenant Whelms," the captain said as he joined them for the transfer. "The CMOD would like to speak to you immediately."

Paden inclined his head before he stepped into a private communications cube to call Merjack and see what the bastard wanted. "Sir?" he asked as soon as Merjack's face came up on the wall. "Lieutenant Whelms here."

There was an evil glint in the man's eyes as he gave him a smug smile. "Lieutenant, I hear congratulations are in order."

"I don't know about that, sir, but Kell is in custody."

"And the others?"

"Dead, sir."

Merjack cocked one arrogant brow at that. "Even the slave?"

"Yes, sir."

Merjack *tsk*ed. "Damn shame. She looked like she would have been fun for a night or two. Oh, well. I'll have to console myself with her sister . . . In the meantime, I want Kell brought to me as soon as you arrive."

"Yes, sir."

With a curt nod, Merjack cut the transmission. Paden leaned his head back as he debated what to do. But in the end, he knew he had no power against someone like Merjack.

Setting Devyn free was going to require a lot more muscle than what he had, and inside, he knew the truth he didn't want to face.

He'd just sent his only brother to prison.

Devyn sat alone in a cell as they flew him toward Ritadaria and a future he really didn't want to face. *Why didn't I tell her I love her?*

He should have. But for some reason, the words wouldn't come.

It figured. He'd never been one for a lot of sweet talk, anyway. It was one of the things that Clotilde had complained about most.

Leaning his head back, he closed his eyes and summoned an image of Alix lying naked in his arms. Yeah, that helped a lot.

"I've never seen anyone look so happy while going to prison."

He opened his eyes to find Paden staring down at him. "I'm not happy."

"You shouldn't be. I just saw the files. What the fuck have you done?"

"I saved my family."

"You're an idiot, Devyn. Have you any idea what they'll do to you?"

"Yeah, I do. I've seen the scars on my father's

back from prison. And I've heard the stories Nero has told that Dad denies. I know exactly what I'm facing. But at least I'm a man and not a child like Dad was when he went in."

Paden cursed. "I don't understand you. You could have handed over the slave and been free."

"Freedom bought on the back of a loved one isn't worth shit."

"She's a slave."

Devyn glared at him. "You better be glad I'm cuffed or you'd be looking for your teeth right now. Alix Gerran isn't a slave. She's a lady, and I would die for her."

He shook his head. "I hope you're still saying that when Merjack executes you."

Alix paced the shuttle floor as they landed on Gouran. Guilt rode her furiously over what Devyn had done.

As soon as they were cleared to leave the ship, she bolted for the door.

Vik caught her before she could get all the way down the ramp. "What are you doing?"

"I have to get to Devyn."

"Alix, there's nothing you can do."

"I have to try. I can't leave him there. You don't understand, Vik. I love him, and I can't let him pay for something I did. I don't care what it takes, we have to save him."

"Those words, little girl, just saved your life."

Alix turned at the woman's voice that came from behind her. Tall, slender and beautiful, she wore a dark blue Armstich suit that hugged her curves in a way that said it had been custom-fitted to her.

And in an instant, she knew that this was Devyn's mother. Though they didn't favor each other much in looks, there was no mistaking the lethal aura or deadly glare.

She involuntarily took a step back.

"You don't have to fear me. If I wanted you dead, you'd already be bleeding." She looked at Vik. "How could you let him do this?"

"I know you're not going to pin this on me, Shay. I didn't raise the embryo. *You* did. It's what you get for teaching him things like honor, love, courage and loyalty." He made a mocking noise. "If you'd left him a scared little snot-nose, he'd still be living in your basement."

"I don't have a basement."

"Yeah, but you'd have built one if he wanted it."

Shahara rolled her eyes. "I am so angry with you right now, Vik, you might want to curb your tongue before I forget how much Syn and Dev love you."

"Grandma!"

Shahara turned as Omari came running. She caught him in a fierce hug that made Alix raise her brow. One, because he dwarfed her, and two, Shahara didn't really look old enough to be Devyn's mother, never mind Omari's grandmother.

She gave Omari a tight squeeze before she

released him. "I swear you get more handsome every time I see you."

"You always say that."

"It's because it's true." She stepped past him as Nero came down the ramp. "Nero, we need a full debriefing. Now."

"What are you planning?"

"To get my baby back and to kill anyone who gets in my way."

Alix listened to Shahara, Nykyrian, Syn, Nero, Jayce, Sway, Vik, Darling Cruel and Devyn's legendary uncle Caillen all argue on how to get Devyn out of custody. But as every minute ticked by, she became more and more concerned about him.

"I can shoot my way out without a problem," Shahara snarled.

Syn shook his head. "The hell you say. You're not that good, baby. They'd mow you down."

"It's quite a show, isn't it?"

Alix jerked her head up at the sound of Zarina's voice. "What are you doing here?"

She crooked her finger for her to join her outside.

Curious, Alix followed her out into the hallway and into a small room.

Her jaw hit the floor.

Her mother and Tempest stood in the middle of the room, looking about nervously. Her heart pounding, she ran to them.

"Alix!" Tempest squealed, pulling her into a tight hug.

Laughing, she looked at the two of them, who didn't appear any worse for the wear. "I don't understand. How did you get here?"

Her mother pointed to Zarina. "She and another lady came and they freed us."

Alix looked at Zarina for an explanation. "While Jayce and DJ went to take care of you guys, Devyn had me, Taryn and DJ's sister take the freedom certificates to the Ritadarion high justice."

No, that wasn't possible. "What?"

Zarina smiled. "Well, you know it's illegal to hold a freed slave as chattel. You can be fined up to ten times their value, and when one of them is a prime virgin female . . . let's just say the warden let them go without a fight."

"I don't understand. They're not freed slaves."

"Oh, yes, they were, too. Your father freed them *and* you five years ago on Kirovar." Zarina winked at her.

Alix finally understood what she was saying. "You forged the documents?"

She blinked innocently. "Forgery's illegal. I would never do anything like that."

Yeah, right. 'Cause that would just be wrong.

"Thank you, Zarina."

"Don't thank me. I'm not that good. Devyn's the one who got the certificates for you." She held out a certified document.

Alix took it and stared at it in amazement. It was her own freedom there. She couldn't believe it.

After all these years, she was free.

But Devyn had bought her freedom with his own.

CHAPTER 15

Paden paced the floor outside the interrogation room as he tried to think of some way to save Devyn's life. For hours Merjack had been torturing him, and with his brother's weakened heart, he knew Devyn couldn't take much more of it.

Merjack no longer wanted a public trial for Devyn. He wanted to torture and kill him, and then send the tape of it to Devyn's parents.

Psycho bastard.

He'd sent Darion on to see if he could get a League transfer to get Devyn out of Merjack's hands. But not a single word had come back from him.

And every second brought Devyn closer to death.

All he could do was wait and pray that his brother held on and didn't have a heart attack before they could save him.

He heard someone approaching.

Hoping it was Darion with good news, he waited until a group of League soldiers appeared. Sure enough, Darion and Jayce were with them. Relief tore through him as they marched past him and into the room with Devyn.

Darion stopped in front of him and winked.

"What did you do?" Paden asked.

"Nothing. I couldn't. No one would listen to me." He indicated the soldiers with his thumb. "This is all from the Overseer's office."

Paden scowled at that. The Overseer was the highest authority in the Ichidian Universe. Her will was law, and she ruled everyone, including The League.

"Why is she involved?"

"Alix is a firecracker. I don't ever want to be on her bad side."

Shaking his head, Paden followed the soldiers into the room to see Devyn pinned and bleeding against the far wall. Merjack had done a number on him.

The soldiers surrounded Merjack and pushed him away from Devyn.

Jayce cornered him. "Uriah Jonas Merjack, you are being remanded into Overseer custody."

Merjack's face flushed with color. "For what?"

"False imprisonment, torture, trafficking in freed slaves and terrorism."

Merjack was aghast at the charges. "What? Who would dare?"

And it was then that Merjack fully understood as he saw the procession behind the guards. Emperors Nykyrian Quiakides and Caillen de Orczy, along with Darling and Ren Cruel. They led Shahara and Syn into the room.

Yeah, that was the power-player brigade that no one in their right mind would cross.

And at the rear of their company was one lowly slave, who ran to comfort Devyn as soon as she saw him.

Paden shook his head in disbelief at how lucky his brother really was. Because in his heart, he knew that if he were the one chained to the wall, there wouldn't be a single soul who'd step forward on his behalf.

Not a one.

Paden watched his father run to Devyn's side while he faded into the crowd. He wasn't a part of this family and yet, he was morbidly curious about them. So much so that he couldn't bring himself to leave even though it hurt him to see Devyn with everything he craved.

Alix ran to Devyn's side while his father released him. "Devyn?"

His eyes were so swollen from his beating that he could barely open them. "Alix?"

She choked on a sob as she hugged him close, grateful that he was still alive. "It's me, baby. I'm sorry it took so long to get here."

"Devyn baby?" His mother brushed the bloody strands of hair back from his face. "Can you hear me?"

"I hear you, Mom."

But his voice was so weak that it made tears sting her eyes. She could kill Merjack for doing this to him.

Syn caught Devyn as Caillan released the hooks that held him to the wall and let him slump against Syn's side. Nykyrian took Devyn's other side, draping his arm around his shoulders, and together they headed for the door.

But they didn't get far before Merjack let out a bloodcurdling scream of rage and indignation. Grabbing the blaster from the soldier nearest him, he leveled it at the three of them.

Alix moved to stand in front of Devyn to protect him at the same time Merjack fired.

But it wasn't Devyn he was aiming for.

It was Syn.

The next few seconds happened in a blur as someone shoved her and Devyn away and tackled Syn. She and Devyn fell to the floor while Nykyrian pulled out his own weapon. The blast that had been intended for Syn landed solidly into the body that had tackled him.

Merjack was brought down hard by Darion and Jayce.

Shahara's face went white as she saw her husband on the floor. "Syn?"

"I'm all right."

As he disentangled himself from his rescuer, Alix gasped as she recognized him. "Paden?"

Syn froze. "What did you say?"

She pointed to the man who'd saved Syn's life. "That's Paden."

Syn carefully rolled him over. His jaw ticced as he saw his son's pain-contorted face.

Paden was bleeding badly. He'd caught the blast through his abdomen.

Syn cursed foully as he examined the ragged wound. "Why did you do that?"

"I couldn't let him kill you."

"Syn!" Shahara shouted. "Devyn's going into cardiac arrest."

Alix felt her stomach hit the floor as she cradled Devyn's head in her lap. Tears blinded her. "Stay with me, Devyn. Don't you dare die. You hear me? Don't you dare leave me."

Syn looked panicked and stricken as he quickly examined Devyn. "The stress has caused another tear in his heart. We've got to get him on life support. Immediately."

Paden reached out and touched Syn's arm. "He needs a donor."

"There isn't one."

"Take mine."

Syn shook his head. "You're not a match."

Paden laughed bitterly. "Yes, I am. We're even the same blood type. Mom lied to you about me. I am your son."

Syn scoffed. "I did the DNA test myself."

"No. Her lover doctored the results. He thought you'd leave her if you found out she was cheating on you and believed I was his. After he learned who you were, he refused to have me in his house. Mom hated me from that point on because I reminded her of you and I'd cost her her next meal ticket."

"Why didn't you ever tell me?"

"I was angry at you for my birth. Angry at you for making Mom hate me. By the time I realized what an idiot I'd been, I was too embarrassed to apologize." He looked over at Devyn. "He's a better man than me and he's your real son, Dad. Save him."

Alix watched as the medics came in and put Devyn and Paden on a lift to get them to surgery. She started to go with them.

"This isn't over!" Merjack shouted, making her pause. "Do you hear me? I'll get all of you if it's the last thing I do!"

Something inside Alix snapped at those words as she looked at Devyn's painful condition. How dare Merjack threaten any of them after all he'd done. There was no way she was going to allow that worthless bastard to hurt or intimidate another innocent person. And before she even realized what she was doing, she grabbed a blaster from the soldier closest to her and opened fire.

The only thing was, she wasn't alone.

As the sound faded and Merjack lay on the floor in a bleeding heap, there were ten blasters aimed at him: Syn, Shahara, Jayce, Darion, Nykyrian, Darling, Caillen, Vik, Sway, and hers.

"Wow," Jayce said, "how's anyone going to prosecute a firing squad? Don't even think they can tell which shot ended his life since I think we all basically hit something fatal."

"Don't worry about it," Nykyrian said in an emotionless tone. "We have a contract for his life. His death is considered a public service by The League."

Darion's eyes widened. "In that case, can I claim it? I want my promotion."

Syn inclined his head to him. "Take it."

Because right now they had something a lot more important to fight over.

Devyn's life.

Alix wiped at the tears in her eyes as she waited for word from Syn about Devyn. They'd been in surgery for hours, and she couldn't stop herself from crying like a baby.

Gah, what is wrong with me?

But then, she knew. The only man she'd ever loved, the only one who'd ever shown her kindness, was lying in surgery and could be taken from her at any moment. Over and over, she saw his smile and felt his touch.

She remembered every detail of him. How could he have come to mean so much to her so quickly?

And yet if he died . . . she wanted to die, too.

She choked on more tears.

"Here."

She looked up as Shahara brought her a mug of

hot cocoa and placed it in her cold hands. Devyn's mother had been amazingly kind and attentive to her. Most of all, she was frighteningly composed. "Thank you."

Shahara inclined her head. "I really hate hospitals."

"Me, too." She took a sip of her cocoa, still awed by Shahara's composure. "How can you be so calm?"

Shahara's gaze burned her. "I know my husband won't let our baby die."

"But what if—"

"Shh, Alix. There are no what-ifs. Syn will move the universe itself to keep Devyn alive. I have faith in him. Besides, he knows if he fails, I'll kill him where he stands."

Now she understood the source of Devyn's morbid humor. "I'm surprised you're even talking to me after everything that's happened."

"Me, too, to be honest. I've never been able to stand any woman my son has brought home."

"Then why me of all people?"

Shahara smiled gently as she smoothed a piece of Alix's hair behind her ear. "Because I see a lot of myself in you, and you're one of us. You put your family first and when Merjack threatened Devyn and Syn, you answered the same way we did. You took the means necessary to stop him. Without hesitation. Most of all, my son and grandson love you. Even Vik and Sway love you, and that's no easy feat. Vik still hates *me* most of the time."

Those words meant a lot to her. "I would laugh if I wasn't so scared."

She rubbed Alix's arm. "I know, baby. But have faith. It took me a long time to learn it. Now I don't know how I ever lived before Syn catapulted into my life."

As if in answer to her words, Syn came out of the OR door. Alix couldn't take her eyes off the specks of blood on his right sleeve.

Devyn's blood from surgery.

But by his relieved demeanor, she knew Devyn was alive. He went to Shahara and hugged her.

"He's fine?"

"You think I'd be out here facing you unarmed if he wasn't?" Syn kissed her forehead. "He's in recovery and will be back on his feet in a few weeks."

For the first time, she saw the chink in Shahara's armor as she wept in happiness.

"What about Paden?" Alix asked.

"I couldn't kill one son to save another. It took a little bit, but we patched him up. He's in recovery, too."

Shahara cleared her throat and regained her composure. "How did you fix Devyn?"

Syn flashed her a grin that reminded Alix so much of Devyn that it sent a chill down her spine. "I am *that* good, baby. I took parts from Vik and reconstructed another chamber for him. His heart should be stronger now."

Shahara leaned into her husband as she looked

at Alix. "I think you're definitely right, Syn. His heart is much stronger now."

Devyn came awake to the worst pain imaginable. He felt as if someone had clawed him into pieces. But as he blinked his eyes open, he was surprised to find Alix beside him, holding his hand.

Her smile dazzled him. "Hey, sweetie."

He grumbled as more pain throbbed. "What did you do to me?"

"That was your father, hon, not me. He had to do some repair work on your heart."

He breathed slowly, trying to mitigate the pain. "I take it I lived, though I don't feel like it right now."

"Bitch, bitch, bitch. Most people would just be grateful they're alive after all you went through."

He laughed until he saw his parents, Vik and Omari in the corner. "Why are you guys being bashful?"

His mother smiled. "We didn't want to intrude."

"Oh, please. When has that ever been your concern?"

His father's gaze went to Alix. "Since you finally found a woman your mother approves of. And me, too, for that matter."

Devyn started to ask how Paden was doing, but before he could get the words out, Paden was leaning against his doorframe. Like him, he wore a blue hospital gown.

"The nurse said you were awake."

Devyn held his hand out to him as he approached

the bed, and Alix made room. "I heard what you said when you were shot. You're such a lying sack of shit, I have no idea what to believe where you're concerned."

Paden turned his head to their father. "I would die for you guys. You know you can believe that. Does anything else really matter?"

Devyn looked at Alix as he realized that he felt the same for her. "No, no, it doesn't."

His mother moved forward and tugged gently at Paden. "We're going to step out and see Paden back to bed before he collapses. You two have some things you need to say to each other and I'm sure you don't want an audience for it."

They carefully took Paden out, along with Omari and Vik.

Alix didn't speak again until they were alone. "Devyn, I want to say—"

"Alix, I've been meaning—"

They laughed as they talked over each other.

"You first," Devyn said. As always, he was a gentleman.

Alix took a deep breath as she stared at him. "I wanted to say thank you for everything you did. Really. Thank you."

Devyn arched a brow as her words cut through him. "That's it?"

She looked confused by his quesion. "What? Were you expecting me to say that I love you?"

Well, yeah. Especially since that was what he'd intended to say to her.

But he'd be damned if he was going to say it if she didn't feel that way toward him.

So he dropped his gaze away. "No. Why would I expect that?"

She wrinkled her nose in an adorable way that actually made him hard. "Maybe because I do?" She leaned forward over him until they were practically nose to nose. "I love you, Devyn Wade Kell, with everything inside me. But it's okay if you don't feel the same. I know I'm just a piece of trash in your world, and I don't expect you to share my feelings."

He cupped her face in his hand and gave her an angry stare. "Don't you *ever* say that to me again."

Alix felt tears sting her eyes at his reaction. Though she'd been scared to tell him how she felt, she'd never thought her love would actually anger him.

When will I learn?

Still, his eyes shredded her soul with his anger. "Trash is something people throw away, Alix. I intend to keep you for the rest of my life."

His words stunned her as her hurt melted away. "What did you say?"

He flashed that disarming grin. "I love you, baby. And I want you to stay with me. Always."

Laughing, she smiled and kissed him soundly. "Believe me, there's no place else I'd rather be."

"Me, either, but I would rather we be naked."

EPILOGUE

One year later

Alix stood aside as Devyn, Paden, Omari, Sway, and Vik helped the rebels at Paradise City unload the supplies they'd brought for their wives and children while her mother helped hand out clothes.

Never in her life had she seen a happier group and she was thrilled to be a part of it.

She understood why Devyn did this for free. There were things in life that no one could put a price on, and with every day she spent with him, she learned that more and more.

Tempest came running up to her, holding a link. "You're buzzing."

"Thanks, runt." She placed it in her ear and answered it while Tempest went to help give out supplies, too.

"How's my daughter doing?"

She smiled at the sound of Shahara's voice in her ear. "Fine, Mom, how are you?"

"Worried about my babies as usual. Am I interrupting?"

She smiled at the two things Shahara always said whenever she called. "You're never intruding, and I'm looking at your babies right now and they're all good."

Devyn came up and kissed her on the cheek. He dropped his hand down to touch her stomach. "Did you tell her the news?"

"News?" Shahara asked.

Alix bit her lip before she spoke. "We're going to have a baby."

The happy shout in her ear almost deafened her. "All right, you guys take care. I have to go make calls. If you thought the wedding was big, wait until you see the baby shower."

Alix laughed as she hung up and put her arms around Devyn. "Thank you."

"For what?"

"For everything."

He rubbed his nose against hers. "Trust me, I'm the one who's thankful. I thought I had everything until you stuck your nose in where it didn't belong."

And she'd had nothing until the day she'd found him. Now . . . now she had a life worth living and she intended to spend the rest of it loving all of them.

Read on for an excerpt from

Sherrilyn Kenyon's

BAD MOON RISING

Available now from Piatkus

"Stay out of it, Fang," Vane said under his breath.

His anger snapping, Fang narrowed his eyes on the Sentinels surrounding Aimee. "It's a threatened female."

"She's not one of ours and we need the bears on our side. You break Omegrion sanctuary laws and they'll refuse to help us. Ever. They'll refuse to help *Anya*."

Fang heard those words and he was willing to abide by them. His sister was the most important thing. . . .

Until he saw the knife.

Vane cursed as he saw it too. Anya or not, it wasn't in their nature to let that go and since the bears seemed to be in over their furry little heads . . .

Vane's hazel gaze locked with Fang's. "I have the asshole in front, you take the one with the woman."

Fury lowered his head in agreement to their suicide run. "We've got your backs."

Vane inclined his head before they teleported to the fight.

* * *

Aimee considered the consequences of head-butting the jackal holding her. But he kept the knife tight to her throat, preventing it. She'd cut her own jugular if she even tried. She looked at her brothers and father, all of whom were standing back, too afraid to move for fear of causing her harm.

Tears of frustration welled in her eyes. She couldn't stand being helpless. The bear in her wanted to taste jackal blood regardless of what it cost her. Even death. But the human side of her knew better.

It wasn't worth the chance.

The jackal grabbed her by the hair and pressed the knife even closer. "Tell us where Constantine is. Now! Or else her blood flows like the mighty Niagara."

Papa opened his mouth, but before he could speak something snatched the knife away from her throat.

Aimee cursed as her head was snapped back and her hair wrenched. Unbalanced, she fell to the floor and landed on her stomach. Sounds exploded all around her as the jackals were quickly and painfully brought down by the wolves. Rubbing her throat where the knife had been, she looked to the jackal who'd been holding her.

Fang had him on the ground, slamming his head repeatedly against the floor as hard as he could. It was as if he were possessed by something that demanded he kill the jackal with his bare hands.

Blood covered both of them.

"Fang!" Vane shouted, pulling him away. "He's out of it."

Growling, Fang rose only to kick the jackal in the ribs. "Cowardly bastard. Pull a knife on a woman." He started back for his victim, but Vane caught him.

"Enough!"

Fang shrugged his brother off before he turned to her with a look so anguished and tormented that it stole her breath. What demon had its spurs sunk deep into his soul? Something tragic lay behind that kind of pain.

It had to.

He turned for the jackal.

Vane spread his arms out to capture him. "He's down. Let it go."

Growling in true wolf fashion, Fang pushed past his brother. "I'll wait outside."

Before Vane could catch him, he got one last kick on the jackal's head on his way to the door.

Fury laughed at Fang's action as he twisted the arm of the jackal he held. "I really should break you in two. It might not brighten your day, but it would definitely make mine."

Vane shook his head at Fang's actions and Fury's words. Turning to Papa, he made his way slowly toward them. "Sorry we broke the covenant." He held money out to Dev. "We'll leave and never come back."

Papa pushed the money back toward Vane. "You don't have to leave. It was my daughter you saved.

Thank you for what you did. So long as we have shelter, you have shelter." That was the highest honor a Were-Hunter could bestow on another. It was their oldest saying and only offered to another species as a show of eternal friendship.

No, more like kinship.

Vane seemed abashed by it.

Aimee watched as her family took the jackals from the wolves and led them away, no doubt to give them an even harsher ass-whipping out of sight of the humans.

"Are you all right?" Remi asked her as he helped her to her feet.

She nodded.

He glared at the one Fang had thrashed, who was still lying on the floor in a bloody heap. "Good, 'cause I'm going to skin me a jackal when he wakes up."

Aimee folded her arms over her chest. "I think the wolf already did."

"Yeah, but it's not good enough. I'm going to add my own head pounding to him. That boy will have bear nightmares for the rest of his life . . . which just might prove to be a lot shorter than he ever dreamed."

Normally Aimee would have smarted back at him, but right now she was as shaken as the rest of them. It was rare anyone got the drop on her family, especially Dev, who was renowned for his fighting prowess. Never in all these centuries had she seen anyone pin him before.

A little beating on the jackals might go a long way in ensuring this never happened again. "What about the humans?"

Papa jerked his chin toward the tall blond who was walking around the crowd. "Max is wiping them even as we speak. It's why they didn't scream or move when the jackals attacked you. He heard the commotion and popped in."

She let out a relieved breath. Maxis was a dragon-were who had the ability to replace human memories. It was one of the reasons they kept him here even though it was hard to accommodate his large dragon form. His talents came in handy at times such as this and it meant they didn't have to kill humans who witnessed things they weren't supposed to know about.

"Should we go get Fang?" Keegan asked Vane as they started past her.

"Let him calm down first. We don't need him starting another fight."

Aimee held her hand out to Vane. "Thanks for the assist. I really appreciate it."

He shook her hand gently. "Anytime."

She smiled up at him and gestured with her thumb toward the kitchen. "I'll go put your orders in and have them out shortly."

Her father inclined his head to Vane. "And don't worry, it's on the house. Whatever you wolves need, just let us know."

"Thank you," Vane said as he led his wolves back to their table.

Dev grinned at her. "Never thought I'd say this about any canine species, but I think I like that group."

Aimee didn't comment as she headed to the kitchen where her mother was waiting.

Her features stern, Maman stepped aside to let her pass. "Constantine sits on the Omegrion as their Arcadian Grand Regis. I don't know him well, however I think we should find him and tell him where his friends are being kept—just to level the field a bit since they seem so eager to meet up with him."

It was a subtle way for Maman to say that she wanted the jackals dead and to be able to justify it to the Omegrion should anyone question her. After all, if the jackals were hunting Constantine so ferociously, it was only fair he know about it.

Aimee might have argued it was a harsh sentence, but given what the jackals had done to her, she was in the same sporting mood as her mother. "I'm sure Dev can arrange that."

Her mother's eyes darkened. "No one threatens my cubs. Are you truly all right, *chérie*?"

"I'm fine, Maman. Thanks to the wolves."

Maman patted her lightly on the arm before she headed back to her office.

Aimee went over to where a rare steak was already up on the order shelf. Handing her orders over to their cooks, she took the plate and grabbed a beer for Fang as she passed by the bar. "I'll be back in a few."

Her older brother Zar, who looked a lot like Dev with short hair, only taller and broader, stopped her. "Are you all right?"

At this point, that question was getting old. She wasn't a fragile doll that would break at the slightest wrong twist. She was a bear with all the strength and abilities inherent in their species. Her family, however, tended to forget that fact. "A little shaken and a lot of pissed off. I don't like anyone getting the drop on me the way the jackals did. But I'm fine now."

A muscle ticked in his jaw, showing her the anger he kept hidden underneath his calm exterior. "I'm sorry we didn't get to you faster."

Those words were haunting as they stirred memories inside her she didn't want to remember. "Really, it's okay, Zar. I'd much rather be the one threatened than to see you hurt." Again. She left that one word unspoken as she saw her own painful memories mirrored in the horror of his gaze.

It was a past they never talked about, but one that scarred them all.

"I love you, Zar."

He offered her a hollow smile before he moved away so that he could continue tending the bar.

Aimee headed out the back door to the alley and then across the street to where Fang was sitting on the sidewalk, waiting for the others. His features troubled, he reminded her of a lost child. Something completely incongruous with his tougher-than-steel aura. Not to mention his prowess at taking down her attacker without even scratching her. His speed and strength were unrivaled and frightening.

Even though he must have used his powers to remove the blood from his clothes, she remembered well the way he'd trounced the jackal.

But what surprised her most was the fact that she wasn't repulsed by his violence. Normally such overkill would have had her showing him the door.

Then again, she'd been the one with the knife at her throat. Personally, she'd like to kick the jackal around a bit herself. Yeah, that had to be it. She was too grateful to him to be angered over his actions.

Fang shot to his feet as soon as he saw her.

For some reason she couldn't name, she was suddenly nervous and self-conscious as she approached him. Hesitant even.

How unlike her. She was always icy cold around men, especially when they were from another species. But with Fang . . .

There was just something different.

Fang swallowed as he saw Aimee pause across the street. She was even more beautiful in the daylight than she'd been inside the dark club. The sunlight sparkled in her hair, turning it into spun gold and making his palm itch to touch its softness. She had to be freezing. All she had on was a thin Sanctuary T-shirt.

He shrugged his jacket off as she finally neared him.

"I wanted to say thank-you again," she said, her voice low and sweet. She scowled as he draped his jacket around her thin shoulders.

Fang lowered his head sheepishly as he realized why it bothered her. "I know I smell like a wolf, but it's too cold to be out here bare-armed."

She frowned even more as she looked at his arms. "You're wearing a T-shirt too."

"Yeah, but I'm used to being outside." He took the food from her. "So I take it I didn't get us banned after all."

She smiled, showing him that beckoning dimple that he would kill to kiss. "Far from it. Anyone who fights for us is always welcome here."

His features relieved, he nodded. "Good. I was afraid I'd have to listen to Vane's shi—stuff for the next few centuries."

Aimee stifled a laugh at the way he caught himself before he cussed in front of her. It was very sweet and charming and also unexpected. "You're not like other wolves, are you?"

He swallowed a drink of beer straight out of the bottle. "How do you mean?"

"I've never been around wolves who were so . . ."

He arched a brow as if daring her to insult him.

"Mannered."

Fang laughed, a warm, rich sound that lacked any hint of mockery. The expression softened his features, making him even more gorgeous and intriguing. And for some reason, she couldn't quite take her gaze off his well-sculpted arms as they flexed with every move he made. He had the best biceps she'd ever seen.

"Our sister's doing," he said after he swallowed a bite. "She has codes we have to follow and Vane enforces them to please her."

"But you don't like them?" There'd been a note in his voice as he spoke.

He didn't answer as he cut the steak with his fork.

Aimee gestured back toward the bar. "You want to eat that inside with the rest?"

"Nah. I don't like being indoors and I can't stand most of them anyway." He jerked his chin toward the saloon-styled door where Dev was standing guard again. "You should probably go back though. I'm sure your brother doesn't want you out here consorting with dogs."

"You're not a dog," she said emphatically, surprised that she actually meant it. An hour ago, she'd have been the one to hurl that insult at him and the rest of his pack.

Now . . .

He truly wasn't like the others and she really wanted to stay out here with him.

Go, Aimee.

She took a step away before she remembered that she wore his jacket. Pulling it off, she held it out to him. "Thanks again."

Fang couldn't speak as he watched her cross the

street and head back into the bar. As he held his
jacket against his chest, her scent hit him full force
with a wave so strong he wanted to howl from it.
Instead, he buried his face against the collar where
her scent was the strongest. Inhaling deep, he felt
his body harden to a level it had only done for one
other female. . . .

He winced as old memories tore through him.

Even though they hadn't been mates, Stephanie
had been his entire world.

And she'd died in his arms from a brutal attack.

That memory shattered the heat in his blood and
brought him back to reality with a fierce reminder
of how dangerous their existence was. It was why
that jackal was lucky to be alive. The one thing
Fang couldn't stomach was to see a woman threatened, never mind harmed.

Any creature cowardly enough to prey on a
woman deserved the most brutal death imaginable.
And if it was delivered to him by Fang's hand, then
all the better.

Shrugging his jacket on, he picked up his plate
and returned to eating.

Once he was finished, he took the dishes to Dev
who thanked him again for saving Aimee.

"You know for a wolf, you don't really stink."

Fang snorted. "And for a bear you don't chafe
my ass."

Dev laughed good-naturedly. "You going back
inside?"

"No. I'd rather stay out and freeze my ass off."

"I hear ya. I like it better outside myself. Too human in there for me."

Fang inclined his head, surprised that the bear understood. Anya had made him human enough, he didn't want any more housebreaking than that. Tucking his hands in his pockets, he headed back to the bikes to wait.

Aimee went outside at Dev's insistent grumblings that kept coming in through the earpiece she wore— all the staff wore them so that the Were-Hunters could appear more human whenever they used their powers to communicate with each other.

"What?" she snapped in the doorway.

He held out an empty plate and beer bottle.

"Oh." She stepped forward to take them from his grasp. Unbidden her gaze went to Fang who was again sitting on the ground with his legs bent and his arms draped over them while he leaned against an old hitching post.

There was something very feral and masculine about that pose. Something about it that made her heart quicken.

He's not the same species, girl. . . .

Yet it didn't matter to her hormones. Gorgeous was gorgeous, regardless of breed or type.

Yeah, that was what she was reacting to. It was nothing more than the fact he was an exceptional specimen of male physiology.

"Something wrong?"

She blinked and looked at Dev who was watching her. "No, why?"

"I dunno. You have this dopey kind of expression that I've never seen from you before."

She made a sound of abrupt disgust. "I don't look dopey."

He snorted. "Yes, you do. Get to a mirror and check it. It's really scary. I definitely wouldn't let Maman see that."

She rolled her eyes at him. "This from a bear who got his ass kicked by a jackal?"

His eyes flared. "I was preoccupied by the knife at your throat."

She gave an exaggerated laugh. "You were on the ground and pinned before I was held."

He started to argue, then stopped. He looked around as if afraid someone might have overheard her. "You think anyone else remembers that part?"

"Depends." She gave him a calculating stare. "How much you gonna pay me to back *your* version?"

His look turned charming and sweet. "I pay you in love, precious little sister. Always."

She scoffed at his offer. "Love don't pay the rent, baby. Only cold hard cash."

He gaped, his expression one of total offense as he held his hand over his heart as if she'd wounded him. "You really turning mercenary on your favorite older brother?"

"No. I would never do that to Alain."

"Ouch!" Dev shook his hand as if he'd burned it. "Bearswan got 'tude."

Laughing, she stepped out to give him a quick hug. "Don't worry, big bro, your secret's safe with me so long as you don't annoy me too much."

He tightened his arms around her and held her close. "You know I love you, sis."

"I love you too." And she did. In spite of their disagreements and quarrels, her family meant everything to her. Stepping away, she turned to glance one last time at Fang. Most likely she'd never see him again. A common occurrence really for their clientele and yet for some reason this time that thought hurt deep inside her.

I have lost what three brain cells I have. . . . Bear, get your butt back to work and forget about him.

Fang stood up as he saw the pack leaving the bar. Vane was the first to reach him.

"Here." Vane tossed him his backpack, then handed him a bag of something sweet and rich. "The bearswan wanted to make sure you got that for Anya. She said there was something in there for you too."

That shocked him completely. No one ever gave him gifts. "For me?"

Vane shrugged. "I don't understand bear thought processes. Most days I barely understand ours."

Fang had to give him that—he didn't understand it either. He tucked the sack into his backpack as the rest of the wolves took up their bikes and headed out. They were silent the entire way back to the bayou where they'd made camp for their females to deliver their pups in peace and protection.

As soon as they'd returned, their father met them in his wolf form. Markus shifted into a human just to sneer at them.

"What took you women so long to return?"

As Fang opened his mouth to smart off, Vane shot him a warning glare. "I toured the clinic and have the contact information should any of our females require help."

Markus curled his lip. Even though he'd sent them there, he had to be an asshole. "In my day we let the wolfswans incapable of birthing our young die."

Fang snorted. "Then it's a good thing we're in the twenty-first century and not the Dark Ages, isn't it?"

Vane shook his head while their father growled at him as if about to attack.

This time Fang refused to back down. "Try it, old man," he said, using a term he knew infuriated his father since Katagaria despised their human natures. "And I'll rip out your throat and usher in a new age of leadership to this pack."

He could see the desire in Markus's eyes to press the issue, but his sire wolf knew what he did. In a fight, Fang would win.

His father wasn't the same wolf who'd killed his own brother to be Regis of their pack. He was weak with age and knew that he didn't have many more years left before either Fang or Vane took over.

One way or another.

Fang preferred it to be over the old man's dead body. But other arrangements would work for him too.

It was another reason their sire hated them. He knew his prime was past and they were only coming into their own.

Markus narrowed his gaze threateningly. "One day, whelp, you're going to cross me and your brother won't be here to stop me from killing you. When that day comes, you better pray for salvation."

Fang's look turned evil. "I don't need salvation. There's not a wolf here I couldn't wipe my ass on. You know it. I know it and most important, they *all* know it."

Vane arched a brow at his comment as if taunting him to prove those words.

Fang gave him a lopsided grin. "You don't count, brother. I think more of you than to even try."

Markus raked them with a repugnant twist to his lips. "You both sicken me."

Fang snorted. "It's what I live for . . . Father." He couldn't resist using the title he knew made the old fart seethe. "Your eternal disgust succors me like mother's milk."

Markus turned back into a wolf and bounded off.

Vane turned on him. "Why do you do that?"

"Do what?"

"Piss off everyone you come into contact with? Just once, couldn't you keep your mouth shut?"

Fang shrugged. "It's a skill."

"Well, it's one I wish you'd unlearn."

Fang let out an irritated breath at the constant bitch-topic that had grown old three hundred years ago. He wasn't the kind of wolf to suck it up. Rather he gave as good as he got, and most times he gave better. "Against the grain is the only way. Stop being such an old woman." He turned and headed for the edge of camp where Anya had chosen to den with her mate Orian.

Fang always had to bite his tongue around them. He hated the wolfswain the Fates had picked for his sister. She deserved so much better than that half-wit, but unfortunately, that wasn't in their hands. The Fates chose their partners and they could either submit or the male would live out his life completely impotent, the woman infertile.

To save their species, most accepted whatever abysmal mate the Fates assigned them. In the case of his parents, his mother had refused and now his father was left impotent and perpetually pissed off.

Not that Fang blamed the old man for that. He'd probably be insufferable too if he had to go centuries without sex. But that was the only part of his father he understood. The rest of the wolf was a complete mystery to him.

Luckily Anya's mate wasn't with his sister. Anya was lying down on the grass in the fading sunlight, her eyes barely open as a light breeze stirred her soft white fur. Her belly was swollen and he could see her pups moving inside her.

It was pretty much gross, but he wouldn't insult her by telling her that.

"*You're back.*"

He smiled at her soft voice in his head. "We are and . . ." He held the bag out toward her.

She sat up immediately and trotted over to him. "*What did you bring?*" She nosed at the sack as if trying to see through it with her snout.

Fang sat down and opened the sack to see what Aimee had given them. The moment he did, his heart quickened. She'd thrown in two steaks, baklava, beignets, and cookies. There was also a small note in the bottom.

He dug out the cookies and held them for Anya while he read Aimee's flowing cursive.

> *I really appreciate what you did and I hope your sister enjoys her food. Brothers like you should always be treasured. Anytime you need a steak, you know where we are.*

He didn't understand why such a short, innocuous note touched him, but it did. He couldn't help smiling at it as an image of her drifted through his mind.

Stop being a head case.

Yeah, something was definitely wrong with him. Maybe he needed to see one of those pet psychics or something. Or maybe have Vane give him a sharp kick to the hindquarters.

"*Do I smell bear?*"

He tucked the note into his pocket. "It's from the Sanctuary staff."

She shook her head and sneezed on the ground. "*Gah, could they stink any worse?*"

Fang had to disagree. He didn't smell bear, he only smelled Aimee and it was a delectable scent. "They probably think the same about us."

Anya paused to look up at him. "*What did you say?*"

Fang cleared his throat as he realized how out of character it was for him to defend another species. "Nothing."

She licked his fingers as he held out more cookies for her.

A shadow fell over them. Looking up, he saw Vane standing there with a stern frown.

"Shouldn't it be her mate doing that for her?"

Fang shrugged. "He was always a selfish asshole."

Anya nipped hard at his fingers. "*Careful, brother, that's the sire of my pups you're talking about.*"

Fang scoffed at her protective tone. "One chosen by a trio of psycho bitches who—*ow!*" He jumped as Anya sank her teeth deep into the fleshy part of his hand. He cursed as he saw the blood dripping from the wound she'd given him.

She narrowed her gaze. "*Again, he's my mate and you will respect him.*"

Vane cocked him on the back of his head. "Boy, don't you ever learn?"

Fang bit his lip to keep from snapping at both of them. He hated how they treated him like their mentally defective distant relation. As if his opinions didn't matter. Anytime he opened his mouth, one of them told him to shut it.

Honestly, he was more than tired of their treatment. All they saw him as was the muscle they needed. A loaded gun to be used against their enemies. The rest of the time, they wanted him kept in a box, completely silent and unobtrusive.

Whatever.

Changing into a wolf, he left them before he said something they'd all regret.

But one day . . .

One day he was going to let them know just how tired he was of being their omega wolf.

Delve into the other titles in Sherrilyn Kenyon's sexy new *League* trilogy and become immersed in futuristic settings and heart-stopping adventure.

Available now from Piatkus…

BORN OF NIGHT

In the Ichidian Universe, the League and their ruthless assassins rule all. Expertly trained and highly valued, the League Assassins are the backbone of the government. But not even the League is immune to corruption…

Command Assassin Nykyrian Quiakides once turned his back on the League – and has been hunted by them ever since. Though many have tried, none can kill him or stop him from completing his current mission: to protect Kiara Zamir, a woman whose father's political alliance has made her a target.

As her world becomes even deadlier, Kiara must entrust her life to the same kind of beast who once killed her mother and left her for dead. Old enemies and new threaten them both and the only way they can survive is to overcome their suspicions and learn to trust in the very ones who threaten them the most: each other.

978-0-7499-3928-1

BORN OF FIRE

In a universe where assassins make the law, everyone lives in fear – except for Syn. Born of an illicit scandal that once rocked a dynasty, he always knew how to survive on the bloodthirsty streets. But that was then, and the future is now…

Raised as a tech-thief until his livelihood uncovered a truth that could end his life, Syn tried to destroy the evidence, and has been on the run ever since. Now trained as an assassin, he allows no one to threaten him. Ever. He is the darkness that swallows his enemies whole.

Shahara Dagan is the best bounty hunter in the universe. When Syn comes back on the radar, she's the only one who can bring him to justice. There's only one problem: Syn is a close family friend who's helped out the Dagans countless times. But if she saves him, both of their lives will be on the line. Is Syn's protection worth the risk? The only hope Shahara has is to find the evidence he buried long ago. Now it's kill or be killed – and they, the predators, have just become the hunted…

978-0-7499-0878-2

Sherrilyn Kenyon's award-winning paranormal romances have topped the *New York Times* bestseller charts, offering readers a world full of dark, dangerous heroes and feisty heroines.

Become immersed in the novels of the *Dark Hunter World*, available now from Piatkus…

DREAM CHASER

Condemned by the gods to live out his existence without emotions, Xypher chose the pursuit of sensations, to feel again in the dreams of humans, only to find himself condemned to death. But he is given one last chance at a reprieve. Made human for a month, he must redeem himself within that time or Hades will return him to Tartarus and his torture.

Simone Dubois is a coroner who isn't scared by much, especially since she's psychic and can see and hear the people she's working on. When they wheel in another victim, she doesn't think much about it, until he gets up from her table and starts to leave.

Xypher doesn't have time to spend with this human woman and her questions. But it's not long before mysterious attempts on Simone's life force Xypher to stand between the woman who is beginning to touch the heart he thought had died a long time ago and the danger that is threatening her life.

978-0-7499-3888-8

ACHERON

Eleven thousand years ago a god was born. Cursed into the body of a human, Acheron endured a lifetime of hatred. His human death unleashed an unspeakable horror that almost destroyed the earth. Brought back against his will, he became the sole defender of mankind. Only it was never that simple...

For centuries, he has fought for our survival and hidden a past he never wants revealed. Now his survival, and ours, hinges on the very woman who threatens him. Old enemies reawaken and unite to kill them both. War has never been more deadly... or more fun.

978-0-7499-0927-7

ONE SILENT NIGHT

It is the Christmas season and all hell's breaking loose.
Literally. While humans are busy shopping, an angry
demon lord is plotting an all-out onslaught against his
enemies, which – unfortunately for us – includes the
human race. But as Stryker gathers his forces, he discovers
a grown daughter he never knew existed and an angry ex,
Zephyra, who's as determined to end his existence as he is
to end ours.

The ultimate predator is about to meet his match as new
battle lines are drawn and the Dark-Hunters are rallied for a
blood bath on Christmas Eve. The only question is this: can
Stryker survive his oldest enemy to fight the ones he really
wants to kill – or will Zephyra finally have her shot at the
husband who abandoned her?

978-0-7499-0891-1

DREAM WARRIOR

Cratus, the son of Warcraft and Hate, spent eternity battling for the ancient gods who birthed him. He was death to any who crossed him. Until the day he laid down his arms and walked into self-imposed exile. Now an ancient enemy has been unleashed and our dreams are his chosen battlefield. And the only hope we have is the one god who swears he will never fight again.

As a Dream-Hunter, Delphine has spent eternity protecting mankind from the predators who prey on our unconscious state. But now that her allies have been turned, she knows in order to survive, the Dream-Hunters need a new leader. Someone who can train them to fight their new enemies. Cratus is her only hope. But she is a bitter reminder of why he chose to lay down his arms.

Time is running out and if she can't win him to her cause, mankind will be slaughtered and the world we know will soon cease to exist.

978-0-7499-0905-5